Starting Over at Halesmere House

Suzanne Snow writes contemporary and uplifting fiction with a vibrant sense of setting and community connecting the lives of her characters. A horticulturist who lives with her family in Lancashire, her books are inspired by a love of landscape, romance and rural life.

Her first novel in the Thorndale series, *The Cottage of New Beginnings*, was a contender for the 2021 RNA Joan Hessayon Award. Suzanne is a member of the Romantic Novelists Association and the Society of Authors.

Also by Suzanne Snow

Welcome to Thorndale

The Cottage of New Beginnings
The Garden of Little Rose
A Summer of Second Chances
A Country Village Christmas

Love in the Lakes

Snowfall Over Halesmere House
Wedding Days at Halesmere House
Starting Over at Halesmere House

SUZANNE SNOW

Starting Over at Halesmere House

CANELO

First published in the United Kingdom in 2023 by

Canelo
Unit 9, 5th Floor
Cargo Works, 1–2 Hatfields
London SE1 9PG
United Kingdom

A CIP catalogue record for this book is available from the British Library.

Print ISBN 978 1 80032 878 5
Ebook ISBN 978 1 80032 877 8

This book is a work of fiction. Names, characters, businesses, organizations, places and events are either the product of the author's imagination or are used fictitiously. Any resemblance to actual persons, living or dead, events or locales is entirely coincidental.

Trigger warning: contains mention and themes of miscarriage.

Cover design by Cherie Chapman

Cover images © Shutterstock

Look for more great books at www.canelo.co

Printed and bound in Great Britain by Clays Ltd, Elcograf S.p.A.

1

To Ali and Jo, with love.

Daughters, sisters, wives, mums and more xx

Chapter One

'Have you thought about dating again, Alice? And why are you driving that old thing and not your car when you said you were giving it up?'

Alice Harvey bristled at these blunt questions from her friend Kelly, who was pretty much the only person bold enough to say them out loud. They'd barely even said hello after Alice had accepted the call and she was already half wishing she hadn't. Kelly didn't take any prisoners when it came to her own love life, and now she had Alice's single status firmly in her sights.

Alice was more focussed on the journey she was about to take rather than thoughts of relationships. She hadn't intended to make the drive from Sheffield to her new home at Halesmere by articulated lorry, but she couldn't resist one last trip in her favourite cab. It had been her former colleague Ray's idea, and when he'd offered to drive her car up and swap vehicles, she'd thanked him gratefully.

'What do you mean, dating again? I've barely even started.' A huff of laughter escaped, raising her voice above the engine as she took in the view of the haulage yard from her seat behind the wheel, as achingly familiar as her own home had once been. 'And don't be rude about my cab; she and I go back a long way.'

'Yeah, yeah. You and your lorries. Nice try, by the way, changing the subject. You're forgetting how well we know each other.'

Alice heard the smile in her friend's voice and swiftly decided that Kelly could have picked a better moment for this conversation. Although knowing her, she probably had done it on purpose while Alice was distracted to get her to agree to some mad idea just so she could end the call and get going.

'Could we possibly leave the question of dating well alone please, at least until I've moved into my new house? It is literally the last thing on my mind. And don't you dare say I'm not getting any younger.'

'You've said it now, so I don't have to. And it's true. Thirty-eight's hardly on the shelf seeing as we're not living in the eighteenth century, but you don't want to be hanging about. Not if you want to meet someone before you're forty.'

'Forty!' A tremor of alarm darted through Alice's mind at the thought. 'That's ages away, thanks very much. And I really don't want to meet someone; I'm doing fine on my own.'

'I know you are.' Kelly's voice had fallen, and Alice sensed her concern now, banishing the frivolity of before. Kelly did have Alice's best interests at heart, but they'd often included persuading Alice to do something she wasn't keen on, like that time on holiday in Santorini when they were supposed to be going on a boat tour. Kelly had booked all-terrain quad vehicles instead and Alice had come home on crutches as a consequence.

Their teasing had always marked their friendship as much as their mutual affection did. They'd been looking out for one another since they'd met at college, the only girls on a mechanics course full of boys. At eighteen, Alice had gone on to work for her dad's haulage firm while Kelly had headed off to university, qualifying as a mechanical engineer and now a partner in a consultancy firm in the north-east. Alice had picked Kelly up whenever she needed it in a life spent serial dating and now it seemed her friend had decided it was time to share the benefits of her experience.

'And I think this move is perfect for you, Al, even though I would've loved you to be closer to me. Think of all the fun we'd have had.'

'I know, and I love you for it. But Durham's not for me; I can't live in a city again. I need to be outdoors, in the landscape. It's part of what got me through this past year. If I hadn't had my garden or the time at Halesmere, I don't know how I would've coped. And the new house is officially all mine now, deal done.'

That produced a happy glow as Alice thought of the converted barn she'd just purchased, a first ever home on her own. The happiness was also followed by a glimmer of nerves; even though she had a relative in her aunt Sandy at Halesmere, and friends she'd made on previous visits, this was still a whole other level of living alone since the end of her marriage. When her ex-husband had left with no warning, she'd swiftly let the guest room to the student daughter of a friend, preferring to have someone else around.

'Well, when you do come and stay, we'll hit all the best places in town.' Kelly wasn't ever down for long, and the merriment was back. 'So, FYI, I've set you up a dating profile online. We just need a banging picture of you to go with it.'

'You've done what?' Alice wailed, so startled she hit the horn by mistake and a passing colleague leaped in alarm. She raised a hurried hand in apology and cut the engine. 'Kelly! Why?'

'Because it was your idea, remember? That weekend at mine, when we were out late drinking cocktails. You said it would probably be the only way you'd meet someone and that you were ready to give it a try once you've moved.'

'I didn't say that! Did I?' Alice tried to drag her mind back to the summer, but the conversation was gone.

'Oh, you did, Alice, you really did. I never forget a thing when it comes to dating. So, let's go through your profile when I come over on Saturday. It needs to sound authentic, like you, not me. You'll probably get plenty of matches if you go with something like, "sexy redhead with curves in all the right places who drives lorries like a boss and knows her way around an engine", but Mr Petrol Head maybe isn't what you're looking for after all those years running the business. You've got to get back out there, have some fun.'

'Fun! That's not a word I've heard you using very often when it comes to dating. Maybe it's still too soon for me? I've obviously wiped our little chat from my mind after that night.'

'Saturday,' Kelly said confidently. 'We'll talk then and if you're still not on board, we'll hide your profile for now, so you can update it again later.'

'Or delete it?' Alice replied hopefully.

'Only if you absolutely insist. Gotta run; I'm meeting Damon, that gorgeous recruiter I told you about.'

'The one who tried to head-hunt you?' Alice was mentally going over their most recent messages. 'That's what, date number six now?'

'Seven. And he's lovely, I really like him. Hope all goes well with the move, take care.'

They said goodbye and Alice was happy to restart the engine, pull out of the yard and forget about the question of dating. It was impossible for her to take the lorry all the way to Halesmere; those final, winding lanes in the remote Cumbrian valley she was about to call home were far too tight. This stately Mercedes-Benz cab had been her dad's favourite and the one that he'd assigned to her when she'd passed her heavy goods vehicle test at twenty-one. He'd assured her then it was the most reliable unit in their yard, and he knew it would take care of her.

They'd both loved that when work was frantic in their haulage business and available drivers in short supply, she'd swap her heels for boots and slip behind the wheel to quite literally keep things moving. This particular cab didn't often get a run out now it was older but that had never changed how Alice felt about it. Ray had brought it out of semi-retirement today just for her and she knew he understood how much she appreciated his gesture.

Four hours later, the main road heading west through Cumbria was quiet now that autumn had fully arrived, the last few days of October draping the landscape with fallen leaves in shades of burnished copper, red and amber. Afternoon sun was low above the fells as she drove, stretching out these final moments behind the wheel for as long as she could.

All too soon her journey was over, and Alice parked up behind a garden centre where she'd arranged to meet Ray. She turned the key in the ignition, trying to ignore her sadness as silence replaced the loud rumble of an engine she knew as well as her own heartbeat. She jumped down to meet Ray when he arrived soon after and got out of her car.

'How was that?'

The quiet understanding in his few words had her nodding fiercely as she tried to hold back the sadness threatening tears for this final goodbye. So much in her life had changed and he had been one of the few constants at her side, along with Kelly, and her family.

'The best. She's a beauty.' Alice steeled herself against the sympathy she saw in his gaze. 'You will let me know if you hear anything? I haven't got a place but if they decide to sell or even scrap her, then I'm first in the queue, okay? I'll find a lock-up somewhere.'

'I will. You know I will. She's had your name on her for a long time; your dad saw to that. Every one of our lads knew they had to look after her or they'd have him to answer to.'

Ray held out a hand, the key to her bright yellow Porsche Boxster sitting on his palm. She stared at it, a fresh wave of sorrow bringing the realisation that this beloved car was the only remaining link between her old life and the new one waiting a few miles down the road.

'Go easy on yourself, Alice. You know where we are if you need anything.'

'Thank you.' This time a single tear did slide down her cheek and she swiped it away to give him a smile. 'And you know where I am if you're ever stuck for a driver.'

'I do.' Ray grinned. 'But I reckon that flower meadow is going to be keeping you busy enough.'

'Not so busy that I can't do the occasional run to Aberdeen or Cornwall if you need me.'

The mention of the meadow had a flurry of doubts rushing into her mind. Was she really doing the right thing, moving north, and taking on land at Halesmere to grow her own flowers and arrange them, teach others to do the same? But it was far too late to allow misgivings now; all decisions were made and this final drive in the lorry had put a physical distance between the past year and now to match the crushing emotional one.

'I know.' Ray jangled the key to her Porsche, and she swapped it for the cab's. 'You're still part of the family, no matter where you are. Keep in touch.'

He held out his arms and she hesitated before walking into them, feeling the familiar, solid kindness of the man who'd been her dad's right hand for as long as she could remember. Ray had watched over her for years, had stepped in at work on the odd occasion when she'd needed him, and his family was her family. The business had been like that, one big family. Until she'd sold it and had let go of everything she'd known and loved. This was it. This was goodbye.

'I know you didn't want a fuss, but we couldn't let you go without something to mark the occasion. So we clubbed together and got you a gift.'

'That's very generous, Ray, thank you. But you've got that look again, the one that means you're very pleased with yourself.' Alice's tone was purposely light as they separated. 'And that makes me suspicious because it's the one you always give me when you're about to tell me something I might not want to hear.'

'You'll just have to wait and see. You'll know when it arrives why we didn't spring it on you at the yard before you left.'

'That sounds ominous.' She was twisting the key between her fingers.

'It's not, nothing to worry about. Something you said you wanted. Just remember, Alice, that you always see things through and that's why we got it. And if you want anyone to blame, it was my idea.'

'Okay. Thank you.' Alice couldn't think what Ray might have chosen for a goodbye present that they couldn't have gifted her in person. A wave of shame followed; she didn't feel deserving of a gift from her colleagues. She'd sold the company and let go of her dad's dream to start this new life.

She wished she could hang on to this moment suspended between her two lives for a bit longer. This was still a day when old decisions were made, and new ones not yet required. She never used to be like this; she'd spent her career making difficult choices and acting on them to keep the haulage business thriving. But when life swerved sharply out of control the way hers had, with her marriage ending almost overnight, worry and uncertainty liked to make themselves apparent in ways they didn't used to.

'Go on, then,' she said lightly. 'You've got a long run and you've already done me a big favour, letting me bring the lorry this far for old times' sake.'

Ray nodded sadly and she really didn't want to watch him drive off and take her favourite cab with him. She settled in the Porsche, battling back tears she swore would be the last, barely noticing the familiar roar of the engine she adored. She raised a hand as she gunned the car down the lane and away from the only life she'd ever known.

Alice couldn't fit many belongings in her two-seater car, and she tried to keep out of the removal men's way when they arrived at her new home soon after she did.

Pear Tree Barn had been named for the crooked and ancient trees that lined one side of the garden, and she wondered if that also accounted for the pale green and white decor throughout the house.

A cosy Lakeland barn conversion was her home now, not the cheerful three-bedroomed house she'd bought new with her ex-husband in a pleasant suburb of Sheffield. Everything about the barn was unfamiliar and, as it had been a much-loved holiday home until now, she'd paid the previous owners to leave everything behind, including all soft furnishings and some of the kitchen equipment. She wanted no shared belongings from her marriage here and her old house had seemed as bereft as she did once her ex-husband had removed all that was his. How easy the practical process and yet so difficult she had found it, dividing their home into two separate ones.

'Any chance of a brew, please?' One of the three removal men paused in her kitchen, a large cardboard box secure in a pair of hefty arms. 'We could do with one for the road before we go.'

'Of course. Sorry, I should've sorted one out sooner.' Alice glanced at the kettle still in its box sitting beside the Aga. 'What would you like?'

'Two teas, one sugar in each and a coffee with none. That all right?'

'Absolutely. Milk?'

'Please.'

'Right. Be as quick as I can.' She unpacked her shiny whistling kettle, filled it and set it on the Aga's boiling plate. She'd never cooked on an Aga before and she was looking forward to trying. She'd bought a few food essentials before leaving Sheffield and was irritated to realise

9

she'd forgotten milk. She removed the kettle from the Aga and shouted up the stairs.

'Just nipping to the shop for milk; I won't be long.'

She closed the front door and shivered the moment she was outside, in a jumper over a vest, wondering about going back for a coat. But the community shop was only up the road, and she didn't want to keep the removal men waiting any longer than she had to; they were nearly done. She'd warm up if she walked quickly enough. Alice hurried down her drive and through an open five-barred farm gate leading onto the lane.

'Oh!' She stopped dead, not expecting six loose sheep nibbling at soggy grass on the verge, picking through hawthorn leaves fallen from a hedge. One sheep raised its head to stare, as though she was the one out of place here, and not them. She recognised the breed as Herdwicks and guessed they'd almost certainly escaped from the farm up the lane, her nearest neighbour, who bred them. The farm was on her way to the shop, so she'd call and let them know about the sheep. She closed the gate before they got in her garden and set off at the same quick pace, startling the sheep, who all shot off in the wrong direction.

'Oh, for pity's sake!' It would be dark soon and she really didn't have time for this. She decided to follow the sheep, overtake and herd them back to the farm. It looked easy enough; she'd seen shepherds doing it. But the closer she got to the sheep, the faster they ran, and they were rounding a bend in the lane in a flash. She'd had no idea they could shift so quickly, and she trailed to a halt.

'Want some help?'

She spun around at the shout to see a van had pulled up behind her and the driver had stuck his head and one elbow out of the window. In all the panicked bleating and the wind whipping her hair across her face, she hadn't heard it approach. Alice wrapped her arms around herself to ward off the chill, the splash of rain cold and unwelcome. 'Would you mind? They're not taking much notice of me.'

He got out, holding a coat she was expecting him to pull on over a dark green T-shirt. Black workwear trousers were edged with reflective strips running down his thighs and calves, a different material padding out the knees. He jogged towards her, dark hair already becoming wet, and as he tossed the coat towards her, her hands automatically flew out to catch it.

'You want to put that on? You look frozen.'

'What about you?' She shivered, already holding it like a shield.

'I'm fine. I got wet at work anyway and I'm heading home to shower.'

'Thanks.' She tugged the coat on gratefully, her gaze meeting eyes as rich and intense as smooth dark chocolate, framed by long lashes. Brows were as dark as his short curls and his beard was sharp, hardly more than a few days' stubble. She noticed a tattoo on the inside of his right forearm, a flash of lilac leaves flowing into green before copper and brown, forming the rough outline of a circle.

'You're not from around here, are you?'

'Why would you say that?' Alice questioned indignantly. She might not be a local quite yet but surely she didn't stick out that much? She zipped up his coat, the scent of lime and something spicier woven into the fabric every bit as distracting as the smile playing around his mouth.

'You're outside in this weather chasing sheep without a coat, plus you're wearing ballet flats. A real farmer would be in boots. So my guess is you're here on holiday?'

'Ballet flats? Most of the men I know would call them shoes.' Her former colleagues had for the most part been great, but she suspected some of the male ones wouldn't have known a high top from a heel.

Alice was trying to remember her management training, what she knew about body language and the supposed meaning behind a bottom lip that was fuller than the top one. Happy-go-lucky, she recalled, someone who liked to have fun. Sensual and spontaneous. All words she already thought suited him.

'Have I got something on my face?' The smile became a grin, and he ignored a phone ringing in a pocket on his right thigh.

'I don't think so.' She was happy to let the wind do its worst with her hair again to hide her embarrassment. She'd worked with dozens of men down the years and she'd had no difficulty in maintaining a professional approach, no matter what they looked like or how they behaved.

So why was this one different? She put it firmly down to her developing determination to have some fun in her life, even if she was seriously out of practice when it came to flirting. Kelly would've had his contact details and made plans for a first date by now, and Alice choked back a laugh.

'Good to know. But I really do have to run.' His voice held plenty of amusement but no trace of an accent to suggest that he was a local. 'What are we going to do about the sheep? They've legged it.'

Sheep? She was still thinking about telephone numbers and first dates, and her hand shot out a second time to catch a set of keys he flicked across.

'I'll go and see if I can turn them. You can drive?'

'Just a bit.'

'Could you back my van up to the farm? Hopefully then the sheep won't be able to get past it.'

'Aren't you worried I might steal it?'

'Are you planning to steal it?' His smile widened again as he edged away.

'No, but I probably wouldn't tell you if I was.'

'You really don't seem like the kind of person who'd steal someone else's van. You don't look devious enough.'

'That's because you don't know me.' Was this flirting? It certainly felt that way, if the new colour on her face was a means of measure. Maybe it was just the wind.

'Just don't run me over if you do steal it, okay?'

'I'll do my best. Although I'd probably turn it round and drive off in the opposite direction.'

'So you have thought about it?'

'Maybe a little,' she replied, and they both laughed.

'So I'd better get running.'

'You really should. Who knows how far those sheep have got by now; they seemed pretty determined.'

The plan sounded simple enough and he disappeared while she reversed the van and blocked the lane as much as she could. It was warm inside and she was tempted to stay put, but a couple of minutes later six sheep were charging towards her with the driver in pursuit. She jumped down, waving her arms wildly for good measure, and at the last minute the sheep swerved sharply into the farmyard. Alice slammed a gate behind them and shared a grin with the driver as he caught her up.

'Nice work.' He raised a hand, and she hesitated before letting hers meet his in a celebratory high five. The briefest of touches, and she felt the sting of it on her palm. 'We made a good team.'

'We did. Thanks.'

'And thanks for not stealing my van; I need it.'

'You're welcome. I could actually do with a van but not one that big, so I decided not to take it.'

'Cheers.' He leaned an elbow on the gate to face her. 'So am I right? You're a tourist visiting out of season?'

This exceptional landscape was her home now and happiness ran through Alice. This wasn't a visit when she'd have to leave and return to Sheffield, to the embers of the life she'd lived there. Halesmere was her new start, and suddenly she couldn't wait.

'I'm not a tourist.' She was surprised to realise how much she was enjoying their continuing conversation. It felt nice for a change, to play this game with a man as attractive as he was.

'Staying with friends?'

'Wouldn't that also count as holiday?'

'I suppose it would.' He stuck one foot on the lowest bar of the gate and Alice remembered he was supposed to be rushing as well. He didn't seem in such a hurry now, and that was a thrill.

'I thought you had to run?' Testing him, trying to discover why he might be lingering.

'I do. But I'm curious.' He straightened, removing the phone from his pocket to check it before fixing his gaze back on hers. 'About everything, and I like answers. So, go on, tell me. What brings you here?'

'Right now?' Alice ignored the quick disappointment that she was unlikely to see him again. At least her flirting skills had gone up a notch. 'Buying milk from the community shop. And I have to run too, before they close. Thanks again for stopping.'

'You're welcome.'

She'd only gone a few yards up the lane before his words, loaded with laughter, were carried by the wind to reach her.

'Do you think I could have my coat back please? And my keys?'

Chapter Two

For a few bleary moments the next morning, Alice thought she was actually on holiday when she woke up. It had been an unsettled night, the first here on her own, and she fumbled for a lamp in the darkness. The silence, too, had been something else. She blinked as the lamp flared into life and her new bedroom was revealed. Pale green walls, a dressing table at the opposite end of her wrought-iron-framed bed, shelves in the alcove on one side topped by a thick oak beam, a narrow chest of drawers in the other. A double wardrobe was crammed into the space beyond her bedside table, the bright colours of a patchwork quilt she'd thrown over her duvet the only other colour.

She sat up, rearranging the pillows to make herself more comfortable. The barn was an upside-down house, with three bedrooms and bathrooms all on the ground floor, the open-plan kitchen and dining area between them. Upstairs was the sitting room, which led onto a garden room and outdoor terrace with stunning south-facing views of the valley. The garden wrapped around three sides of the barn, and it was one of the reasons why she had fallen in love with the house.

She'd spent her life until now in Sheffield, and through her career Alice was as familiar with the entire motorway network as she had been with her own office. Losing her dad suddenly two and a half years ago had been a terrible shock and she still felt his loss every day. He'd been the heart and centre of a business he'd grown from a rough breaker's yard and a couple of vans until it offered state-of-the-art haulage solutions for their many clients.

They'd always been close, sharing a love of cars, and after college she'd made herself at home in the yard and learned the business from the ground up. Her dad had offered no short cuts or concessions for being the boss's daughter, and she hadn't wanted any as she shadowed the mechanics, admin staff and the drivers, and drove the huge HGVs he sent out all over the country.

Her dad had lived for his family, work and his cars, and his last restoration project had been the yellow Porsche Boxster for her. Alice couldn't part with it, no matter how impractical it was, especially now with her move to this Cumbrian valley, with narrow lanes and challenging winter conditions unsuited to a sports car. But sense didn't come into how she felt about the Porsche, and she adored driving it, never closer to her dad than when she was behind the wheel and revelling in its power.

Each new morning brought a sharp reminder that her busy, capable dad was gone, as though it was a lesson she had to keep on learning and couldn't quite grasp. He'd always told Alice he wouldn't be going anywhere until she had her own family he could dote on, just like her younger brother, Steven. That thought was another stab of sorrow and as she sat in bed, she waited for the hurt to pass.

Her dad's sister, Sandy, was the rector of the church at Halesmere and one of the reasons why Alice had decided to make the move here. Ten years younger than her dad, Sandy's relationship with Alice fell somewhere between a doting aunt and a fun-loving friend who shared her other passion for gardening. Sandy had wanted to call last night after a parish meeting, but Alice had told her not to worry when it ran on late and that she was ready to crash into bed after a long day.

She was desperate for tea so pushed back the duvet and got out of bed. Kelly was always trying to persuade her to make the switch to green tea, but Alice simply couldn't face it first thing, a legacy from those morning-brew-and-briefing meetings at the yard. Everything was unfamiliar here and even the carpet beneath her feet felt different. It was like being on holiday, as though in a week she'd go back to Sheffield and pick up her life where she'd left off.

Thoughts of holiday reminded her of yesterday and herding sheep with the driver who'd stopped to help: their laughter and conversation, the curiosity he'd expressed in why she was at Halesmere. But she wasn't likely to see him again and she wouldn't be sitting around all day feeling sorry for herself. She had a new business to run and, along with it, her family and the friends she'd already made here; they would be all she needed to rebuild her life and start over.

Alice left her bedroom and stopped dead, trying to get her bearings. In front was the smallest of the barn's three bedrooms, a bathroom shared between this room and the master, with an en-suite shower in hers. She crossed the narrow passageway and opened a door into the kitchen.

It was slightly bigger than the one in her old house, with units lining three walls and a staircase to the sitting room leading from it. She loved the blue Aga and pale grey cupboards, matching those in the compact utility room. Shelving was carved into the walls above white granite worktops and doors opened onto a small patio and shady garden on this side of the barn. A dining table with chairs for six sat around the corner, an empty Welsh dresser at one end.

Her stomach was already rumbling, and she thought longingly of the community shop up the road, the plentiful breakfasts on offer, and decided to make the walk again for something more inspiring than cereal. Last night had been beans on toast for dinner and her appetite was never stronger than when she was at Halesmere. Alice put that down to good company and the bracing country walks she loved to take, sometimes on her own, sometimes with Sandy or Marta, who lived on the farm next door with her partner, Luke.

Outside, Alice reminded herself that she needn't rush as she usually would. The morning air was sharp, and she breathed deeply as she locked the door, the squeeze of anxiety about her move lessening. She pulled on a beanie, covering shoulder-length auburn hair, trying to hold on to that feeling of calm, a moment of hope and happiness. She'd always felt the cold and since the end of her marriage she seemed to be even more chilled, as though nothing less than scorching heat could properly warm her.

The walk up the lane was mercifully free of loose sheep and another reminder of the man who'd stopped to help, making her smile. Alice was soon at the shop, and a bell tinkled as she opened the door. The delicious aromas of coffee and bacon did her hunger pangs no good, and she wished she'd brought a bigger carrier bag; she was likely to need one.

'Welcome back, Alice, it's grand to see you.'

The woman behind the counter paused sliding chunky chocolate brownies onto a tray. Grey hair was curling and short, her face welcoming and attractive with clear blue eyes. 'Sandy said you were moving into the barn this week.'

'Hi, Pearl. Thank you.' Alice picked up a wicker basket, ignoring the tremor in her voice. Everyone had been so kind since her divorce, and she would be very glad to get these infuriating moments of emotion firmly behind her. 'Mince pies! Surely it's too soon; it's not even November yet.' She didn't want to think about Christmas, not until she'd settled into the barn and found her feet at work.

'Don't let Stan hear you say that.' The tray was empty of brownies now and Pearl reached for two mince pies, dusted with pale icing sugar, and wrapped them in a small paper bag. 'As far as he's concerned, it's never too early for mince pies. He'd eat them all year round if he could.'

She held the package over the counter and Alice accepted it. The pastry was still warm, and her mouth watered greedily. Breakfast, she mulled. She promised herself she wouldn't make a habit of such things.

'One for you and one for him, on me. I take it you'll be at Halesmere later? Stan's been sorting out that shed for you. Said he's never seen so much rubbish and that's saying something, given the state of those old stables when Max bought the place.'

Stan was Pearl's husband of more than forty years, and he was also Halesmere House's resident carpenter, handyman and agony aunt, or soft touch, as Alice had heard him say with a wink. He could turn his hand to just about anything and was at the centre of all that went on at Halesmere. The door to his workshop was perman-ently open for a brew, a listening ear and a kind word in between the bluster and the banter.

Halesmere was less than a mile from Alice's new home, and she'd spent time there during her increasingly frequent weekend visits to Sandy after the end of her marriage. Part family home, part holiday business, the house had a range of artists' studios in the old stables set around a cobbled courtyard. Halesmere was run by Ella Grant and her partner, Max Bentley, alongside his flourishing landscape architecture practice. Ella and Max were expecting their first child together next month and Ella was already a stepmum to Lily and Arlo, Max's children from his marriage before he was widowed three years ago.

A keen ceramist who sold much of her work, Sandy also had a studio at Halesmere and back in the summer had suggested to Alice that she might find a way to combine her passion for gardening with a future in Cumbria, and Alice had fallen in love with the idea at once. The haulage business was already in the process of being sold as she searched for a new opportunity, and Halesmere made perfect sense. She loved the community there and had already taken a couple of courses as well as enjoyed mindfulness sessions in the large barn used for events.

Alice had approached Max with a tentative request to take on the flower meadow he'd planted last spring after redesigning the gardens. He'd accepted at once and also offered her the use of a shabby old corner building attached to the stables, known as The Shed, and a part-time role looking after the gardens at Halesmere, with a view to her supplying and arranging the flowers in the house once the meadow was more established.

'Yes, I'm going down as soon as I've had breakfast.' Alice dropped a couple of homemade frozen ready meals into her basket to tide her over until a first online shop arrived tomorrow. She couldn't wait to get started at Halesmere and sort out The Shed. She'd always worked long hours and didn't plan to reduce them by much now she was here. 'I'll take Stan's mince pie with me.'

'Thanks, Alice. He's already been in for his bacon butty.' Someone else arrived and Pearl went to the coffee machine to make the Americano they'd ordered. 'How about a nice chai latte to take away,' she said to Alice over her shoulder. 'It'll warm you up; you look perished.'

'That sounds lovely, thanks.' And a perfect accompaniment to the mince pie. Alice could almost taste both already, she was so hungry.

'Don't tell Stan about the latte,' Pearl said cheerfully. 'He's a stickler for his tea or hot Bovril. You should've seen his face when I tried him on the chai and told him it was tea. I thought he was going to spit it out and most of it went down the sink.'

'I won't say a word,' Alice promised. She'd been invited into Stan's workshop on previous visits and had once ventured to try the Bovril, which she'd found as disgusting to drink as Stan obviously did chai lattes.

'How's your mum, is she still down in Cambridge near your brother?'

'She is, yes. Steven works from home now and his wife has just got a job in a primary school, so they don't plan to move again.'

Alice ignored the pang of guilt. She'd meant to spend a few days with Steven and her sister-in-law, Jenna, before her move, but she'd run out of time once the house sale was complete. It had taken a while to wrap up her role in the haulage business and she'd clung to it for as long as she could, dreading making that final goodbye.

She and her mum weren't especially close, not like her mum was to her brother and his family. Alice had been her dad's little shadow, interested in everything cars.

Steven had been the musical one, playing the violin and saxophone through his teenage years, which had suited her mum's interests more than Alice and her cars had. Alice had more or less grown up in her dad's workshop, covered in grease and oil as she'd learned about restoration and how to change a set of spark plugs.

Within a month of losing her dad, the family home went up for sale and her mum bought a bungalow a couple of miles from Steven and Jenna. Alice knew they appreciated the support with a young family, even if they sometimes did find the attention and expectation of near-daily visits smothering as her mum tried to settle into a new community.

Nothing important between her and her mum was ever really put into words, and yet Alice had been surprised to find the move more hurtful than she'd expected. Still coming to terms with not having the family she'd longed for after a diagnosis of polycystic ovaries in her twenties, followed by years of treatment and two IVF failures, it felt as though her mum had made Alice's heartbreak just a little bit louder by moving so close to her only grandchildren. Not for her mum a home between son and daughter, where she could travel between the two and spend time with both. Steven was the one with the grandchildren and down to Cambridge she had gone.

'Good that she's settled, after your dad an' all,' Pearl said kindly as she popped a lid on the latte. 'Takes time, more than you think, when someone passes.'

'It does.' Alice was still wandering around the shop, adding all sorts of treats to her basket she never normally bought. 'Steven and Jenna are coming up next month for a weekend, and I'm seeing them at Christmas with Mum. We've booked Center Parcs for a few days.'

She adored her little nieces and was looking forward to sharing their excitement over the holidays. Her basket was heavy now that she'd added more milk and three soy candles that Marta from the farm made in her studio at Halesmere, and Alice placed it on the counter.

'That sounds very nice. An' you know where me an' Stan are if you need us, Alice. He's dead set on getting that shed straight for you.' The shopping was flying through the till as Pearl scanned it faster than Alice could pack it into the extra bag she'd requested. 'Come down an' have a meal with us one night, when you're ready. You can message me on Instagram; I'm following your new account for the meadow.'

Alice knew that Pearl managed the social media for the shop and Halesmere brilliantly, and also kept everyone at the house supplied with goodies that Stan brought in fresh every morning.

'I will, thanks. And that's lovely of you, Pearl, the follow. There's not much to see in the meadow yet but I want to show it through the seasons.' Alice gulped back the emotion clutching at her voice. For all that she'd loved Sheffield, she already felt part of Halesmere, and that was down to Sandy, Ella and Max, as well as Pearl and Stan. 'And then you must come to me. I promise not to give Stan a latte, chai or otherwise.'

Pearl's laugh was merry as Alice tapped her card against the machine and the bell tinkled again as she left the shop. This place was her home now and she was going to make a real, happy life here. She wasn't alone, not totally. Alone was only a feeling lodged in her heart and she would keep the fears about how she would cope to herself.

She hurried back to the barn and settled at the breakfast bar with the latte and the mince pie. Underfloor heating was welcome, and one foot dangled from her stool to reach it, toasting her toes as she ate, the crumbly short-crust pastry and chunky fruit every bit as delicious as she'd anticipated. Behind her a door led to the second bedroom, across the kitchen from the other two, and one she planned to use as a guest room.

Alice knew she really shouldn't be eating breakfast like this, not after porridge at her desk for so long. She'd always preferred to be at the haulage yard first thing as drivers set out on long runs or returned from overnight trips. She'd loved those times then, sharing banter with colleagues she'd known for years, and she missed it. Hopefully in time she would learn not to, and maybe the guilt she still felt about selling the company would ease as well.

Staring through the window, she focussed on the view instead of her thoughts. There wasn't an awful lot of her new garden to see from here; most of it lay on the south side of the barn. The lawn would have benefitted from a final cut, but it was too late now, with the temperature dropping and the weather wet. A green wooden shed stood beyond the patio, a row of bedraggled and dying conifers further on disguising a view of fell ponies on the farm next door she'd seen from the sitting room upstairs.

The conifers had to go. They were turning brown, and a couple were leaning at an alarming angle over the boundary wall, ready to topple over in a stiff breeze, never mind a rough storm. And once Alice had seen to that job, then she could plant another hedge. Maybe hawthorn that would blossom in spring and berry in autumn. Just the thought of new plants and the wildlife they would attract was enough to make her smile.

Her garden could use some attention and probably a redesign but that was work she'd put on hold until next year. She would nurture it and fill her home with colour and scent, and the healthy, delicious produce she planned to grow. This new life was a long-term project, not something she'd have boxed off for Christmas. And the business needed her time before the garden did, and for that she needed to be at Halesmere.

Alice finished the latte, left the cup in the utility room to recycle and put her shopping away. Rain was due later and she went in search of her new waterproofs. She had a feeling they were going to be her constant companions, and she laughed, the soft sound floating through the silence of the barn. One of the joys of working outside was returning indoors when jobs were done, and tonight she'd light the stove in the sitting room and stay cosy. Wintering was also a time of retreat and repair, and Alice planned to be good to herself when she needed it.

–

'Welcome back, lass. I'm very 'appy you've taken on T'Shed. It'll be just right for what you want.'

'Stan, hi!' Alice was unlocking her new studio, trying to dodge the rain, when she heard Stan's voice call out. She backed through the door, peering beneath a hood pulled low. 'I've got something for you. Are you coming in?'

'That makes two of us, then, cos I've got summat for you.' Stan was strolling across the courtyard, hands pushed into the pockets of a dark donkey jacket, shoulders outlined in a shade of orange that clashed with his bright pink bobble hat. She wasn't sure she'd ever seen him without a hat and his collection was famous, knitted by Pearl, who was an expert in all things wool and sold her creations in the shop almost faster than she could produce them. He was stocky, a couple of tattoos inked on his hands, and one of the kindest people Alice knew.

'Oh?' She hadn't got any outstanding orders for the business yet and Amazon already knew she'd moved for the personal ones. 'Have you got time for a cuppa?'

'Thought you'd never ask.'

'Tea?' For a second she was tempted to offer chai instead until she remembered she hadn't got any supplies here, of anything. 'Please can I borrow some stuff? Sorry, I'm not very organised yet. That's my plan for today, to make The Shed a bit more homely.'

'Get that fire lit an' I'll fetch us a brew over.' He nodded at the black stove at the far end of the room. 'It's turnin' proper nasty out there.'

'On it. Oh, and by the way' – Alice gave him a beam when she noticed the kindling and logs he had no doubt left ready for her – 'it looks amazing in here, thank you. You're a superstar; I can't believe the difference now all the rubbish has gone, and the walls have been painted.'

'You're very welcome, an' I 'ad some 'elp.' Stan's chest seemed to broaden just a smidge and he coughed. 'An' before we get started, proper like, I'm just gonna say that you'll be all right 'ere, Alice. We look after each other an' my door's always open.'

'Thanks.' Her eyes were threatening to water, and she wasn't sure she trusted herself to say much more without her voice cracking. 'So's mine.'

'Back in a minute.' He stomped out and she blinked the dampness away so she could see to light the stove.

The Shed was bigger than the other studios, apart from the forge at the far end of the courtyard, where local blacksmith Cal Sutherland was based. Alice had met him and his fiancée, Lizzie, on a previous visit. Lizzie was an events planner and photographer, and she managed all the retreats and events at Halesmere for Ella and Max. They'd recently moved out of a flat above the old dairy opposite The Shed and were busy renovating a cottage they'd bought. Sandy had mentioned that they were having a party to celebrate their engagement soon, and Alice was already invited.

L-shaped, The Shed had a tiny kitchen and larger sitting area to the right of the door, and two squashy sofas that Alice had ordered, one green, one copper, were already in place. Exposed beams met in the apex of the roof, making the room feel large and airy, and the long line of the L formed a practical space where guests could take part in the courses she was planning to offer. So far, she had arranged several wreath-making days leading up to Christmas as a trial run and to learn how she might improve for next year. She was busy with the stove, coaxing kindling into life, when Stan returned.

''Ere you go.' He held out a mug and Alice stood up to accept it, glancing warily at the contents, which appeared suspiciously dark even though it smelled like tea.

'It's not Bovril?'

'No, just a proper brew.' He plonked himself on a sofa and sighed contentedly. 'I can see I'll 'ave to try again to induct you into the benefits of drinkin' Bovril, lass. Sets me up for t'day.'

Alice settled on the other sofa to his right. 'I wanted to thank you for the shelves, too.' She glanced at neat rows of oak lining the walls above the kitchen. 'They're so beautiful and practical – I can't wait to fill them up. I thought I'd search out a few local antique shops for inspiration.'

'You're welcome, lass; I was 'appy to 'elp. Oh, there's this too.' He reached into a carrier bag at his feet and brought out a flat piece of wood, passing it to Alice.

'What is it?' She turned it over and a thrill of surprise and pleasure quickly followed. Carved into the varnished oak were the words *The Flower Shed*, outlined in pale grey. 'Oh Stan, it's gorgeous, thank you! You made this for me?'

'Aye. Call it a welcome present. This place 'as bin The Shed for as long as ever I can remember, an' I thought a new sign would be useful for remindin' folk what you're callin' it now. "Flower Shed" sounds a bit smarter than some old glory 'ole used for dumpin' stuff.'

'I love it.' She swallowed. 'Thank you so much.'

'Grand. I'll put it up for you later if you show me where you want it to go.'

'Thank you. Oh, sorry, I nearly forgot.' Alice was rummaging in the waterproof rucksack she'd brought. 'Pearl sent a mince pie for you. I can confirm they're outstanding; I had mine for breakfast.'

'I can see you an' me are goin' to get along like an 'ouse on fire, Alice.' Stan beamed as he unwrapped the little package she handed over.

He finished the mince pie quickly, scrunching up the paper to throw it into the stove. Alice leaned back on the sofa, the mug of tea between her fingers, the room heating up nicely and Stan's company adding to the feeling of cheer.

She started as the door was suddenly flung open, bringing a blast of cold air and the appearance of someone whose face she recognised. Bright spots of colour rushed into hers as she leaped up, waterproof trousers flapping like wings around her legs. Her fellow sheep rescuer from yesterday swung the door shut and his incredulous stare went from Stan back to Alice.

'This looks very cosy,' he said with a grin. 'Room for a little one?'

Chapter Three

'Trust you to know where to find a brew, lad; I reckon you can sniff 'em out at twenty paces. An' we're all out of mince pies.' Stan delivered this to the new arrival with a look Alice recognised was kindly meant. 'What are you doin' back 'ere? It's not even dinnertime yet.'

'Picking up something from the yard; shame about the mince pies. Are you going to introduce us, Stan?'

That same amusement from yesterday was back, the mischievous glint in the younger man's eye letting her know he was surprised, maybe even pleased, to see her too.

'Alice, this is Zac, a mate of Max's who's stayin' in t'flat across courtyard an' workin' with 'im, supposedly.'

'I am working, Stan; I'm on my way.' The rain had flattened Zac's short dark hair and he was wearing the coat he'd lent her, a very insignificant link that she found unexpectedly thrilling. It was unzipped and Alice marvelled how he didn't seem to feel the cold. She'd layered up for walking here; a thermal vest was comforting beneath a thick wool jumper and dungarees, her waterproof trousers the final nail in the coffin of chic.

'Or at least I was, until I got waylaid by a driver with a delivery for someone called Harvey. I'm guessing that's you. Hello. Again.' Zac stuck out a hand. 'So am I really living next door to Alice?'

'I haven't heard that song for ages. Hi.' The touch of his fingers was brief around her hand. Was that her own voice and where had it come from? She cleared her throat. 'I've just taken over the flower meadow and this studio.' A simple explanation that suddenly felt huge and maybe even beyond her capabilities. She straightened her shoulders, refusing to be daunted by doubts about her new role.

'Ah, so you're the horticulturist Max told me about.' Zac's smile widened. 'Welcome to Halesmere.'

'Thanks.' 'Horticulturist' sounded awfully grand, and Alice wasn't sure her qualifications achieved part-time at college in between work over the past three years warranted it, especially given her lack of practical paid experience. 'But this is my first professional job.'

''Ave you two already met?' Stan threw Zac a puzzled glance.

'Briefly.' She really hoped her expression wasn't betraying that she'd thought about Zac since last night. The teasing, the laughter they'd shared, his plea for her not to steal his van. She'd forgotten how to flirt; running the haulage business and being married for ten years and together for fifteen with the same man had seen to that. She'd been out of the game so long she had no idea what the rules were any more.

At work she'd always fended off those men who'd wanted to flirt. She'd faced down the hostile ones who'd doubted her with unwavering politeness and a resolve honed from experience and confidence in her own abilities, and made friends with a few, like Ray. But no longer did she have to set the rules and abide by them for the people in her working life. It felt nice, new, to loosen the shackles a little and enjoy a conversation with someone she wasn't required to manage.

'Yesterday, near the farm,' Alice said. 'A few of Luke's sheep had escaped and Zac helped me get them back. He even gave me his coat.'

'Well, you were very unsuitably dressed for herding sheep, and it was the gentlemanly thing to do, even if you were already soaked.' Zac's mouth curled into a grin. 'Nice boots, by the way. You look much better prepared for being outdoors today. If it wasn't for your hair and those green eyes, I'm not sure I'd have recognised you.'

His words might have been playful but she caught the compliment in his own eyes as they held hers, beginning to think that maybe Kelly had it right after all when it came to conversing with a man like Zac. It really could be fun.

'Gentleman!' Stan scoffed. 'You're no gentleman, lad. Cheeky bugger an' full of 'imself more like. Watch out for 'im, Alice; don't take any notice of a word 'e says.'

'Hey,' Zac protested. 'You're giving Alice totally the wrong impression about me. I'm friendly and sociable, that's all.' He turned a shoulder to the door. 'So do you want me to bring that delivery in? It's a bike.'

A bike? Alice was about to say *no thanks* and that there had been a mistake because she definitely hadn't ordered a bike, but a parting comment from Ray yesterday dropped into her mind and she gripped the back of a sofa as her mouth fell open.

'You all right, lass?' Stan clambered to his feet. 'Only you've gone a bit pale.'

'I'm fine. Thank you.' Her knuckles were white too and she took a calming, slow breath. 'Does it say who it's from?'

'Not that I can see.' Zac hadn't budged and the play-fulness had been replaced with a suggestion of concern. Alice didn't want him to wonder at her startled reaction and she released her grasp on the sofa. 'What would you like me to do with it?'

'Bring it in, thanks.' It couldn't stay outside, not with her own name on the box, and she definitely couldn't send it back. Not if it was her promised farewell gift from Ray and her old colleagues. But she really didn't want to set eyes on the bike now and think about what it represented, and why. What she had promised to do, and for whom.

Zac disappeared and Alice busied herself washing up the two dirty cups for Stan. Zac returned moments later with a large cardboard box, unwieldy in his arms. It was unmistakably a bike, going by the name of a large company she recognised splashed across it. She thanked him stiffly as he propped it against a wall. She would deal with it later and decide what to do once she was alone. It wasn't Zac's fault the delivery had caught her by surprise and dragged a piece of her past in with it.

'Do you want me to run it down to your new place?' Stan was looking at her feet now, and she couldn't see why her steel toe-capped wellies were so interesting. 'You don't look like you could ride it back to t'barn, not in them boots.'

'I think I'll just leave it here for now, thanks, Stan.' Alice flashed him a grateful smile to soften her refusal, blinking away the reminder of her dad in Stan's cheerful nature. The box certainly wouldn't fit in her car, and she didn't want it in the house anyway. 'I'd need to order a helmet before I could ride it.'

'You mean the barn that's just been sold, near Luke's farm?' Zac had already made the connection. 'So you're the one with the conifers that need sorting out? Max asked me to take a look at them.'

'Conifers?' Alice forced her mind away from the bike and back to her new house. She'd totally forgotten that Max had been kind enough to view the garden back in late summer once her purchase of the barn was progressing. He'd offered some expert professional advice, advice she was planning to take when time allowed. But first she needed to find her feet with the new business. 'Oh, those. I don't think they're going anywhere for now.'

'Are you sure? Max said they'd had it, and they should come out before the weather takes them out. And I'm a tree surgeon, a really good one, according to him.'

'But aren't you too busy? I heard there's a lot to do at the hotel.' Alice knew about the huge landscaping project Max was leading, and the team working alongside him. Her waterproofs rustled irritatingly as she dried Stan's two mugs with kitchen roll and handed them back. Tea towels were something else she needed in here.

'I'm not so busy that I can't sort out those conifers before they become more of a problem for you.' Zac glanced around the studio, taking in the bright glow of the fire, the pair of comfortable sofas. 'Can we sort a time?'

'Do you mean in the evening, after work?' The jump in her pulse at the thought of making plans to see him again, even in a professional sense, was a surprise. Unhelpful too, for considering his suggestion to meet. And now she'd made her reply sound like she'd meant something more intimate, like the pub. She really ought to be writing all this down and emailing it to Kelly for interpretation.

'Actually I was thinking during the day as I'm not great at sizing up jobs in the dark with a torch.' Zac's mouth quirked in that grin again and Alice's face was pink as he raised a brow. 'But if you're suggesting…'

'Maybe pop in when I'm around and you have a minute, so we can arrange it,' she added quickly, reaching for the tone she'd used at work, and failing. 'I'll be here most days.'

'Throw in a brew and you're on.'

'Okay. I just need to buy some supplies first. Stan brought the tea.'

'You still don't have any milk?' Zac crossed one ankle over the other as he regarded her.

'I'm all out,' she said smoothly, lips twitching and aware of Stan watching on in puzzlement. It was like having two conversations at the same time, one with words and an entirely separate one with Zac's eyes, flashing now with laughter.

'Not having much luck with that, are you?'

'Come on, lad, time to leave Alice to it.' Stan gave Zac a pointed look as he made for the door. 'Some of us, namin' no names, might 'ave time to stand around all day an' some of us 'aven't. I'd better get on before anyone thinks I'm skivin' or summat.'

'I could put the bike together for you, if you want?' Zac rested a hand on the box. 'Save you buying tools if you don't have any.'

Politely made, his offer still irritated Alice. It had been quite some time since she'd had to resist assumptions that she needed someone else to fight her battles, or even build her a bloody bike. She could probably put it together quicker than him, given her experience, and was half tempted to suggest it until she remembered that she hadn't kept her dad's old tools. It had been hard, letting go of that connection to him, but she wasn't planning to restore any more cars in the future.

'Thank you but it won't be necessary.' She could order whatever she needed online if there wasn't a nearby shop.

Zac nodded and outside he casually pointed to a door at the top of a flight of stone steps across the courtyard. 'So that's me. See you, Alice.'

'Right. Bye.' She couldn't think of a single reason why she would ever set foot in his flat. They were directly opposite one another; every time he opened his curtains he'd be staring down at her studio. She wasn't sure how *that* made her feel, but the thought of him being her neighbour had her smile lingering as she closed the door.

Sighing, Alice brushed against the box before dropping on the sofa. She picked up her phone, put it down again. She needed to find the words to thank Ray and her old colleagues for the gift and soon, but right now she had no idea what they would be.

There was some admin to do, including writing the final content for her new website and ordering supplies for the wreath-making courses, but she wanted, *needed*, to be outside, and she could take care of the admin at the barn. The fire was only embers now and she put her coat on and locked up.

Tending her garden and spending every spare moment outdoors had been a necessary balm to the pace of running her own business and the anguish over her failure to have a family of her own. She'd sometimes wondered if the two went hand in hand, one success and the hours she put in exacerbating problems with the other. But there was no definitive answer and as the distance grew between her and her ex-husband, Gareth, being outside became ever more important.

When her marriage had finally collapsed, she'd been utterly crushed and her dreams of a family in the future had fled with her ex-husband. He'd stormed out, informing her that he couldn't live with her expectations and sorrows for another minute. The crash of his car door slamming and the engine roaring as he drove away had reverberated through her mind like gunshots, each separate sound brittle and sharp as they'd sliced through her heart.

Afterwards she'd done what she always had when all else seemed lost: worked, forcing herself into the yard every day, determined to hide her distress and continue as normal. Within three months of Gareth's leaving, she was running on empty.

Closer in distance – geographically and emotionally – than Alice's mum, her aunt Sandy had been a constant support. She'd asked Alice to come and stay at Halesmere and each time Alice had refused, until the day Sandy turned up in Sheffield and pretty much dragged Alice back with her. Sandy welcomed her with good food, time alone or company when she wanted it, plenty of rest and, when she was ready, a listening ear.

It was during one of those visits, as she'd wandered around Sandy's garden and taken long walks immersed in the landscape she'd already fallen in love with, that Alice had realised she didn't want to go back to Sheffield. She didn't want to leave this place and other than the business there was nothing much to keep her there now. Some friends had drifted away; others she could keep in touch with online and meet when time and opportunity for everyone allowed, which seemed to be less and less these days. Kelly was a brilliant emotional support too, but her career often took her overseas and time together was rare.

During a mindfulness session at Halesmere – which Sandy encouraged her to try on one of the weekend visits that were becoming more frequent – Alice had discovered forest bathing and her mental load had finally begun to lift. Encouraged to walk slowly, let her senses take over and 'bathe' herself in beauty and nature, she'd felt a powerful, unexpected sense of connection to the ancient wood and the strange wisdom of the age-old trees around her.

She'd stood still, alone, for the first time aware of the scent of the earth beneath her feet, leaves rustling, light twinkling as it fell through the canopy, birdsong. This time her eye drew her mind to tiny details she'd never noticed before: a perfect pinecone she'd brought home as a reminder of all she'd felt; gnarled and twisted roots anchoring the trees to the ground; the soft, springy touch of moss on bark, like a blanket beneath her fingers.

That day she'd slumped to the ground and howled, releasing all the emotions she'd kept pent up for months as she'd tried to keep going, keep working. When the tears were spent and she was still leaning against a solid trunk, she felt almost as though the wood was holding her, letting her know that the worst was over, and she'd be okay.

Alice couldn't be in the office any longer. She needed to be outdoors and realised it was essential to her well-being. She'd also never lived properly on her own and it was a leap she was going to have to make. Back in Sheffield there was some shock among the staff when she shared her plans, but there was encouragement too, and the company was in very good shape. It wasn't long before a buyer was found and the transition to new ownership underway.

Every single day now, she made time to notice a detail in nature. It might be the smell of the earth after rain, a bird calling or the feel of a breeze on her face, each enough to lift her mood and restore some energy. All of it brought calm and happiness; all reminded her that life did indeed go on and she would somehow survive this newly single one just fine.

–

Alice tugged her hood up and slid her phone into a pocket as she left the courtyard and headed down a track towards the meadow. At the gate she took a deep breath, as well as a few images for social media, trying to quell a moment of panic. Why did such a small-sounding plot on paper look so huge in real life? This acre of land was her responsibility now and it was so very different to her previous career. Signal wasn't great and she decided to upload her images to Instagram later. She didn't mind the conditions when she was wrapped up; the rain was easing and working outside was her reality now, making her feel more alive. Her days would be dominated by nature and the weather, and both would bring their own challenges.

The meadow was very different to when she'd last seen it a few weeks ago, as summer had been drawing to a close. She forced away nerves at the thought of the work ahead to make it a viable space to grow flowers. Weeds were still evident but with temperatures dropping, no more would appear for now. The meadow was surrounded by post and rail fencing, and firmly hemmed in with chicken wire, which Max had explained also ran underground in an attempt to keep rabbits out and away from the plants. He'd left a wide space for wildlife beyond the fence, letting nature take over as it chose.

Alice had upended her life for this land and its promise of healing, sweeping her old one away in the wake of her divorce. As she opened the gate, she allowed herself a merry little dream of next summer, of the days when the meadow would be bursting with bright colour, and full of beautiful flowers she would collect and share.

Walking the boundary was something she planned to do every day if she could, and she set out slowly. She needed to understand this plot, to recognise where the sun landed the longest and the water held before draining away. All would affect what she planted and where, and getting in the hundreds of spring bulbs she'd bought was top of her list of jobs, along with sowing seeds in the new polytunnel. She kept to neat paths covered in chipped bark as she strolled, not wanting to disturb the soil in these wet conditions and risk damaging its structure, already thinking of extending the herbaceous perennial planting next year.

After her walk, she spent a happy couple of hours reorganising the polytunnel and cleared a corner ready for a small table and couple of chairs, so she had somewhere cosy to retreat if – when – the weather turned really nasty. It was almost winter but there was still so much to do, and a laugh escaped into the cold and damp air. She would be okay. She was finally here and would make the life she wanted.

–

By Saturday, Alice was making good progress. Max had arranged for a delivery of manure to mulch the soil in the meadow and improve it. The bags were piled up neatly in the polytunnel, along with a wheelbarrow Stan had fetched down. She'd emptied twenty bags so far and it was smelly, dirty work. Still, she relished it, cleaning herself up in the studio as best she could and walking back to the barn each day.

Every morning, her body liked to remind her that it wasn't yet used to this type of work, and she stretched before she set out. She'd already caught up with Ana, who was a jeweller based at Halesmere and ran early morning yoga sessions in the barn, and she planned to join Ana for one next week. Alice would have loved a long, hot bath each night but there wasn't one right now as replacing the bathroom was the final job on a list the previous owners of the barn had almost completed, and work was due to start again in a few weeks. She couldn't wait and made do with hot showers for now.

She'd ordered far too many packets of sweet pea seeds, but she simply couldn't resist them, which maybe wasn't a sensible prospect for the financial future of her new business. But then her mind would catch on the image of the flowers clambering around the meadow next summer and she filled cell after cell with compost and plump seeds. They would overwinter in the polytunnel and she could plant more in spring to ensure a good supply of her favourite flowers, which smelled divine. They reminded Alice of sunshine, of the heady scents of long, hot days – a distant dream in the mist and moods of a Cumbrian autumn.

Last night, Ella and Max had joined her at the barn for dinner. Ella had just returned from a visit to her parents in Scotland before they moved to Halesmere to help with the growing family and the holiday business. Alice had known Ella was pregnant, with the baby due in less than a month, but the reality of seeing her huge bump after a few weeks' distance was a shock, which she'd done her best to conceal as she congratulated both of them again.

Ella chatted about the nursery they'd decorated for the baby and their daughter Lily's plans for another chicken to add to their flock of four the moment the baby was born. Alice made sure to be happy for them; she refused to mourn her own circumstances forever or hide away from everyone else's families because she didn't have her own.

'If I'd remembered about you being such a brilliant chef before coming to Halesmere, Ella, I would probably have booked a table at the pub and invited you both there instead,' Alice said. They were upstairs in the sitting room, cradling coffees after a dessert of Eton mess, with peppermint tea for Ella. A few lights were twinkling in homes scattered about the valley and for Alice it was a welcome change from the blare of the city.

'Oh, your risotto was gorgeous, Alice, thank you. Loved it, and it's so nice to be cooked for. Max does his best but Arlo's never impressed when it's his dad's turn in the kitchen.' Ella nudged Max with a foot and he laughed.

'Just another reason why we all love you so much,' he replied to Ella softly. 'And this one.' He reached across to cover her hand on her bump with his and Alice gulped. 'Halesmere might have gained a brilliant new manager when my mother schemed to bring you here without telling me, but I'm thankful every day that she did.'

He glanced from Ella to Alice. 'Just don't tell her I said so, although I'm sure she knows it. We're so pleased you're here, Alice. Ella and I think the Flower Shed and you will add so much to Halesmere, and Lizzie's looking forward to extending your courses to guests next year.'

'Thanks, Max, I really appreciate all the support and help you've both given me. I'm excited to see what the future holds now I've finally made the move.'

The three of them chatted about Halesmere and how best to manage Max's new design for the gardens now it was built. It was late when Ella and Max left to relieve Pearl, who was babysitting, and Alice had fallen into bed, slowly getting used to the silence of living here alone.

She'd emailed Ray and thanked him for the mountain bike he'd sent her, a very generous gift she didn't feel deserving of after selling the company. The bike in its box was still sitting, ignored, in her studio and Alice felt unsteady every time she caught sight of it, reminded of the challenge she had set herself. But it couldn't stay there forever and she'd made herself order a cycling helmet and checked which tools she needed to build the bike.

This afternoon, Kelly was arriving from Durham for an overnight stay and Alice hadn't given the dating app or her profile another thought since they'd last spoken. She'd only been on a couple of dates since her divorce, introduced to someone who was a friend of a friend, but it was clear from the start they had little in common beyond an interest in cars. They'd politely parted ways after a drink and one dinner.

Back at the barn after a morning spent sowing the last of her sweet peas, Alice just had time to grab a shower and make up the bed in the guest room before Kelly arrived, bringing her usual energy and a small case that she kept on standby for when she might be required to travel with little notice.

'Love it, Al, the pictures don't do it justice. It's so cosy.'

'Thanks, Kelly.' Alice had made indulgent hot chocolates and, after a tour of the barn, they were enjoying the view from the terrace, wrapped up against the cold, cheeks stinging from the sharp breeze. 'I wasn't sure it would be quite your thing. A bit too rural maybe.'

'It's certainly that but I can totally see why you love it, after Sheffield.' Kelly tugged her chunky scarf a little higher. 'And you're okay, on your own?'

'Fine,' Alice replied determinedly. She didn't always feel fine, especially when she woke in the middle of the night in a strange house, but she'd get there. She had to. 'Anyway, you haven't come over to listen to me blathering on again. I'm much better than I was and being here is helping. Everyone's been great.'

'I'm so pleased. And I'll listen to you any time you want, you know that.'

'I do, and thanks.' Alice shot her a grateful smile. 'But I'd much rather hear all about your hot head-hunter guy. Tell me the latest.'

'Sure you want to hear it?'

'Hey, this is me! I'm your oldest friend and if you think I begrudge you happiness because I had a rotten break-up, then I'm doing something wrong. Of course I want to hear it!'

'So things have moved on since you and I last spoke. The weekend away before that went brilliantly and the dates have been nothing short of spectacular. I'm still trying to get my head around it, to be honest. Damon's amazing and he feels the same way. In fact...' Kelly put her half empty mug of chocolate down. 'We're planning to move in together next month, after I get back from Munich.'

Alice was about to offer concern and some words of caution and swiftly changed her mind. She and Gareth had dated for five steady years before sliding into marriage. She'd thought she'd known him and could read him better than any book, but she'd got that totally wrong and didn't think she was in any position to counsel someone else about relationships. Like her, Kelly was approaching forty, so instead she got up to hug her friend tightly through their layers.

'I'm thrilled, for both of you. I can't wait to meet him. You'll have to bring him over when you're ready.'

'We'd love that.' Kelly settled back in her seat, reaching for her mug of chocolate before it went cold. 'He can't wait to meet you too. And you know me, always pragmatic with a plan B. There'll still be dating apps if we crash and burn.'

'Doesn't sound like you'll need a plan B. It's wonderful.' Alice glanced towards the sitting room. 'It's probably time to get changed and head out for dinner.'

She'd booked a table at the White Hart, the pub close to the barn. They strolled down in time for a drink before their meal, settling at the bar to wait with glasses of wine. Each of the pub's three rooms was a warming shade of red, with paintings by local artists on the walls, and Kelly was busy taking images to share on Instagram and with Damon.

'Great place, Al, totally different vibe to city bars. It's so cute and you couldn't have picked a more picture-perfect pub for my first visit to Cumbria.'

'As long as it's not your last. The food's amazing too, and I haven't stopped eating since I arrived.' Alice was checking out the pub too, and spotted Zac sitting at a table, laughing with a young blonde woman. Her pulse spiked when his gaze landed on hers and he tipped his head in acknowledgement. She smiled stiffly back, ignoring the flare of disappointment that he and the woman seemed as though they were on a date.

46

Chapter Four

'Who's that, Alice?' It hadn't taken Kelly more than a moment to pick up on the exchange. 'Is there something you're not telling me? I saw the way he was looking at you. And more to the point, how you were looking at him. What's the story?'

'There is no story,' Alice protested, still thinking about that swift, loaded glance he'd given her and trying to avoid Kelly's sharp scrutiny. 'Zac's a tree surgeon based at Halesmere and that's all I know.'

It wasn't quite everything, though. She also knew he had the most expressive eyes of any man she'd ever met, and they were as dangerous as the rest of him, from the tall frame to the intriguing leaf tattoo on his right arm. He liked to laugh, understood flirting much better than she did and confidence came naturally to him. Alice wanted to reassure herself that he wasn't as striking as she remembered, and another glimpse confirmed she'd got that all wrong as well.

'A tree surgeon?' Kelly nudged her with a foot tucked into a knee-length black boot. 'How very earthy; that's right up your street. Maybe he could be your perfect next date, if he's single, of course. I bet he'd be up for it.'

'And how can you tell that from a five-second appraisal?' Alice knocked back a hasty mouthful of Sauvignon Blanc. She probably would be better off on some singles app, with all the potential for complications and confusion, than dating Zac. Not that he would want to date her even if he was single and she wasn't about to let Kelly think the thought had even crossed her mind. Because it hadn't. It was a crazy idea.

'Experience,' Kelly said airily, giving him a grin, which Alice saw he quickly returned. 'When you've been dating as long as I have, you just know.'

'So you don't think that's a girlfriend he's with?' Alice was working hard to keep a casual note in her voice.

'Why?' Kelly raised a brow. 'Are you interested?'

'Of course not.' Alice was busy swirling the wine in her glass as though she was meant to be taking notes for a tasting. Kelly was like a bloodhound with her nose to the ground when it came to dating. She'd be on to Zac in a flash and Alice needed to knock that notion firmly on its head. 'I've literally met him twice so can you please stop making something out of nothing? Plus he's obviously younger than me.'

'So? He's early thirties at least. Are you saying you're not going to ask him to have a drink with you?' Kelly produced her phone with a flourish. 'Because if so, we should decide on your final profile and get it out there. You said after you'd moved, remember.'

Alice realised too late she'd walked right into that one and there was a tremor of panic in her voice. 'Kelly, can we please slow down; I've never done this before! I met Gareth through work and other than those two rubbish dates in the summer, he's the only person I've been out with in fifteen years. I don't know how to be around someone else who I might be attracted to. I've literally no idea how all this stuff works now.'

She wondered if that was why those two dates had been so drab. Always quieter when she was nervous, her date had roared his way through one average joke after another, trying to plug the awkward gaps in conversation. Online matches or even mutual friends' recommendations did not equate to chemistry or connection in person for Alice, and those evenings had been irrefutable proof.

'And that's precisely why you need to do this. You'll catch up quickly, I promise.' Kelly turned her phone to Alice. 'What do you think of that? Your hair's gorgeous and you look all natural, like you've just come in from a walk.'

'It'll do, I suppose.' Alice stared at the photo, reminded of Zac and his amusement over her waterproofs the other day. She'd been laughing at something Kelly had said as she'd turned in the door of the pub, her red hair spilling to her shoulders beneath a green bobble hat. It wasn't the worst image of herself she'd ever seen and if it put some potential dates off and kept Kelly happy at the same time, then all to the good.

'So you're up for it?'

'Maybe.' Alice pressed a hand to her temple. 'I know you're trying to encourage me to move on and have some fun, but so much of the past year has been about the divorce, selling the company and relocating, and I need to focus on the business. Give me a month and let's talk again, okay? Then I might be ready for Mr Right Now.'

'Fair enough. But maybe he's already sitting across from you. Even if you don't see it, you are luscious, and he keeps looking over. I love how you embrace your curves. I was born with angles, and they've never gone away.'

'That's very sweet of you, especially as my skincare routine now consists of getting it wet outdoors and then slathering on moisturiser after a shower.' Alice's gaze darted across the pub to check the truth of her friend's comment, but Zac was laughing again with the woman as she leaned towards him. 'And never forget that no one can rock killer heels like you. I'd fall over.'

'You wouldn't, not with a bit of practice. But whatever you're doing, it suits you. It's the happiest I've seen you in ages and the shadows under your eyes are gone.' Kelly leaned forward to grip Alice's hand. 'Starting the new business is obviously helping bring back your self-confidence and you've come such a long way since Gareth left the way he did, Al. A first relationship after divorce probably won't last but you can spend time with someone you like without having to make room for them in every part of your life. It's just dating, not signing up to a permanent commitment. Try not to overthink it; you're not going to fall in love with the first man you meet.'

Alice nodded; statistically, she knew Kelly was right. Gareth had been only her second serious boyfriend and they'd both made mistakes. Alice had been oblivious to them at times, pushing ahead with her dream of a family and assuming he was right there beside her. But when the end of their marriage came, it had shocked her to the core and she still sometimes felt blindsided by the betrayal.

'And what about you?' Alice took in their linked hands. It had always been this way between her and Kelly; they'd been on different paths for years. Alice coming home to Gareth every night and planning a family while Kelly rose in her chosen profession and refused to settle for second best in her personal life. For Alice, this move and the new career had been the final changes in a life that had become almost unrecognisable as her own. 'Does it really make you happy, all that dating?'

'Not always.' Kelly raised a shoulder. 'But I've had a lot of fun along the way and it's the easiest way to meet people, especially when you work long hours or travel. And I like being able to cut out some of the crap before I even get as far as a date.'

'I suppose.' Alice was still doubtful. 'But I'm not sure how I'll create a connection with someone through an app or messages. You don't really know anyone until you spend time with them in real life.'

'True. So that's why I think you should seriously consider your sexy tree surgeon, once you've established if he's single, of course. You clearly have a connection already.'

'We do not!'

'Well, we'll find out. He's coming over.'

Alice froze, aware of Zac crossing the pub and halting between them, a couple of steps back.

'Hey, Harvey. This a nice surprise.'

'Ooh, delicious, you two are on second-name terms already.' Kelly held out a hand to Zac. 'Hi, I'm Kelly, Alice's best friend and dating guru.'

'Zac. Nice to meet you, Kelly.' Zac shook her hand and then his look was back on Alice. 'You need a guru to date?'

'I don't date so the answer's no.' Alice flashed Kelly a glare that dared her to say otherwise.

'That's why I'm here, to help Alice remedy that situation.' Kelly was toying with her almost-empty glass and looking up at Zac through long lashes. Alice had to admit, Kelly was a pro. Maybe she really could learn something here.

'Oh?' Zac caught the barman's attention and Alice wondered if he was making that word sound like a question just to be polite. 'Can I get either of you another drink?'

'Won't your date mind?' Kelly asked smoothly, running her fingers through short blonde hair swept up and back from her face.

'I don't think so, seeing as we're not actually on a date.' He removed a wallet from the back pocket of his jeans and Alice noticed the tattoo again, wondering what it represented and why he'd chosen it. 'It's more of a work thing.'

'On a Saturday night?' Alice hadn't meant to sound so disbelieving.

'Some of the people I work with are friends and some-times we get together outside of work.'

'So you're single then? Asking for a friend who's not looking for anything complicated.' Kelly shifted on the stool to rest one booted foot on the floor.

Alice jerked her head up at such a blatant question, praying her interest in his response wasn't plastered all over her face.

'You can let your friend know that I'm single, but I don't usually date.' Zac's reply was for Kelly and Alice simply wasn't ready for a glimpse of apology in his eyes when they found hers, maybe even a trace of regret. She was so out of the game she was probably reading far too much into this.

'You don't date?' Kelly hadn't quite recovered from her surprise either and her voice had risen. 'Why not?'

'I like things that way.'

'Surely you're talking about relationships, not seeing people or hook-ups!'

'Kelly.' Alice placed her hand on Kelly's arm and gave Zac an apologetic look. 'Just leave it.'

'What would you like to drink?' Zac was ready to order, and he was keeping the barman waiting so they could decide.

'Our table will be ready soon and we're going to choose from the wine list.' Alice put her glass down. 'But thank you for the offer, Zac.' His name felt unfamiliar on her lips, in her mind. Sharp, quick, direct, those few letters formed a whole that suited him.

He nodded, ordering a bottle of non-alcoholic beer and a large glass of Chardonnay.

'So I've heard you're a tree surgeon, Zac. That must be interesting.' Kelly still hadn't quite given in.

'It is – I love it. Keeps me fit and I like working outside.'

'You sound like Alice.' Kelly's smile seemed to be trying to make up for her searching questions a minute ago. 'I can't wait to see her new studio; she's showing me around tomorrow.'

'Yeah, we're neighbours, for now. I'll be finished with Max's project at Christmas and then I'm moving on. Halesmere's only temporary for me.'

'Oh, that's a shame.' Kelly pursed her lips. 'Isn't it, Alice?'

'It's just work, Kelly,' she said calmly. 'It happens. You travel all the time; we barely get to see each other.'

Was that another message from Zac, letting her know there was no point in taking the mild flirting they'd shared any further? Her heart was far too bruised to be feeling any kind of disappointment at that news. Relief, then. Her sister-in-law, Jenna, was much more understanding than Kelly about Alice wanting to take her time in the search for a potential new partner.

'So you won't be coming back? Ever?' Kelly's natural default was direct.

'Maybe not for work but Max and I are mates, so sometimes, yeah.' Zac shrugged as he looked at Alice. 'So how's it going with the bike? Have you been out yet?'

'Bike? You've actually gone and got one? You never said.' Kelly's voice found another level and Alice's toes were curling under their joint scrutiny. The bike was still imprisoned in its box propped against the wall in her studio where Zac had left it.

'So you've done it, then, signed up for the triathlon?' Kelly squeezed her hand. 'That's brilliant, Al, well done.'

'Kelly...' Alice couldn't look at Zac as he reached past her to pay for his drinks.

But Kelly hadn't finished, and she carried blithely on. 'I know entering was a big decision for you, given the circumstances, and that you've not cycled for years or swum in open water.'

'So why do it, then?' Zac slid the wallet back into his pocket and picked up the two drinks. 'Or do you just like giving yourself a hard time?'

Alice was fumbling with her bag to hide her face before she revealed any more distress in front of him. She had to stop doing this every time the triathlon was mentioned and someone attempted to uncover her reason for entering the race.

'Send me the link to your page and I'll sponsor you right now. Are you still doing it for the same charity, the miscarriage one?' Kelly was back on her phone and her face turned pink as she suddenly realised what she'd said. 'Al, I'm sorry,' she whispered. Her hand was back on Alice's arm as she darted a glance at Zac.

A waitress was beckoning over Kelly's shoulder and Alice nodded faintly. 'I'll tell you later,' she said quietly. She hadn't yet created a sponsor page or made her intentions public. She hadn't even got any further than telling Ray one day at work that she'd entered a triathlon because she knew it would be tough and she wanted somehow to pay back the support she'd had. It had to be difficult, a challenge that required effort, commitment and couldn't be ticked off in five minutes. She needed her own circumstances to count for something and this was one way of helping to achieve it. 'We'd better move, before they think we've changed our minds and give the table to someone else.'

Alice was relieved to be escaping Zac and a need to explain herself. She didn't dare so much as glance at him, still waiting with the two drinks he'd bought, and risk finding sympathy or even pity for what Kelly had clumsily given away in her attempt to offer support. Those sorts of looks were part of the reason she'd wanted to start over at Halesmere, where fewer people knew her history. Sometimes she felt like an outline of her own self, as though the middle, her heart, her centre, had fled.

Kelly nodded at Zac as she walked off to claim their table. He touched his free hand to Alice's arm, delaying her, his fingers already gone as he dipped his head closer to hers. 'Are you okay? I'm sorry if I said something that upset you.'

'Of course you didn't.' Denying it was her only defence. 'Thanks again for offering to buy drinks. I hope you have a nice evening.' She stepped around him to join Kelly and pulled out a chair when she reached their table.

'I'm so sorry, Alice, truly. Me and my big mouth. I just didn't think, and I should've done.' Kelly slipped her phone into her bag without looking at it. 'Are you all right?'

'Yes.' There was no point in being anything else. Alice had cried enough tears and lain awake too many nights wondering what might have been if she hadn't lost her baby eighteen months ago. That final round of IVF had worked but still her tiny baby had slipped away just a few weeks later.

'So why you do think a man like Zac doesn't want to date? His phone would be on fire if he was online.' Kelly was studying a menu and Alice knew she was trying to move away from more awkward moments.

'How should I know? You really are asking the wrong person.' Alice was trying to read the menu too, but Zac was still in her thoughts. Her line of sight too, if she looked up and slightly left. 'The most likely answer is that he's been hurt before and doesn't want a relationship. Or maybe he's gay and didn't want to say so. Why should he have to explain himself to us?'

'Trust me, he's not gay. I saw him looking at you, remember? But you are attracted to him. You might be out of practice, but all that eyelash-batting and furtive glances tell their own story.'

Had Alice really done that? She'd definitely have to be more careful, especially when Kelly was around. 'It's not as though he's going to notice me.'

'Don't kid yourself; he already has. And he likes you too, whatever you both might be trying to tell yourselves about dating. Why else would he make a point of coming to the bar to buy you a drink and explain that he's not on a date?'

'Whether or not I'm attracted to him is irrelevant.' Having decided what to order, Alice set the menu down. 'Can you imagine how awkward it would be if I asked him to have a drink and he said no?'

'Well, he's just asked if you'd like a drink, and you said no.'

'That was totally different! That's good manners and most people do it. I've met loads of attractive people in my time and have never been tempted to ask any of them out, especially ones that are guaranteed to say no. You heard what he said about not dating as clearly as I did. He literally spelled it out!'

'You and Gareth were together far too long. Nice guy or not, until he proved he wasn't, you have to admit he was incredibly steady.' Kelly leaned closer. 'In fact, I didn't think he had it in him to have an affair the way he did. The old dog. Time you learned a few new tricks as well.'

Alice couldn't hold back a gasp of laughter. The hurt over her marriage was getting easier and more distant with every day. It was the ache of losing her baby she couldn't quite shake off in the same way. 'Maybe that's what we were missing: a bit of passion and excitement.'

'Exactly.' Kelly's grin faded as her voice lowered. 'I know you loved him, and you were happy together for most of your marriage. I just want to see you having a good time, living life a bit more freely. I had a quick look at Instagram while you were still at the bar with Zac, but I couldn't find him on social media via Halesmere. Any idea where he hangs out?'

'None.' Alice was only just getting started again with social media after avoiding it for months. Too many posts popping up from old friends or acquaintances who didn't know she and Gareth weren't still together. 'Here's a thought. Maybe he just doesn't do social media?'

Kelly looked as nonplussed as anyone had a right to these days. Her phone almost never left her hand and nearly her entire life was contained inside it. 'So what do you really have to lose if you ask Zac to have one drink? He's practically perfect for you right now. Single, gorgeous, seems nice. And moving on so you both know there's an end point. I mean, come on! How many profiles do you think you'd need to swipe through to find that?'

Alice was grateful to be saved a reply by the waitress returning to take their order, and conversation shifted to safer subjects over their meal. After they'd finished and the table had been cleared, she noticed Ana arriving with her girlfriend, Rachael. Alice waved and the two women came over to join them. A couple of extra chairs were shuffled up and introductions made as more drinks were ordered.

Sandy arrived soon after, surprising Alice, and they stood up to share a hug. She'd had supper with her aunt at the rectory a couple of nights ago, and she was happy to see her again. Like her dad, Sandy too had inherited the auburn hair he'd passed on to his children and the style Sandy preferred, short with choppy layers and turning grey as she neared her sixtieth birthday, suited her. She'd brought two baskets stuffed with baking apples from her garden, and paper bags so everyone could help themselves.

She couldn't stay too long, Sandy explained, as she was expecting a call from a friend in Australia and had only popped in to offload the apples. She settled next to Alice on the chair Ana had just vacated to chat with someone she knew at the bar. Alice felt a sharp longing for her dad; this was just the sort of jolly evening he used to love, and she hated that she couldn't ever bring him here for a cheerful pint or a hearty Sunday lunch.

During the next round, Marta and Luke, Alice's nearest neighbours, turned up with another couple who both looked fresh and glowing, and Alice introduced Kelly to everyone. Lizzie and Cal were based at Halesmere and just back from a couple of days wild camping on the fells, having vacated the courtyard flat for Zac a few weeks ago. Lizzie said, with a grin as Cal laughed, that the cottage they were renovating was so basic it was like camping indoors.

Alice explained to Kelly that Lizzie planned the events and retreats at Halesmere alongside her photography and that Cal was a blacksmith, with a workshop in the old forge. Alice had already admired his work in the gardens in the form of two stunning, life-sized hares sculpted in steel. Next Saturday they were holding their engagement party in the Hart and Alice learned it was also where they'd first met twelve years ago before they'd both moved away.

Cal looked every inch the qualified mountain leader he also was, and Luke was soon teasing him about his latest client, a reality TV star used to every comfort who was now trying his hand at living off-grid for an upcoming production. Alice connected to everyone on Instagram, chatting to Marta and Lizzie as more drinks were ordered while Kelly was talking with Rachael. Lizzie offered to take some images of the flower meadow for Alice's Instagram, and Marta invited Alice to the farm for supper next week.

Then Sandy was saying good night, ready to catch up online with her friend, and Alice moved to make way for her aunt to leave. It was her turn for drinks, so she asked the others what they'd like and made her way to the bar. She noticed Zac and the blonde woman across the pub sharing what looked like a goodbye as she found a spot and Alice turned away as he dipped his head to kiss her cheek, focussing on her order instead as the barman approached.

'I thought you might want some help with those.' A couple of minutes later, Zac had positioned himself at the bar, tilting his head to the tray starting to fill up. She liked that he hadn't attempted to crowd her, leaving a space between them.

'I'll be fine, but thanks for the thought.' She was determinedly avoiding any suggestion of eyelash action, if she had indeed even been doing that earlier. Did it come naturally, she wondered, or were you supposed to practise? She stifled a smile. One drink with this man would be like inviting a tiger to tea and expecting not to be gobbled up.

'What's so funny?'

'It was nothing, I promise. Just something Kelly said.'

'Your friend is very direct.' He glanced across to the Halesmere table, where Kelly was talking with Ana now, heads bent together.

'She is; it's just her way. I'm sorry if she was intrusive.'

'It's okay. It wasn't your fault.'

Alice had already recognised his cologne; it was the same one woven into the coat he'd given her the other day chasing sheep. Notes of lime and juniper, fresh and fragrant on his skin. Her gaze caught on a chain around his neck, a tag inscribed with numbers hanging from it.

'So I'm guessing you were the friend she was asking me if I'm single for?' Someone had moved behind Zac, and he was forced to inch closer to her.

'It was her kindly meant but far-too-early attempt to get me dating again after my divorce.' Alice made herself hold his gaze. 'But I think we're in the clear because you and I feel the same way about dating.' She was curious why he didn't date too, but she certainly wasn't about to quiz him the way Kelly had. 'Not that we would have dated anyway!'

'We wouldn't?' The lazy smile was back, and Alice couldn't fault his flirting skills. Her skin was already tingling, and her pulse was threatening to skip a beat. 'Why not, theoretically speaking, if both of us were into dating?'

'Because Halesmere is a new start for me and I'm all about keeping things simple.' Alice thanked the barman as he fetched a second tray and set a bottle of red and three glasses on it.

'I understand. I like my life that way too.' Zac was holding her again with just a look and she forced her attention back to the barman when he told her how much she owed for the drinks. She took her purse from her bag and waited for the card machine to arrive.

'If you want any help with a training plan for the bike, let me know,' he said casually. 'I ride whenever I can, and I know my way around here.'

'Why would you do that?' She placed her card on the machine to pay for the drinks, suddenly realising she hadn't offered to buy him one. Walking and yoga was the extent of her exercise and even they had taken a back seat since the divorce. It was another reason why Halesmere, with all it had to offer outdoors, had appealed to her so much. And she was definitely going to need some sort of plan for the triathlon.

'Maybe I know what it's like to need a target to keep you going,' he offered quietly, and then the wide grin was back. 'Looks like I'll have to buy my own drink, Harvey. You owe me.'

Chapter Five

On Monday morning, Alice was still in her pyjamas when a knock landed on her door just after eight. Relieved that her expected delivery of wreath-making supplies had turned up so early, she went to answer it. Now she didn't have to wait in and could head down to Halesmere for work before the rain forecast for this afternoon arrived.

She opened the front door, a *thank you* already on her lips until she saw Zac leaning against the frame. The sight had her thoughts racing back to those last few moments with him in the pub on Saturday night, his quiet offer to help her with the bike if he could.

'Morning. Brought you this.' She couldn't help but return his grin when he held out a pint of milk. 'Just in case you've run out again.'

'Actually, I already have milk. But thanks for the thought – that's very kind of you.' Her dressing gown was a grey fluffy one, covered in stars, her auburn hair scraped into a messy knot at the nape of her neck. The fresh air was cool, and she could already feel it filtering into the narrow hall. 'Are you doing special deliveries now?'

'Only for you.'

'Oh!' What did that mean? Being around Zac was like learning a whole other language, one without a dictionary at hand.

'Heads up, I'm hoping you're going to make me a cup of tea while I check out those conifers in your garden.'

'You are?' Monday was already more fun. 'It was very good of Max to ask you but it's not urgent. I'm sure you must be busy at the hotel.'

'Not so busy that I can't find time to at least have a look. From what Max said it won't be a big job and I'm here now.' Zac straightened up and shook the carton in his hand. 'It's cold out here, Harvey. What's it to be?'

'You could try wearing a coat; I don't know how you do it.' Alice wanted to shiver just looking at him, but that maybe wasn't down to the weather. She folded her arms firmly. 'How do you like your tea?' Why did that simple question suddenly sound so intimate, as though she was asking it the morning after the night before?

'Strong, no sugar thanks.' He pointed to his booted feet. 'Shall I take these off or go around the back?'

'Probably easiest to go around the back. There's a gate beside the garage; the conifers are through there.'

In the kitchen, she filled the kettle and put it on the Aga, staring at Zac's pint of milk sitting on the worktop. That carton implied planning, that he'd intended to surprise her and had gone to the community shop first, had been thinking about her. She ignored the flutter in her stomach and dropped tea bags into two mugs. She didn't have time to run into her bedroom and change, and almost everything he'd seen her in so far was hardly flattering anyway.

It was a dry, crisp morning and she'd planned time in the garden at Halesmere later to help keep it ticking over until spring, then she'd switch to planting seeds in the polytunnel when the rain came. Zac tapped on the patio door a few minutes later and she let him in. He was bending to unlace his boots and she spoke first.

'Don't worry about them; it's a hard floor and they're not dirty.'

'Are you sure?'

'Absolutely. So what's the verdict on the conifers?' Alice passed him a steaming mug and he thanked her as she retreated to the Aga, leaning against the rail to appreciate the warmth. She realised she had actually used his milk and now she didn't know whether to hand it back or put it in the fridge. Her kitchen felt different with him inside it, his presence filling the space in a way she wasn't used to.

'They need to come down. At least two of them are about to fall and they'll probably take part of the wall with them if they do. It's a day's work and I could do it on Thursday.'

'So soon?'

Zac nodded, a hand around his mug, another green T-shirt matching the one she'd first seen him in. 'Better to get on with it before the weather and the ground get any worse. I'm pretty much booked up with Max until I leave but I can fit in a day. He's good with it.'

It made sense and Alice knew it. 'How do you never seem to feel the cold?' she rushed out. 'I'm already planning to light a fire tonight and curl up beside it.' It was part of her new wintering ritual: to be outside and really feel the season before snuggling indoors again.

'Don't know. Never have, I suppose.' His free hand was on the chain around his neck, and he tucked it out of sight beneath the T-shirt. A buzzing noise started emanating from a trouser pocket on his right thigh – his phone, she assumed – but he ignored it. 'How are you settling in? Halesmere's great; I love the landscape here.'

'So do I. And fine thanks, getting there. I'm lucky to have Sandy so close.'

'She's your aunt, right?'

'Yes. It's because of her that I discovered Halesmere and met Ella and Max. They've been really good, giving me a chance here.'

'The meadow is a lot of work.' Zac finished his tea and put the empty mug in the sink. 'Max was ready to turn it back to wildflowers if he couldn't find someone to take it on. But from what I've seen of you, I think that meadow's met its match.' He slid the phone from his pocket to check it. 'I've got to head off. See you Thursday.'

'Zac?'

'What?'

'Don't you want the rest of your milk back?' Alice felt lighter as she smiled. She was doing it more every day.

'Keep it.' The grin was still there as he opened the door. 'Then hopefully you'll still have enough left for Thursday.'

–

Alice gradually settled into the beginnings of a new working routine as the week went on. She was at Halesmere early on Wednesday to join Ana and Rachael for a yoga session and loved it, promising to take part as often as she could. Stan had bustled past as Alice was leaving the barn with Ana, calling over that he'd have the kettle on if they wanted a proper brew to put right all that bending and breathing malarkey, which he was sure would be very bad for him if he ever attempted it.

Ana didn't have time to stay but Alice took him up on the offer, sitting in his comfortable workshop, full of the array of tools he used for his carpentry and chatting together like old friends. Down in the meadow later she found plenty to do, glad that the gardens were in good shape and just needed an eye and a few hours each week to keep them tidy for the winter. Spring was the season when she'd be busiest, and she would be welcoming her first guests to the Flower Shed in three weeks.

Ella was on maternity leave and Alice saw her most mornings with the children, feeding the chickens and the guinea pigs before they walked down to school with Prim, their lively English pointer. Ella's parents were moving into their cottage soon and her mum would be taking over housekeeping responsibilities for the holiday business.

Stan liked to pop his head into Alice's studio to ask if she needed anything, and he could usually be enticed in for a brew, nattering as she filled the shelves with vintage china and the array of pretty vases she'd picked up second-hand.

She'd seen Zac a couple of times, but they didn't speak again until Thursday. He arrived at the barn promptly at eight a.m., just as darkness had given over to daylight. She was already at a small desk she'd set up in a corner of the dining area off the kitchen and planned to spend the morning finalising content for her new website. Through the window she saw his van pull up and when a second man followed him out, the similarities between them were too obvious to miss.

Both tall, sporting the same short curls, although the older man's hair was grey and he didn't have Zac's breadth of chest. His grin, as Zac said something to him while he unhitched a commercial woodchipper, was unmistakeable and she was certain he must be Zac's dad. He opened the van and began unloading tools into a wheelbarrow while

Zac moved the chipper to one side of her drive. Alice was caught watching when he looked over and he raised a hand. She waved back and retreated to the kitchen to put the kettle on.

The two men were in the garden by the time she opened the patio doors and stepped outside. Zac was carefully pushing a machine that resembled an over-sized lawnmower onto a tarpaulin already spread over part of the lawn.

'Morning. Tea will be ready in a minute.' She looked at the older man with a smile. 'Unless you'd like something else?'

'No, tea will hit the spot, thanks.' He came over, holding out an arm. 'You must be Alice. I'm Neil Blake, Zac's dad. Nice to meet you.'

'Hi, Neil. It's lovely to meet you too.' Their handshake was brief. Zac approached, running a hand through his hair and messing up the curls some more.

'Morning.' His eyes narrowed and she couldn't help liking how it emphasised the playfulness in his expression.

'Hello. Wow, it must be cold – you're wearing a coat.' Alice noticed it was the same one he had lent her that first day chasing sheep.

'It's coming off; I'm already too hot.' He shrugged the coat from his shoulders and draped it over a garden chair, revealing the tattoo on his right arm. 'So you've met my dad. He arrived last night and he's staying with me for a bit. I've brought him along so he can make himself useful. Take everything he says with a very large pinch of salt.'

'Hey,' Neil protested, and she noticed the merry glint was a match for his son's. 'I was just about to let Alice know not to listen to a word you say about me.'

Zac was back on the lawn and pulling protective safety gear on, a chainsaw at his feet. 'Well, at least if you're working with me, I should get to hear the nonsense you come out with.'

'How you do like your tea, Neil?' The kettle in the kitchen behind Alice was whistling its cheerful tune.

'Plenty of milk please, no sugar.' Neil's voice was also similar to Zac's, with the same deep resonance, although his accent was a northern one.

'Have you got enough milk?' Zac's grin was evident, even behind a safety visor. His foot was on the bar of the chainsaw, keeping it steady before he removed the saw cover to start it up.

'Lots, actually,' she said smoothly. 'I seem to be receiving extra deliveries and I made sure to stock up at the shop just in case.'

'Perfect.' Their eyes held before he glanced up at clouds hovering. 'I'd better make a start; I'm not sure the forecasters have got it right.'

Neil was putting on ear defenders and Alice returned to the kitchen to make the tea. She filled a plate with some of the treats she'd picked up on her early morning dart to the shop. In the garden, Zac was already slicing branches from the conifers with smooth, efficient strokes and Neil raised a hand in thanks when he saw her place the tray down.

Alice returned to her desk, re-reading the email from her clever and technically gifted cousin Marcus, Sandy's son. He was pushing for Alice to send over the last few details for her website so he could finalise everything. She was thrilled with the concept he had produced: an elegant, simple design with a white background interspersed with pastels and pretty images of colourful flowers.

Having a live website would make it all official and she was suddenly nervous about launching the Flower Shed. She'd bumped into Lizzie at Halesmere yesterday and Lizzie had suggested holding an event to celebrate the occasion before Christmas, maybe as part of the Artisan Open Day planned for December. Alice loved the idea, and they arranged to meet for lunch to discuss it. With so much coming up, she really needed to get a move on with the website and keep her Instagram relevant.

She heard the whine of the chainsaw as she worked, and from her desk she saw Neil feeding branches into the woodchipper, which spat them out in bits at the other end. She strongly suspected that both men ran on buckets of tea, and she had the kettle back on the Aga a couple of hours later, website content finalised and emailed to Marcus. Sandy arrived soon after, bringing more baking apples and fat orange butternut squash from her garden.

'Oh, how lovely, thank you.' Alice took the bag and deposited the contents on the worktop in the kitchen. She loved having Sandy so close and able to pop round for visits instead of having to make weekend plans.

'I remembered you said you were intending to make soup for your studio guests once you've done your food hygiene certificate. I've got more squash than I know what to do with so I thought you might like some. I really must give away more plants next year.'

'So you're suggesting I use it up?' Alice was already imagining thick, spicy soup for lunch. Good, nourishing food was also going to be part of her winter routine and she loved to eat seasonally if she could. 'I bought sourdough this morning so if you've got time to stay and join me…?'

'I hoped you'd say that. You're much better in the kitchen than me.' Sandy shrugged out of her coat and went to the patio doors to look outside. 'Those two are hard at it. Is that Zac's dad? I heard he was coming for a visit; I think he's staying in the flat with Zac. It's tiny so one of them must be on the sofa.'

'Yes, Neil arrived yesterday.' Sandy's interest gave Alice an excuse to watch too, and she was surprised to see that two conifers were already gone, with Zac halfway down a third, which looked strangely bald and thin. 'They certainly don't mess around. I wasn't going to bother before spring, but Max had already asked Zac to have a look and he apparently had time to do it this week.'

'Did he now?' Sandy slid a gentle elbow into Alice's side. 'Because I know Max is flat out with the clearance at the hotel, and he wants Zac to start on the woodland at Halesmere as well before he leaves. There's some work to do in there before they can replant more trees.'

'That's nothing to do with me,' Alice protested as she edged away. The last thing she needed was anyone other than Kelly suspecting she found Zac attractive. Especially her aunt, with whom she usually shared most things and who had taken care of Alice during one of the worst times of her life. 'Zac offered to do it and I said yes. One less problem for me to sort out later on.'

She busied herself arranging the apples Sandy had brought into a bowl. 'Are we still having lunch after church on Sunday? I could return the favour and bring these back to you in a crumble if you like?'

'Yes, and yes please, that would be brilliant. There's bound to be a couple of extras, though, so do you think you can stretch it to serve eight?' Sandy shared the rectory for now with a family from Ukraine, a young woman and her two children, both at the primary school next door to the church.

'Sure can.' Alice was thinking over baking ingredients in her cupboard. She'd been buying everything she could at the community shop and had topped up online; she just needed some oats and demerara sugar for the crumble. She bet the shop would have both; she'd nip down and check later.

'Can I help?' Sandy turned back to the kitchen as Alice quickly diced the squash and put it in the top oven to roast. She loved cooking but it still felt strange, preparing a meal in this kitchen that didn't yet feel like home. Everything was unfamiliar, from the cupboard where her new wine glasses lived to the pans hanging above the Aga instead of sitting in a drawer.

'Could you make some more tea and take it outside please? I'm sure they'll be ready for another, and I'll be getting a bad reputation as a host if I don't keep the drinks coming.'

Alice sliced onions, garlic and chilli and slid them into a pan, filling the kitchen with a gorgeous aroma as they softened. Sandy was taking her time in the garden and Alice saw her chatting to Neil, who'd stopped stacking branches on his wheelbarrow and was nodding at some-thing she was saying. Alice turned away to stir the contents of the pan and Sandy was back a few minutes later.

'What a nice man; we had a lovely chat,' Sandy exclaimed as she closed the patio doors against the chill. 'Turns out he loves walking too and he's planning to do Grey Friar and Dow Crag while he's here.' She picked up her mug of tea and tried it, pulling a face. 'Cold. I'll stick it in the microwave – no point wasting it.'

'Maybe you should go with him, Sandy. Neil might appreciate a bit of local knowledge and some company.'

The microwave pinged and Sandy carefully removed the mug. 'Well, he's already suggested it and I said I would.'

'How brilliant!'

Her aunt was a lively and attractive woman who'd had her share of dates down the years. She refused to settle for companionship just yet, especially with five parishes to look after. She'd always said to Alice if she met someone they'd have to be understanding, patient and kind as she simply didn't have time to be a glorified housekeeper for a person incapable of looking after themselves.

'When are you going?'

'We thought Saturday. Maybe I'll see if Neil would like a drink in the pub afterwards.'

'Why not? You'll have fun.' It sounded so easy to Alice, and she wondered why she seemed to be creating her own complications when it came to dating. Was it just as straightforward as saying *Hey, we both like walking, let's do it together one day*? It didn't quite feel that way for her.

'As long as he doesn't mind the company of a rector pushing sixty with a *Strictly* addiction and a passion for pottery.' Sandy was leaning against the sink as she sipped her tea.

'I doubt he'd have suggested you go walking together if he did. Just enjoy it; he seems very nice. And go for that drink.'

'What about you?'

Alice was pouring boiling water over a stock cube in a jug. 'What about me?' She had an uncomfortable feeling she knew what was coming. Sandy was very perceptive and shrewd, especially when it came to people. Alice lifted the tray of squash from the oven and slid it into the pan.

She added the stock, stirring everything together before putting the pan in the simmering oven and removing a pot of crème fraîche from the fridge.

'I saw the way you and Zac were looking at each other the other night, in the pub.'

'I wasn't looking at him in any way and he definitely wasn't looking at me either,' Alice protested. She yanked the plastic lid from the pot and a blob of crème fraîche shot onto the workshop. Sandy tossed her a cloth from the sink and Alice caught it.

'This is me, remember? Don't forget I've known you all your life and you're incapable of telling tales. What are you going to do about it?'

'What am I going to do about what, exactly! Sandy, are you seriously trying to set me up with a man who is younger than me and leaving Halesmere at Christmas?'

'No, I'm just suggesting you have some fun for a change. Zac's good company, the life and soul of everything I've ever seen him at. Not that I don't believe there's more to him than he lets on. There's a story some-where, one I don't think he wants to share.'

'You sound like Kelly now.' Alice ignored that last bit; she had enough emotional history of her own and she didn't want to barge right into someone else's as well.

'We'd both like to see you happy again, although I'm not for one minute suggesting dating is the key to that. Happiness and contentment are something I think you need to find for yourself.'

'Agreed.' She was determined to get her aunt off the subject of dating with one final comment. 'And when, *if*, I ever start dating again it'll probably have to be online like everyone else. Not with someone I know vaguely and am likely to keep bumping into.'

'I'm not sure online dating would suit you. All that swiping and delving through the dross in search of a pearl.'

Alice laughed as she chucked the cloth back into the sink. 'Knowing me, I'd probably land a clam, not an oyster.'

Sandy roared, before continuing more gently. 'You're so like your dad, Alice. Kind, like he was, trying to see the best in everyone. He always stepped in when somebody needed him and you're the same. That's why you had such great people working in the business; they knew it was a two-way street and you'd both support them if you could.'

Alice was about to refute it, saying she'd done nothing more than anyone else might have but her dad had been special, and she'd made sure to continue his legacy of looking after his staff like they were family. They'd both gone to more weddings, christenings, funerals and parties than they could count. With each year that passed, she'd felt more acutely aware of time slipping away, her own family life standing still as others around her expanded.

She'd often sent a driver home to sort out a family concern or a poorly child and taken their place behind the wheel to get a lorry and its load to where it needed to be. Those long hours driving were always a reset after days behind a desk with a laptop, and she missed them.

'Alice?' Sandy's fingers were light on her shoulder. 'Please don't doubt your intuition. What happened with Gareth was extraordinary and no one saw it coming, least of all those of us who thought they knew him. I know how difficult the IVF treatment was for you both, but he didn't give you any reason to suspect you weren't on the same page.'

Chapter Six

Alice's mind leaped back twelve months to the overnight stay she and Gareth had planned. They were due to meet friends at a hotel in Derbyshire and at the last minute he'd cried off, pleading a virus that had been plaguing him for a day or two. She wasn't sure she wanted to go on her own but he persuaded her, saying he was going to lie low and there was no point in wasting two places instead of just one.

But the evening turned out less than ideal, with their friends leaving in a taxi straight after dinner to attend to their poorly child at home. So instead of staying over, Alice decided to drive back as well, feeling guilty about the room they'd booked. She hadn't drunk more than a glass of wine and she was home in an hour. The house was dark, and she crept in, unwilling to wake Gareth sleeping off his illness.

He was in bed, and he wasn't alone. A woman she knew as a business acquaintance of his was with him. On Alice's side of the bed. The side that held the paperback she'd forgotten to pack and the antihistamines she sometimes needed in spring and early summer. The shock was staggering.

She remembered stumbling backwards onto the landing as the door crashed against the wall, startling Gareth, who'd leaped up and grabbed some clothes. He'd shot across the room, trying to waylay her. She was already downstairs and desperately searching for the car keys she'd only just put down. In the row that raged through the house and onto the drive before he left, she knew only one thing. Her marriage was over; she would never trust or love him again.

–

Alice jumped as Sandy squeezed her shoulder, jolting her back to now. This different kitchen; the barn; her new life at Halesmere.

'Alice? How are you finding it here, on your own?' Ever the practical one, Sandy understood her well. 'I know it's not been very long.'

'Yeah.' Alice smiled, pushing away thoughts of that night. Those memories had no place here. 'Getting there, slowly. Do you remember what you said when I first came to stay, about how the little things came sometimes make the biggest difference? Working outdoors helps, cosying up beside the fire after a meal at night. Planting, feeling the wind on my face, the sun, even the rain. It reminds me that I'm alive, moving on. Being without company in the house is strange but I think in some ways I lived inside my own head for a long time.' She was staring through the window without really seeing the view this time. 'I'm not sure how often I really let Gareth in. I was so fixated on having a family and keeping the business going. Looking back, it feels like I was dragging myself along because I thought if I fell, I might not get up again.'

Sandy was alongside her and she tightened an arm across Alice's shoulders. 'I'm so proud of you,' she said softly. 'It takes courage, to do what you've done.'

'Doesn't feel that way.' She sniffed, reaching for kitchen roll. 'Dad would…'

'Your dad would tell you to do what makes you happy, not look back and doubt yourself every day. He was the most decisive person I've ever known and if he was here, he'd be saying, "Get that meadow planted, Alice my girl, and don't forget to smell the roses." He thought the world of you.'

Alice's laugh was quick; she knew Sandy was right. 'I wish he was here.' She was used to him not being around, in a way, but there were still things she wanted to tell him, things she wished she could share.

'I know. We all do. And we only miss him because we love him.' Sandy's arm slid away. 'It looks like the workers are stopping to eat. I take it you're going to offer them lunch as well?'

'You did bring plenty of squash so that's my excuse.' Alice exchanged a smile with Sandy before her aunt opened the door to Neil's knock.

'Any chance of a cuppa please? We're going to eat in the van.'

'Would you like to join us instead?' Sandy caught her eye and Alice wondered if she'd imagined the wink. 'Alice has made some gorgeous soup and there's plenty.'

'Are you sure?' Neil's eyes lit up. 'That's a big improvement on the butties Zac knocked up for us earlier. Thanks very much, I'll give him a shout.'

Sandy set the table as Alice blitzed the soup until it was smooth and creamy, and stirred the crème fraîche through it. She put four bowls to warm in the bottom oven and carved thick slices of sourdough, carrying them to the table with the salted farmhouse butter she'd also bought this morning at the community shop. She'd have to watch it; all these goodies she never normally ate were far too tempting and close at hand.

Back in the kitchen, she saw Zac securing the chainsaw before removing his ear defenders and the helmet and visor covering his face. His black and orange protective clothing was splattered with sawdust, and he brushed most of it away. On the patio, he took off his gloves and ran a hand through unruly hair before lifting his T-shirt to wipe his face. Alice wasn't expecting the flutter in her stomach as she wrenched her gaze away before he caught her staring.

She ladled soup into bowls as Sandy opened the door and pointed out the utility room. Both men disappeared to wash their hands and Sandy helped Alice carry the bowls to the table. Zac was finished first, and Alice almost bumped into him on her way back to the kitchen. Her gaze snagged on the T-shirt damp with sweat, a trace of sawdust clinging to his short beard.

'What?' His smile was wry, and she wondered if he was looking puzzled on purpose. 'Have I got something on my face again?'

'Your cheek.' She swallowed. 'It's just some dust.'

'Where?'

'There, above your chin.' She pointed, hoping she was being helpful. But her skin didn't usually tingle this way when she was being helpful.

He raised a hand to swipe at it and she shook her head. 'You do it, then.'

'Really?'

He nodded. Pulse clattering, Alice touched his face and a swift kick of desire landed straight in her stomach. She brushed the dust away, trying hard not to sweep away with it her pretence that this wasn't one of the most sensual experiences of her life. Kelly had been right; she did need to learn a few new things. Alice was aware of the heat of his skin against her palm, light on his jaw, their eyes fastened together. She flinched as the door behind him sprang open, and Neil emerged as her hand fell away.

'Where do you want us, Alice?' he asked cheerfully.

'At the table – it's all ready. I'll bring some water.'

'Cheers.' Neil turned to the dining area but Zac hadn't moved.

'Thanks.' His fingers against hers were so light she thought it must have been an accident.

Chairs were being scraped across the stone floor and Sandy was back to carry the second pair of glasses to the table with Alice. She was still flushed after those few moments with Zac. Did he know, could he tell, how she felt? Almost certainly – she was sure he would have so much more experience at this sort of thing than she did.

A wave of love for Sandy, chatting easily, made Alice smile. Thank goodness for her aunt; she really didn't know where she'd be right now without her, Kelly and her sister-in-law, Jenna, who was in daily touch with cherry messages and whatever long-distance support she could offer.

'We never usually get fed like this at work. Sometimes we're lucky if we even get a drink, never mind homemade soup.' Neil had settled opposite Sandy, leaving Alice facing Zac. She didn't know whether to hold his gaze as though nothing had happened or ignore it. The careful boundaries she'd built since her divorce seemed to be diminishing more every day since she'd arrived.

'Neil was just saying he's only been working with Zac since he retired in the summer, Alice.' Sandy was offering the sourdough around; everyone helped themselves to a thick slice and Neil was first to delve into the butter after Sandy refused.

'Oh?' Alice glanced at him. 'What did you do before?'

'CID, for my sins.' Neil rolled his eyes, sourdough halfway to his mouth. 'When I wasn't looking after Zac and his sister, Hayley. I was a single parent,' he clarified. 'Hayley's my eldest. She lives in Chester with her partner and their two little ones; they're both in the fire service. I love having grandchildren – they're the light of my life. You get to do all the best bits of parenting again without all the sleepless nights and the madness. I'm lucky because Hayley isn't far from me. Do you have children, Sandy?'

'Just the one. Marcus, he's a web designer. No grand-children, though; he and his partner have moved to Paris and they're in no rush. Have you decided which day you're going to do Dow Crag?' Sandy caught Alice's eye as she changed the subject away from children.

'I was thinking next week. Have you done it before?'

'Yes, a few times. The views down to the coast are exceptional from the summit on a good day.'

'So you wouldn't mind doing it again?' Neil seemed hopeful and Alice shared a brief smile with Zac. Something was definitely afoot between their two relatives.

'Oh, definitely not. There's always something new to see.'

'Maybe if you're free we could tackle it together? Long as Zac doesn't need me for a job?'

'Dad, you're meant to be here for a break! You know how much I appreciate the time you put in but you're free to come and go as you please.'

'Are you sure?'

'Certain. Go hike.' Zac nudged Neil's shoulder with his and his dad laughed.

'Marvellous.' Neil glanced at Sandy again. 'Is there a day that works best for you, Sandy?'

'Wednesday? Monday is my regular day off, but I've swapped it around this week. Perhaps I could show you my pottery studio as well before you leave?'

'I'd really like that.' Neil looked a bit like Christmas had come early. 'Maybe I could have a go; I'm making time for new hobbies since I retired. That working malarkey's hard going.'

'Definitely you should have a try. I'm usually in the studio in the afternoons when I can get away. If my light is on, pop over.'

'I will, thanks very much.'

'I was thinking how you and I have had similar careers, Neil,' Sandy remarked. 'I was a prison officer for twenty-five years before I retrained for the ministry.'

'A prison officer to the church? That's quite the switch.' Neil paused eating and Sandy laughed.

'Unexpected but here I am, and I love it.'

'So how long have you been at Halesmere?'

'Two years next March. It's my first parish after curacy in the Scottish Borders and I always knew I wanted a rural one. I love being outdoors, gardening or walking.' She gave Alice a loving look. 'Gardening's something Alice and I share a passion for, but she's far more gifted and creative than me. I'm very grateful to have her living so close now.'

'Zac tells me you moved here from Sheffield, Alice?' Neil clearly loved making conversation and she nodded, after giving Sandy a smile for the compliment she really wasn't sure she deserved.

'Yes, I ran a haulage company with my dad but after he passed, eventually I was ready for a change. Max has been kind enough to offer me the flower meadow at Halesmere and let me loose in their gardens.'

'I'm sorry for your loss.'

Alice caught the glimpse of understanding in Neil's eyes; everyone knew what loss felt like. 'Thank you. It was very sudden but somehow you do get used to it.' She noticed Zac's bowl was empty. 'Would you like more, Zac? There's plenty left.'

'Please, it's so good. But I'll get it; you haven't finished yet.' Zac shoved his chair back. 'If you don't mind me helping myself?'

'No, go ahead. It's in the Aga – the oven gloves should be there somewhere.'

'Anyone else?' Zac looked from Sandy to his dad, and they thanked him and refused.

'Haulage must have been very interesting, Alice?' Neil was buttering another slice of sourdough.

'It was; I loved it.' She ignored the wistful note in her voice. 'My dad started the company years ago and I joined him straight after college, when I was eighteen.'

'Alice is an expert driver too,' Sandy said loyally. 'Drove lorries all over the country for years.'

'Is that right?' Neil gave her a grin. 'You and Zac should get together, swap a few stories. He loves his cars.' Zac returned with another bowl of soup and gave his dad a quizzical look. 'I was just saying to Alice about you and your cars, Zac. You should take Alice out.'

'In my van?' He flashed her a smile and she wondered about the engagement party at the pub tomorrow night and whether he would be there. She hoped he would. 'I don't think that would be very interesting for you.'

'Maybe I should take you out in my car instead.' She'd barely driven since she'd moved; her car was tucked up in the garage out of the worst of the weather. She definitely needed something more practical, though, a vehicle that would cope with her new job and the coming winter conditions.

'Yeah? What do you drive?'

'A Porsche Boxster.' She was thinking of her dad's excitement when he'd found it for her, the work he'd done himself. Happy memories didn't fade; they just meant even more now she couldn't add to them. 'An original 986. It's not the quickest but I love it.'

'Nice. I'd love to see it.' The smile Zac had given Alice quickly disappeared. 'Dad, we need to get back to work in a minute. There's definitely rain on the way, and I'd like to be done before then.'

'Time for a cup of tea before you go?' Sandy asked.

'We'd better take it outside, thanks.' Zac's second helping of soup was almost gone as well.

He collected the bowl when he left the table to pull his boots back on. Neil followed more slowly and they both thanked Alice again for the meal. Sandy helped her clear up and then she left for Halesmere to remove pots from the kiln, with a reminder about lunch after church on Sunday and the crumble Alice had promised to make.

Alice made more tea for Zac and Neil, then took hers up to the sitting room. She still hadn't unpacked the books she'd brought from her old home, and it was hard to ignore a little sadness as she emptied boxes. Some books from her childhood, some of her dad's old car manuals she simply couldn't part with, not to mention favourite novels that seemed to land her straight back at the moment in her past when she'd read them.

By mid-afternoon the sky was darkening, and she was at the breakfast bar, flipping through a seed catalogue, thinking happily of spring and all the gorgeous new plants she'd be growing. Zac knocked on the patio doors, his safety gear gone, and she went to open it.

'We're done; Dad's just loading the van. Do you want to have a look?'

'Please.' Unlike Zac, Alice needed a coat. She grabbed one from the utility room and stuffed her feet into wellies to follow him into the garden. 'Oh, wow!'

The view Zac had opened up by removing the conifers was stunning. The valley stretched before her, dotted with ancient farms and stone cottages among clumps of browning bracken and green meadows. The pair of fell ponies in the field next door had wandered over and she couldn't resist stepping through the uneven border to stroke one across the wall.

'This looks so much better, thank you. I can't wait to plant a new hedge and make sure the birds have somewhere to roost and nest again.'

'You're very welcome. The view is pretty amazing.' He pointed to the hollowed-out ground where the conifers had been, scattered with sawdust and bits of timber. 'So the stumps are gone as well. The roots are quite shallow, and I've got out as much as I can, but some of them are just too thin for me to grind.'

'That's okay, I can work on the rest before I put the hedge in.' The pony raised its head to nudge her shoulder and she pulled a face as it deposited a blob of green slime on her coat.

'Are you planning to plant the hedge now or wait until spring?' Zac had joined her and was rubbing the other pony's neck beneath its thick dark mane, and it curled a hairy top lip in pleasure. Neil was behind them, tidying away the tarpaulin and the last of the tools on the lawn. 'I can recommend a nursery if you want; it's the same one Max uses and they have plenty of bare root stock right now.'

'Thanks, Zac, he's already mentioned it. Visiting the nursery is another job on my list; I'm going to need more perennials for the meadow, but I'll buy most of them in the spring. I hope I can plant this hedge soon – I'll keep an eye on the weather. Thank you for sorting out the conifers; I appreciate you taking care of it so promptly.'

'That wasn't what you said when I came round on Monday.' His familiar grin was back, and the splash of rain was cool on her face. 'You tried to put me off and said it didn't need doing yet.'

'I didn't want to keep you from more important work. I know the hotel is a big project and it's going to take months to complete.'

'Yeah, it's reopening in May and there's a lot to do before then.' Zac's phone was in his hand. 'Can I take your contact details, so I can email you my invoice.'

'Absolutely.' Alice reeled off her email and she included her number for good measure. Now she was completely contactable to Zac, and she watched him adding her details on his phone. She stifled a smile; Kelly would be proud of her, and she hadn't even had to swipe right to get this far. 'I'll pay your invoice as soon as you send it.'

'There's no rush. I don't think you're going anywhere, and I know where to find you.'

'You're right, I'm not going anywhere.' That felt wonderful as she took another moment to enjoy her new surroundings. Both ponies were bored now and wandered off. Alice stepped out of the border, back onto the lawn, stamping her feet to remove some of the mud before she trailed it into the house, with Zac following.

'Zac? Sorry. Can I have your keys? I'll shift the van and hitch up the chipper.'

'Thanks.' Zac found his keys and tossed them to Neil, who disappeared from the garden. 'Thanks for the lunch; that was a bonus. If there'd been homemade cake as well I'm not sure I'd have got my dad back to work.'

'Maybe next time – I'd hate to disappoint your dad twice. Who doesn't love cake?' Rain was falling steadily, so she pulled her hood up, making it harder to see Zac's face.

'Next time? Do you have more trees in need of my services?'

'Nothing came up on the survey, but it wouldn't hurt to have a look over them,' she replied casually. 'Some of the pears are very old.'

'You want me to check them out? I don't mean to presume; I know you're a qualified horticulturist.'

'On paper at least – I still have a lot to learn.' They'd reached the patio and Alice paused outside the door. 'And I'm no expert when it comes to trees.'

'I could find a couple of hours next week, if that works for you?'

She was fairly sure her trees were okay, but she nodded, just as nonchalantly as he had. 'That sounds great, thanks, if you're sure. You've got my number so maybe you could message me when you have a date in mind.'

'A date?'

She didn't need to see him to recognise the amusement in those two words, and her face flushed. 'You know what I mean. A meeting, then.'

'Right. A meeting. Doesn't sound quite so much fun, though. I probably won't bring my dad; it sounds like he's going to be busy with Sandy anyway. He used to walk with a men's group, but they disbanded after a while so I'm sure he'll love the company.'

'Sandy doesn't walk with just anyone so they must have really hit it off. And if your dad won't be here then I don't need to bother with the cake,' Alice finished, and Zac laughed.

'Luckily I don't find cake much of an incentive.'

'An incentive for what?' She really ought to have L plates when it came to navigating a newly single life with someone like Zac making plans to see her again, even if it was only in a professional capacity. He was clearly in the fast lane while she was trundling in the learners'; how would she ever catch him up?

'To come back and check out those trees.' He turned and she had to tilt her head to see his face, making her hood fall back. 'I think you might be all the incentive I need.'

He slowly raised both hands and Alice stilled, realising he was going to touch her. And more than that, she was going to let him. 'May I?' Her breath caught as she nodded, and he carefully slid her hood back up. 'No point in you getting soaked as well.'

'Thanks.' She was trying to process his words, the intimacy of those last few seconds. She might be out of practice, but she knew what desire looked like when it was mirrored in someone else's eyes. 'Do you want to come back in for more tea before you go?'

He glanced at the T-shirt sticking to his chest, the trousers darkened by rain still sliding down his face. 'Better not – I need a shower,' he said ruefully. 'And my dad's waiting.'

'Of course!' How had Alice so easily forgotten about Neil? 'Both of you would be welcome, but obviously you need to leave and…' And what? She'd very nearly said he could shower here. 'Thanks again for today.'

'You're welcome.' He paused, shoving both hands into his pockets. 'Alice?'

'What?'

'Sorry, doesn't matter. I'll find a couple of hours next week and let you know, yeah?'

'Thank you.'

Zac nodded once before heading around the side of the house and Alice went inside, dumping her wet things in the utility room. What had he been going to say? Why hadn't she simply asked him? Why did any of this with Zac matter, when she knew she'd never fall in love again? And definitely not with a man younger than her who might one day want to settle. Like Kelly had said, couldn't she just have some fun without overthinking it?

She made coffee and took it upstairs. Darkness wouldn't be long in following and the day was nearly done. It was too wet to work in the gardens now the rain had set in and even sowing in the polytunnel didn't appeal. She'd make something nice for dinner instead and have an early night.

Her phone was nearby, and she went through her notifications, landing on a message from Zac with a rush of anticipation.

> So I don't date, Harvey, and neither do you. But you owe me a drink

Alice laughed, her fingers already composing a reply. This sounded exactly like flirting, and she was going with it. She needed the practice, and sent the message before she changed her mind. She'd had enough of being sensible for once, always the decision-maker, the one in charge and keeping everything in the air. Gareth had mostly been great, but she'd done the heavy lifting in their relationship.

> It seems that I do. Did you have a date in mind for that as well?

She settled back, waiting for a reply.

> Don't you mean a meeting?

> Is that what they call it when two people get together for a drink?

> I think it can be called lots of things. ☺ Are you going to Lizzie and Cal's party tomorrow night?

> I am.

She had no idea why she added the dancing emoji as well.

> Are you?

She'd socialised so little this past year, trying to navigate old friendships that had altered now she was single again, whether they were friends of her own before Gareth, like Kelly, friends of his or ones they'd made together. Not all of them had stuck; for some she was the wrong fit, no longer half of a couple. But she'd been made so welcome by everyone at Halesmere that she was looking forward to sharing in Lizzie and Cal's celebration.

> Are you asking me to dance? Just want to be sure

> Maybe. What would you say if I was?

> I guess you'll find out tomorrow if you do. See you there. It's not a date, btw

> Cool. I was just about to say the same.

Was the emoji sticking out its tongue too much? She added it anyway, mentally giving herself a pat on the back. She was getting better at this and her fingers kept typing.

> FYI, I'd say no if you ever asked me. On a date

> So would I. I'll be at the bar, come find me

Zac finished with a laughing emoji and Alice was still smiling when she went down to make dinner. She'd had no idea that messaging someone you weren't dating could be so much fun.

Chapter Seven

Alice had spent the morning adding more mulch to the meadow, which left her with a slight ache in her back and cheeks tinted pink from the cold. Max had had the foresight to plant a tapestry hedge of different species around the boundary fence, but it was still in its infancy and couldn't do much yet to deflect wind that seemed to sneak under every layer to rattle her bones.

After lunch, chatting with some of the visitors browsing the courtyard and interested in her studio, she'd borrowed some tools from Stan and finally unpacked and built the bike. Alice had googled the make and model, and learned it was a drop-handled gravel bike that would enable her to ride over different surfaces. Its tyres were wider than a traditional road bike, and it had a sportier geometry and lower gears that would take her off-road as well.

She really liked the bit she'd read about the frame cushioning the ride and offering a little more comfort in the saddle. It didn't take her long to put the bike together, soon fastening on her new helmet and taking it for a first spin. The saddle didn't feel that cushioned when she set off and there really wasn't much wriggle room to get comfy.

She bumped into Max, Ella, Lily, Arlo and Prim out for a walk and, breathless when she stopped after riding harder than she'd meant to, Alice was cross to feel her legs wobble when she put a foot down to balance. Ella's due date was just past, but despite the imminency of birth she told Alice they'd see her later for the party. Lily merrily informed Alice that her grandmother was babysitting as she and Arlo were staying home and keeping Prim company.

Max laughed, tugging Lily close to give her a quick hug. 'My mother's just back from painting in Tuscany and the three of them can't seem to get us out of the house quick enough. They're up to something, and I can't decide if I'd rather know what they're planning or not. My mother has a worrying habit of pre-empting me with her schemes and likes to keep all of us on our toes.'

Alice had heard about Max's mother from Stan, and he'd been at pains to warn her that Noelle was a portrait artist and often on the hunt for new sitters. He'd advised Alice to make herself scarce when Noelle was around, otherwise she'd likely find herself draped half undressed or worse across a chaise longue in Noelle's studio, part of her flat in the house.

Alice had assured Stan she was looking forward to meeting Noelle, confident she could resist any advances. She said goodbye to Ella, Max and the children and got back on the bike. The return ride was even harder after the short break, and she was glad to get off again.

Thankfully there was no sign of Zac around the court-yard. She'd much prefer to see him this evening, when she was more presentable and not red-faced and sweaty after the ride. She tugged the helmet off and left the bike in her studio. Back at the barn, she would have loved a long, hot bath to recover but that was out of the question right now and she made do with a shower instead.

Afterwards she sat at the dressing table in her bedroom to get ready. A party needed a dress and Alice knew exactly which one she was going to wear for Lizzie and Cal's celebration at the White Hart. It was a dress she'd worn once before, green and floral bodycon, mid-length with three-quarter sleeves and a V neck. Elegant, the slit on one thigh added a sexier note to the overall effect. In the summer she'd worn it with white pumps; tonight she'd chosen a pair of black kitten-heeled ankle boots.

Alice had never used much make-up, so eyeshadow, liner, mascara and lipstick would have to be enough for tonight. She drew her auburn hair into an elegant knot on top of her head and left some loose strands framing her face. Checking out her reflection in a long mirror, she was pleased with the end result; her ankle boots looked good with the dress and the whole effect was stylish without looking like she'd tried too hard.

Sandy had offered to drive to the barn and meet her so they could walk down to the pub together. On the way, Alice was surprised to learn Neil had been to Sandy's ceramics studio today, and that they'd made plans to call in at the pub after hiking together tomorrow.

'Wow, Sandy.' Alice leaned into her playfully. 'You two don't waste much time. I take it you like him, then?'

'I do; he's good company and we both enjoy a laugh.'

'And?'

'And we'll see. He's attractive of course, but he might not view me in the same way, and he doesn't live here. I'm happy to be making a friend with whom I share some interests and an occasional walking buddy would be nice.'

'Then I hope your friendship makes you both happy.' Alice was delighted for her aunt, however sensibly Sandy was approaching this new connection. 'You've been divorced for ages; you deserve a lovely time with someone else.'

Inside the pub, the buzz and live music was different from the usual atmosphere. Alice quickly checked out each room in turn but other than seeing Lizzie and Cal at the bar with people she didn't know, there was no sign of Zac yet.

Sandy raised a hand to Stan and Pearl, who were waving them over to a table in the centre of the pub's three rooms, and she tucked her arm through Alice's. 'Come on, looks like they've saved us a place. My feet will thank them later.'

Ella was there too, and Stan was hovering, making sure she had enough room for her bump. She caught Alice's eye, and they shared a grin. Regular dining had been suspended for tonight, and the pub was packed. The smallest room had been taken over by a buffet and Alice recognised most of the artists from Halesmere scattered through the building. Luke, Marta and Max were also at the bar, and everyone was trying to catch Lizzie and Cal's attention so they could congratulate them. Alice offered to go and fetch drinks for her table, and she joined the throng. A few people moved away and she managed to congratulate Lizzie and Cal, raising her voice over the band playing in a corner.

Lizzie, with her long blonde hair swept up, was stunning in a blue dress and Cal was in a kilt. His dad's Sutherland tartan, he explained with a grin, pointing out a tall, craggy man further along the bar, and the resemblance was clear. Cal's reality TV star client had also just arrived and was causing a bit of a stir as he live-streamed his way to the bar, and Lizzie was laughing as Cal pulled a wry face.

Alice had checked with Sandy earlier about gifts, and she'd told her that Lizzie and Cal would like donations, if anyone wanted to make one in lieu of presents, to a charity supporting young people coming out of care. Sandy had explained the connection, that Cal had grown up partly in care in Belfast and had met Lizzie at the Hart when he'd first moved to Cumbria over ten years ago.

A heady sense of new adventure was filling Alice with anticipation, and she found it easier than she'd expected to get swept up in the joyous and lively atmosphere. She'd carried the company's load for so long and she was still getting used to the realisation it had gone. No longer did she have eighty employees to manage, clients' demands to meet and a hefty budget to balance. But awareness that she was far from alone at Halesmere brought another flare of happiness. No matter how hushed the barn was when she came home every night, she had friends here and was determined to make a success of this move. She was part of this place, and tonight she wanted to enjoy every second.

When Max set off for their table with a tray of drinks, she caught his eye.

'Sorry, Alice,' he called over the din. 'I didn't realise you were there. Next one's on us.'

'It's fine,' she shouted back. 'Another time. And I really ought to be buying you a drink to say thanks for giving me a chance with a garden.'

'No thanks required – it's a load off my mind.' Max was holding his tray aloft and he grinned as the crowd swallowed him up.

'Your turn, Harvey. I've been looking for you.' Zac's voice above her left shoulder sent a quiver racing down her back and she looked up at him without moving her head to see laughter dancing in his eyes.

'That makes two of us, because I've been looking for you,' she replied boldly. She'd re-read his messages this morning and the meaning was clear. They were flirting, and she needed only this greeting to understand he was picking up right where they'd left off last night.

'So are you going to buy me that drink?'

'I think the first one's on Lizzie and Cal.' Alice instinctively leaned closer to make sure he'd heard. It was three deep at the bar and still more people were arriving. 'But tell me what you want, and I'll pay for it now. It'll be ages before we get served again.'

'What I want?' He quirked a brow and her breath caught.

'To drink.' Her heart was hammering, and she couldn't look away.

'A bottle of that, please.' He pointed to something in a fridge behind the bar.

'Right. Don't you ever drink alcohol?' All those messages and searching her out here for one inexpensive bottle of non-alcoholic beer? Anticipation raced through her mind again.

He shrugged. 'I'm driving.'

'From Halesmere?' She hadn't been expecting that. 'I thought you'd have walked.'

'I'm supposed to be dropping a couple of people back, so, no. Not tonight.'

'Okay. So is my next drink on you?'

'Definitely. Are you planning to leave early?'

'No. I'm having too much fun to go back to an empty house on my own.'

Zac had one elbow on the bar, and when someone crashed into him from behind, he was sent staggering into Alice. She couldn't have moved out of his way even if she'd seen it coming; a woman pressed in the space to her right kept knocking her arm and muttering apologies.

Desire was a blast racing through her as his body connected with hers, firing her senses in a way she hadn't even thought possible. Alice wasn't expecting the firm press of his chest against her breasts, eyes level with his jaw, and her smile fled. She tilted her head to see his gaze lingering on her mouth and her lips parted, issuing their own invitation about what she wanted.

'Sorry.' He caught her elbow to steady her.

'It's fine.' Those two words were all she had right now, his fingers gentle through the thin material.

When had she last – *ever* – felt like this from contact so unintended and yet already significant? She'd lived with the sameness of her marriage for years, the familiar touch that had been good but nothing close to this. Zac represented everything new and daring. His hold on her was light and Alice could separate them at least a little if she chose, and so could he.

Although she was treading very unfamiliar territory, she felt completely secure. There was no danger that they might want more than the other could give. This was a game for both of them, and she no longer needed or wanted tomorrow. He was her first serious attraction, her practice lap, a chance to up her skills and learn the new rules.

The person responsible for bumping into Zac was holding up a hand in apology and Alice nodded a vague, distracted acceptance. Zac couldn't have seen or heard; he'd pinned her in place with just a look and she knew the decision over their next move was all hers. With this one accidental, exhilarating touch it seemed she had dumped her L plates and roared right into the fast lane alongside him.

'I wondered if you'd be wearing a coat. I've never seen anyone rock a waterproof hood like you.' He let go of her elbow, but it made little difference to the desire spinning in her stomach.

'Of course I'm wearing a coat.' Heat from his body was transferring to hers and she didn't know if it was that responsible for the tingle on her skin, or having him so close, and she laughed. 'Just not right now.'

'I noticed.' He dipped his mouth to her ear, skimming it with a light breath, and she held in a gasp.

'I noticed you too.' She really wasn't sure where this other Alice had come from. Had she been hiding in plain sight all these years, waiting for someone who made her feel this way to be unleashed? Tonight she was bold, unafraid, even playful. She wouldn't let herself regret anything; he would be gone in a couple of months, and she would steady herself again, better prepared for next time.

'You have the most gorgeous laugh, Harvey. It's kind of happy and sexy all at once.' Murmured words Zac dropped into her ear. 'I'd like you hear you laugh a lot more.'

'What can I get you?'

Startled, Alice's head whipped around to see a harassed-looking barman waiting impatiently. She rushed out the first drink in her mind – the bottle of beer Zac wanted – and leaned against the bar. It took a few minutes to gather everything for her table and she was shocked how quickly she'd forgotten why she was even queueing. She ordered two rounds as well, paying for the second and reminding herself to thank Lizzie and Cal later.

The band paused for a break while the buffet was served, and the sudden lack of sound was a shock after those intimate moments with Zac. Alice needed both hands just for one tray while he picked up the second, following her to the table. Everyone greeted him merrily, and Stan was soon wanting to know when it was actually Zac's turn to buy a round. Another chair was dragged into their circle, and she was seated apart from him. Still, she was able to catch his gaze drifting across, feel that quiver of anticipation whenever he was near.

A little later, she joined Sandy in the buffet queue, but she wasn't very hungry, adding some salad and a slice of quiche to her plate. Neil was behind them, and Alice moved away so he and Sandy could chat. Zac had left the table by the time she returned, and she ignored the disappointment when she saw him laughing with the blonde woman from last weekend. Alice took a deep breath. It seemed he played the same game with everyone, and she couldn't take it too seriously or let herself get burned.

Her neighbour Marta brought over a local WI member interested in the Flower Shed and Alice was delighted as she promised to email details and a link to her brand-new website, due to go live next week. She thanked Marta when the woman left, grateful for the new opportunity. Community connections would be vital for spreading the word about what she was planning, and Alice was thinking of an introductory evening in the Flower Shed, with some drinks and nibbles to welcome people.

The band, mostly made up of a group of old mates of Lizzie and Cal's, who'd got back together again for tonight, were ready to restart after the buffet. Rachael had joined them to sing lead vocals and she blew Ana a kiss as the first track began, an old party classic that got lots of people up, including, Alice noted with a grin, Sandy and Neil. Her aunt's enthusiasm for *Strictly* didn't quite match her skills on the floor but she was all about enjoying herself and encouraging those around her to do the same.

The reality TV star had brought an entourage and they were still with Lizzie and Cal at the bar. Alice noticed Zac and the blonde woman with them too, clustering together for a social media shot, everyone's phones except Zac's out to get their own take on the moment.

Sandy wasn't going to let Alice away with not dancing and the band shifted to Strip the Willow, which Alice knew only vaguely. Everyone formed a line, including Lizzie and Cal in his kilt hauled from the bar, and they were off. It was fairly steady, and Alice realised she'd remembered more than she'd thought as the dance progressed, laughing through the dizziness all the spins produced.

The band carried on with more ceilidh dances and she was loving it, especially when Pearl and Stan joined in to show off a few neat moves. Lizzie had brought two women and their partners into the line, and Sandy, opposite Neil, shouted over that they were Lizzie's bridesmaids and that she'd married one of them, Gemma, back in the summer.

When the Scottish dances were over, Alice was desperate for a drink and she excused herself to pour a glass of water at the table. All those happy chemicals she'd released couldn't stop her being breathless so she sat down, content to watch the others for a few minutes. The reality TV star was making an exit, for once not recording himself as he said goodbye to Lizzie and Cal, who both hugged him. Ella and Max offered a good night as well and left the party.

Rachael was a fantastic singer and Ana was dancing with Marta, who'd had no success in persuading Luke to join them. He was at the bar, propping it up with Will, who led Max's landscaping team, as Zac made his way over to the band. The track finished and the opening guitar chords of the next had Alice's gaze catching his in astonishment as she recognised 'Living Next Door to Alice'. He was walking towards her, lips pursed in a lazy smile, and he slowly crooked an index finger, letting her know he wanted her to join him.

'You're not serious!'

'I thought you were going to ask me to dance but you didn't, so...' He held out an arm. 'Coming?'

She could stay right where she was and pretend he hadn't requested this song for her. She could ignore their messages and the flirting, and she'd be just as she was when she'd arrived at Halesmere. Still sad sometimes, trying to view her future through a different lens as she fought her way back to happiness. She desperately didn't want her marriage to be the relationship that defined her whole life; it was enough that the end of it had altered the course of the rest of her days. So she should stand up, accept the invitation Zac was offering and just go with it. It was only a dance.

She held out her hand and his curled around it, thumb lightly brushing her palm and sending more sparks leaping in her stomach. He led her to the dance floor and gently he brought her closer, his free hand going to her back.

'Okay?'

'Yes.' More than okay – it felt amazing to be held and she was melting in his arms. Even though it was a tricky song and she'd wouldn't have chosen it for a first time, if she'd ever danced like this before she couldn't remember when. Zac's palm was flat on her back, warm through the fabric of her dress. Her own hand was on his shoulder, the cord of muscles moving beneath her fingers. The chorus was a little easier and their feet were moving in time, their bodies following, not quite touching.

'So are you going to compliment me?' His jaw, roughened from the short beard, was against her temple and a quiver darted through her.

'What?'

'Before, when I told you how much I like your laugh. Surely you can find something you like about me?'

'You're greedy,' she whispered, reaching up to place the words against his ear. She was flying down the fast lane and she hadn't hit the brakes yet.

'You have no idea,' he murmured, his lips brushing her skin in a smile. 'So what's it going to be? My dancing or my skills as a tree surgeon? Or something else?'

'Maybe I need more time to think.'

'To decide which one?'

'To find one.' She laughed, buzzing with confidence, knowing now he liked it. The hand on her back tightened and she let him drawer her closer, their bodies in sync with the music and learning about each other. 'I'll tell you later.'

Lizzie, Cal, and most of their friends were dancing too, and as Rachael sang the final line, Alice and Zac slowly separated, fingers still linked until the clapping began. The party was coming to an end and the switch into 'New York, New York' kept everyone on the floor, joining hands to make a big circle. Rachael led three cheers and well wishes for Lizzie and Cal, and those nearest to them let go so they could take their place at the centre.

At the end, Rachael offered the microphone and Cal accepted it, Lizzie at his side, arms around each other. He thanked everyone for coming and the many donations to the care charity, which had also had a great evening. He finished by saying they hoped to see everyone at the wedding and Stan shouted out that they'd better get a move on and set a date because with his workload he needed something to look forward to.

Sandy came over to say that Neil would be happy to walk them back to the barn for her car. Alice thanked her and refused as the barn was so close. They said good night, and she and Zac and strolled off together.

'I'm driving, so I could drop you?'

'Thanks, Zac, but it's only a few minutes' walk. And I might give Sandy and your dad time to get back for her car.' Alice found her coat slung on the back of a bench seat, and Zac joined her to thank Lizzie and Cal for the party.

At the door, Alice slipped her coat on, shivering as the night air met her and still warm after dancing with Zac the way they had. He was at her side, keys in hand, as she fastened the zip and wound a scarf around her neck. 'It was a lovely evening, thank you. I had a lot of fun and it's been a while.'

'So did I. Would you mind if I walked back with you?'

'Why?' Her heart bounced in surprise. Was he thinking of some kind of hook-up now, their evening not over? Did she want it to be?

'Just to make sure you get home safely.'

'Thanks, Zac, but I can almost see my gate from here.'

'Okay.' Two people behind them were trying to leave and Alice and Zac moved out of the way, stepping into the lane. 'I wasn't suggesting something else, if you were wondering.'

'Of course not.' So that was clear and maybe it wasn't quite the relief she'd thought it would be. 'Forgive me if I find it hard to keep up sometimes; this is all new for me.'

'And me.'

'What?' She spun around and her laugh was almost disbelieving. 'You're a natural flirt – you could give lessons! I'm certainly learning.'

'Alice, I don't date because…' He hesitated. 'Because it's complicated and I'm not great at sharing my life. Most of my friends know me, but there aren't many who really understand. Max and Ella are two of them.'

'Why are you telling me this?' Alice crossed her arms, as though the gesture could fend off his words as well as the chill.

'I suppose because I want you to know how much I like you but I'm not sure what to do about it.' Zac slowly shook his head. 'I did say this was new for me. But I'm leaving at Christmas and maybe you're not ready for something else either? Something that has to end.'

'And if I was?' Her breath caught as she waited, trapped between two desires. One to keep her safe, another that would carry her away to a place she'd never been before. 'I think you know I like you too.'

'Yeah.' His smile was a gleam in the dark. 'So, what do we do?'

'Maybe nothing, like you said. The flirting is fun.'

'For sure. It's just that, when I'm with you…' He stepped closer, gently taking her hands to unfold them. 'Touching you is all I can think about.'

'That isn't going to help,' she whispered. They weren't as close as they had been at the bar and still she was tingling. Why did it seem their bodies were saying the same thing and their words quite another? In tune, but not quite.

'I know.' His head was lowering with every second and she held her breath. 'I promise I don't want to hurt you.'

'It doesn't mean you won't.' Alice couldn't close her eyes; she wanted to remember every moment.

'I know that too. And it works both ways.' His mouth was against her cheek, beard skimming her jaw, desire slamming into her stomach. 'I don't want to get hurt again either.'

'I don't know if I can do this, Zac, much as right now I think I want to,' she muttered hoarsely. His hands were trembling in hers and she let them go to step back. Allowing someone else in meant being vulnerable, and she was done with feeling vulnerable ever again. 'I don't want to share my life either; it's absolutely not why I'm here. I need to start over, on my own. I need to know I'm strong enough by myself.'

'I understand. I know what that's like, Alice.' Zac raised her hand to his lips and kissed it. 'Take care. I'll see you around.'

Chapter Eight

Alice already felt flat on Saturday morning after last night. The party had been brilliant, exciting, at least until the way she and Zac had parted at the end. She didn't mind the horrid weather matching her low mood as she worked in the meadow, planting dozens of the hundreds of bulbs still left to go in the ground.

She'd only realised the significance of today's date when an email had arrived earlier and coping with the weather had helped to keep her thoughts occupied. She wanted none of them, only to focus on the work on front of her. Having ordered daffodils, snowdrops and crocuses, she needed to get them in and soon, but it wasn't really cold enough for the tulips yet. She retreated to the polytunnel when rain arrived to join the gale catching at the plastic fastened to the metal frame.

Even her waterproofs were flapping noisily as she trudged back to her studio, thinking longingly of a shower, a hot drink, the blazing fire, pyjamas and a cheering dose of *Strictly* on TV. The courtyard was deserted; everyone else clearly had more sense than to be out in this and even Arlo's sheep were huddled against a wall. Alice let herself into the Flower Shed and switched on a lamp, brightening the room and chasing away some of the darkness.

Tea was her default so she put the kettle on, hoping a hot brew would warm her up some; she seriously needed to buy more thermals. There didn't seem any point in lighting the stove; she just needed a quick blast of heat, then she would go home and let *Strictly* steal her mind away to something more heartening than her memories. Sandy had set up a group chat with Alice and her sister-in-law, Jenna, so they could message during the programme and shout out their favourite dances. A cosy night in was all Alice craved to see out this day and tomorrow she would start again. This first anniversary would be over.

Once the tea was made, she dragged off her sopping waterproofs, leaving them to dry on the back of a chair. Stan was building her a table, large enough to seat ten, to use for guests, and last night at the party he'd promised it was nearly ready. Her muddy boots came off too and she stood them on some old newspaper she kept for the stove. She ran a hand through her damp hair, needing no mirror to picture what it must look like. She'd purposely left her phone in here all day, and she'd be safe to look at it now. Evening was almost here and no one else would have remembered what this date had once meant.

Clicking on the usual daily message from Jenna, Alice was expecting a merry update about the girls or more information about their upcoming weekend in the Lakes. But instead a single red heart was flashing at her like a beacon, and the phone slid from her grasp to crash at her feet. Tears were skittering down her cheeks, and her legs suddenly felt like string. Incapable now of keeping her upright, she sank to the stone floor as though she'd been felled.

She was trembling, the heartbreak in her mind being played out through her body, all of it unequal to the love and concern behind Jenna's image. If she could see her now, Alice knew her sister-in-law would not have sent it, and she'd probably deliberated before pressing send anyway. But Jenna meant well, as ever. She was the only one who had remembered the importance of this date and voiced that memory with love. She knew what it meant to Alice, what might have been, had Alice given birth to her baby exactly one year ago today.

It was still her first thought on waking. The wondering, the anguish, and the never-ending sense of failure. Where had she gone wrong? What had she done to deserve it and why had it happened? What could, should, she have done differently? And the answers were always the same. Nothing, because no one knew. These things happen. No one could ever say why. The baby had slipped away and with it her dreams of lavishing her child with love.

Her mum probably hadn't remembered, and Alice couldn't blame her. She'd sympathised, rallied round in the days after Alice's miscarriage, and assured her there was no point in looking back. Alice had known she was right but none of that practical sense went any distance to healing her heart, and it was barely ever mentioned between them. Her body recovered fairly quickly, and she was assured she could try again when she was ready. But that time with Gareth had never come and Alice, wrapped up in mourning, hadn't noticed the fracture lines between them until it was too late.

'Alice?'

The door had opened and her appalled gaze flew up to see Zac appear around it, quickly taking in the sight of her hunched on the hard floor in near darkness. She was too shocked, too slow, to hide her dirty and tear-stained face before he saw, and she swiped at it with hands she'd forgotten to wash as she dropped her head to rest it on bent knees.

'Hey, what is it?' Cautious footsteps were nearing, and she wrapped her arms around her body, trying to ward off him as much as the hurt.

'I'm fine.' The words were a whisper, loaded with the memory of her loss and hauled out from somewhere deep inside her. She was the same woman he'd danced with last night, whose hand he'd kissed when she'd looked and behaved so very differently. Today, now, she was back to the broken one and she'd never imagined or wanted him to see her like this. 'You should go.'

'Are you hurt?'

'No.' Not in the way he'd meant.

'Is there something you need?' Zac turned a hesitant shoulder to the door. 'Should I call Sandy?'

'I just need to be alone for a while, that's all.'

'I'm not sure you should be alone, not like this. Alice, please, let me help you.'

'You can't. No one can.' She closed her eyes as he inched closer, feet quiet and sure on the hard stone, the cold rising to seep into her bones and chill her some more. She curled into herself, trying to make her body smaller still.

'You're shaking. Let me drive you home or come over to the flat and get warm. There's no heat in here.'

'Please don't touch me,' she whispered, opening her eyes to see his hand hovering between them. Her voice was hoarse, as though with her tears she'd cried away its softness, too.

'I won't touch you, I promise,' he said quietly.

Just a fingertip might be enough to shatter the ice she'd built around herself after losing the baby, and he couldn't be the one to crack it. With him she was supposed to be the other Alice, the one who was free and funny, with a laugh he found sexy. How would he ever look at her again without sympathy after witnessing her like this? Dirty, tearstained, broken by an image and dreams of what today might have been.

Her phone was still on the floor, and it hadn't yet reverted to screensaver. He must have noticed the red heart still blaring, bringing her thoughts straight back to how she might have celebrated this day at home in Sheffield if everything had been different.

Might she have baked a cake and invited friends and family over to unwrap presents with a giggling baby, safely cocooned in the love and the life she'd been ready to give it? Instead she was here, sitting on the floor in the dark with a stranger who probably pitied her just like Gareth had. What was it he'd said, that last day when he'd stormed out of their home and left her alone? That her life had become a shadow and he didn't want to live in it any longer.

She glimpsed Zac's arms rising and then his hoodie was off. He draped it across her, tucking the sleeves around her body as best he could without making contact. 'I can't see anything else dry.' He straightened and moved to the door. 'I'll be in the flat if you need me. Please don't walk home alone like this.'

The door clicked quietly shut behind him and she had nothing to add. No thanks for his kindness, the hoodie around her that smelled of him and still contained his own body heat, as though he was able to warm her even from a distance. She had to move; she couldn't stay here all night. The worst was over; the shock of Jenna's message had passed.

Alice was stiff when she clambered to her feet, staring at the phone in her hand. She'd message Jenna later, when she was back at the barn and could think more clearly. She put Zac's hoodie on and her coat over the top, switched off the light and locked up. The lane was darker than ink and she splashed through puddles, trying not to notice the other-worldly shapes and solid trees shuddering in the woodland alongside her. She hadn't got a torch and didn't want to soak her phone. When lights approached from behind, she stepped onto a soggy verge as the vehicle pulled up next to her.

Zac wound down the window and Alice opened her mouth. 'Don't even think it,' he said sharply. 'Get in. If I were Stan, you'd have said yes in the first place, not set out in the dark like bloody Wonder Woman. I've put the heated seat on.' He leaned across and the door sprang open.

She scrambled inside, feeling nothing like Wonder Woman and more like a scarecrow in her gardening clothes. 'Thank you,' she said quietly. 'I hope I don't make a mess of your van.'

'It'll cope; it's seen worse.'

'How did you know I'd gone?'

'I saw the light go out and I thought you'd do this. I was worried about you.'

'Sorry. There's no need.'

'Do you want to talk about it?' he asked, and she almost laughed until she remembered the party and how close they'd become so soon, his words before they'd parted. No, she wouldn't laugh. He had his own story, and she knew none of the details. Who was she to assume her hurt was worse than anyone else's?

They were at the barn already and the gate was closed. She had to get out to open it and there was no point in climbing back in the van for the final few yards. Her hand on the door, she went to push it.

'Can I message you later, to see if you're okay?'

'If you want to. But I will be, I am, fine.' Alice hesitated. 'It was an anniversary, that's all. A first. I didn't think anyone else had remembered and then my sister-in-law sent me a message. We're very close and she's probably the only one who really understands. But it's nearly over now and it won't hurt so much next time.' Not a birthday but she would always hold it in her heart and think of the baby with love.

'I'm sorry. I know what those can be like. Make sure you get warm; you were freezing when I found you.'

'I will.' The second she opened the door, the wind caught it, and her thanks was spun away into the air. Clutching at her hood, she tried to keep it on as she found her key and swung the gate shut. She wasn't surprised when the van's lights faded only after she'd closed the front door. She was home, and she dragged off her wet things and dumped them in the utility room. If it kept on raining like this, she'd be converting a bedroom into a drying room soon and investing in a pair of waders.

Her shower had never felt better and later, curled up on the sofa with *Strictly* and a ready meal on a tray, she found her phone. Alice thanked Jenna for her message, however much it had unbalanced her when she'd seen it. She didn't have to carry her loss alone and Jenna had helped by remembering. As Alice watched an ex-cricketer ace the most gorgeous Viennese waltz, she knew the worst was over and she would be okay.

When her phone buzzed again, she was expecting plaudits from Sandy about the dance. But it was Zac's name she saw, and she scanned his brief message.

> This is me, checking in. You okay?

Alice was about to reply until she caught sight of her feet, cosy in cashmere cream socks on the sofa. In a moment of impulse she took the image and sent it, and his next came quickly back.

> Are you sexting me, Harvey?

He'd added a pair of wide eyes emoji and another one crying with laughter, and she grinned.

> Hadn't intended to but if bed socks are your thing...

> Maybe one day you'll find out. Long as you're okay?

> Thank you, I am x

Alice added the kiss at the end as automatically as she would to anyone she usually messaged, hoping he read no more into it than she'd meant.

–

Sandy's parish church was only a mile or so from Alice and in the morning, she walked down in time for the ten thirty start of the service. Before Halesmere she'd driven almost everywhere, and she loved the extra exercise she was fitting into her days. Trees were bright shades of copper, orange and red, hedges sprinkled with scarlet berries and the cold air was sharp on her face now that the wind had fled and taken the rain with it. Not that her body wasn't making its protests known occasionally, with aching muscles and shoulders sore from lifting. But it would all get easier, and decent weather in spring would help.

The small parish church sat squarely in the centre of a generous plot bequeathed by a local landed family hundreds of years ago, the village school plonked next door, and each had a gorgeous view of the valley spread out before them. The church, its adjoining hall out of action due to a dodgy roof, was busier than Alice expected as people enjoyed a simple breakfast before the service began. She helped herself to tea and chatted with a couple of people she'd met on her previous visits to Sandy.

There had been some surprise in the family when her aunt had left her career in the prison service and retrained for the ministry. Once qualified, Sandy had considered prison chaplaincy before deciding to seek a parish role instead. Alice had always enjoyed Sandy's services, and her care for people was exactly as it had always been as she opened worship with a heartfelt welcome and a lively song led by a small band.

An hour later, as people wandered off after the service or hung back for more refreshment, Alice strolled outside. Sandy was likely to be busy for a little while yet and she could go to the rectory and get on with the lunch. Surprised, she saw Neil and Zac chatting with Pearl in the churchyard. Had they actually been in church? Alice had sat near the front and hadn't noticed them before now.

She flushed as her mind raced back to last night when Zac had discovered her chilled and huddled on the floor of her studio. Did he pity her, distraught by that first anniversary? He'd seen her at her worst, brought low by loss. But then he'd set out into the night to find her, so she didn't have to walk home alone in the dark, soaking and frozen. He'd thought to check in later and they'd made each other laugh with their messages, that image of her socks. This was all leading her down a road she'd never intended to navigate when she'd moved here, and she reflexively took a few steps back, straight into a large plant pot that tumbled over with a crash. Heads turned, including Zac's, and he grinned as she swiftly righted it.

'Doesn't matter, Alice, that shrub is on its last legs. If it's broken, you've probably done me a favour.' Sandy was at her side, and she offered a quick goodbye to another parishioner on their way past. 'How lovely that Neil came to the service; I really wasn't sure he would when I invited him. And he brought Zac with him too – I wasn't expecting that either.' Sandy linked an arm through Alice's. 'Let's go and say hello.'

Alice felt almost naked in front of Zac now, stripped bare by his gaze after he'd witnessed her distress last night. Their messages didn't feel quite so larky as she avoided his eyes and what she might find in them. Only her family and a very few close friends had ever seen her like that. But she couldn't forget his concern, too, and the hoodie he'd draped over her. He had seen so much and in the sharp autumn day that felt even more revealing than it had in her darkened studio or on her phone back at the barn.

'Neil, Zac, how wonderful to see you!' Sandy offered a hand, and they shook hers in turn. 'I'm so glad you both came.'

'It was a great service, Sandy; I really enjoyed it. And we couldn't say no to another lunch, could we?' Neil grinned at Zac, and he nodded, his gaze drifting back to Alice's.

'You don't mind if Neil and Zac join us, do you, Alice?' Sandy said blithely. 'Sorry, I forgot to mention it. We only arranged it last night, after *Strictly*. Turns out Neil likes dancing too.'

'Of course not.' There was no other reply Alice could give without arousing Sandy's suspicions. Her thoughts were on Zac again, wondering what he made of her now.

'Alice? Did you hear me? Did you bring the crumble?'

'What?' Alice blinked and more dismay for letting Sandy down this time swiftly followed. 'Sandy, I'm so sorry, I was going to do it last night when I came back from the studio. I was later than planned and forgot all about it.' She still couldn't look at Zac. 'I'll nip down to the shop and pick something up before they close.'

'I don't mind making a crumble if you have more apples, Sandy?' Neil was looking at her hopefully. 'I enjoy a bit of baking and a crumble is easy enough. Won't take me long.'

'Oh, would you? That would be marvellous, thank you! Anyone prepared to cook in my kitchen is always welcome to get stuck in.' Sandy beamed at Alice. 'Why don't you three go on ahead and I'll be along shortly? I've got a few things to do here first, and you were about to leave, anyway, Alice. And it's just the four of us; my Ukrainian family have gone to a friend from school. They'll be back around teatime.'

It was ten minutes' walk to the rectory and thankfully Neil kept the conversation going at a cheerful pace, with the odd reply or comment from Alice and Zac. She unlocked the front door and pointed to her right.

'That's the sitting room, Zac, if you'd like to make yourself comfortable. There's a cloakroom through that door for coats.'

'And the kitchen?' Neil looked as though he couldn't wait to get stuck in and Alice was expecting him to roll up his sleeves any second. 'I'd better get on with that crumble, if I won't be in your way.'

'Through the dining room, straight ahead then left.'

'Righto. Something smells delicious already.' Neil thrust his coat at Zac, who had none to hang up.

'Sandy left a chicken in the oven,' Alice said, glancing at Zac. 'Shall I take your dad's coat?'

'I can do it.' Neil had already disappeared, and Zac touched her arm before she could follow and keep herself busy. 'Are you okay?'

'I'm fine,' she told him brightly. 'There's a nice view of the garden from the conservatory.' She sounded like an estate agent now. 'Why don't you go and sit in there and I'll bring you a drink.' At least that would keep him out of the kitchen while she got on with the lunch. Neil was whistling now, and she heard water running.

'I'd rather make myself useful. Is there anything I can do?'

'Not really.' She was on her way to the kitchen after Neil. She wouldn't be surprised if he had the crumble mixed and the apples sliced by now.

'At least let me set the table?'

'Thanks. I'll show you where everything is.' Alice desperately didn't want to give away that she'd fallen asleep thinking about him and his kindness last night.

In the kitchen, she helped Neil find the ingredients he needed to make the crumble, and he set to work as she made a cheese sauce for cauliflower and left the roasted chicken to rest while Zac did the table. Sandy hadn't got quite enough apples picked for the crumble so Neil sent Zac out into the garden to fetch a few more. Alice had already recognised that Neil was one of those jolly people who didn't need any encouragement to talk, and she checked on the potatoes roasting nicely in the oven.

'It's great staying here with Zac and having some time together.' Neil was mixing flour, butter, oats and sugar to make the crumble topping. 'He was sharing with me until he moved, and he's looking for a house ready for when he starts his new job in January. It was very good of Max to offer him some work to see him through, and the flat, of course. He was a late starter, Zac. Not like his sister, Hayley – she never came back after university. And I was in no rush to pack him off. I knew he'd go eventually, when he found the right place, not that I'm sure he has yet. He thought the world of that fiancée of his and it turned out she couldn't see further than his four wheels.'

'Neil, I don't think…' Shocked, Alice didn't want to learn any of this but if Neil had heard her, he gave no sign as he carried blithely on. She lifted the cauliflower from a steamer and layered it in a dish, pouring the hot cheese sauce over the top, trying to make as much distracting noise as she could.

'How do you get over a thing like that, when your mum took off too?' Neil caught Alice's eye and his were suddenly full of anguish. 'I'll never forget him crying himself to sleep every night after she'd gone. What do you tell a little lad who just wants his mum why she's not there? Me sitting on the floor in his bedroom and both of us pretending I wasn't because he didn't want me to know he was upset. I thought he'd found what he wanted when he and Serena got engaged but she went off after someone else the minute it suited her better.'

'Right, I think I've got enough apples now.' Zac dumped a bowl on the worktop and his gaze slid from Neil to Alice and back again. 'What?'

'Nothing.' Neil dropped his eyes guiltily.

'What's he been saying about me, Alice?' Zac's face was taut, and she really didn't want to be in the middle of this.

'I was telling her about Serena, that's all,' Neil said defiantly.

'That's over, Dad.' Zac's voice was very level and Alice glimpsed the tension in a muscle flickering in his cheek. 'There's nothing else to say. And I would really prefer it if you didn't talk about me as though I was still some little kid lost.'

'But you wouldn't be in this position if it wasn't for her. Serena,' Neil replied angrily.

'Dad, please... Just leave it, okay. I'm done with it.'

Chapter Nine

Despite the tension earlier in the kitchen, it was a nice lunch and Alice was certain Sandy hadn't missed the slightly strained atmosphere between her and Zac. Neil's remarks had seemed to sit heavy on Zac and he was the most subdued Alice had ever seen him. And she wasn't much better, after last night. Zac was the first to excuse himself as he'd arranged to take Lily and Arlo out for a couple of hours. Alice left not long after and Neil decided to stay for the second coffee Sandy suggested, making plans for their hike during the week.

Back at the barn, Alice had a jolly video call with her two little nieces, who wanted to share their latest Star of the Week awards from school and insisted on trying on the brand-new swimming goggles they'd got for Center Parcs at Christmas. Alice adored them and no matter how much she might mourn her own loss, these two gorgeous girls were her touchstone to family life with youngsters. She promised faithfully to ride every wave in the pool together when they met for the holidays. She'd already bought their Christmas presents and was looking forward to sharing them on the day.

At Halesmere on Monday, Alice was back planting bulbs until it was time to meet Lizzie in her office above the forge for the lunch they'd arranged. Alice had meant to join Ana for yoga as well but had slept in. She didn't usually need to set an alarm but maybe she'd have to, if she wanted to make that regular seven a.m. start. Early mornings in the haulage business, where she'd hit the ground running every day to keep pace with all that was going on, were over.

Already she could feel her fitness increasing, even though her muscles still ached. Her sleep, disrupted since Gareth had left, was slowly improving and she put some of it down to all the hours she was spending in the fresh air. She felt connected to this place and the landscape around her, often distracted by the views of fells in the distance, brown with bracken, or the ripple of dark water in the tarn beyond the field where Arlo's sheep grazed.

Lizzie was busy planning the Artisan Open Day, set for the first Saturday in December. Over sausage rolls from the shop, she suggested to Alice that the open day would be the perfect opportunity to officially launch the Flower Shed and show off Alice's plans for the meadow and her courses next year, as the studios would already be busy with extra visitors.

Alice was very happy to agree and as they ate the muffins she'd quickly made this morning, Lizzie filled Alice in on some of her own history at Halesmere and how she and Cal had met before going their separate ways for more than decade. They'd bumped into each other in the spring when Lizzie had helped plan her best friend Gemma's wedding at Halesmere, and a brand launch involving Cal, who worked with a sustainable Cumbrian clothing company. They chatted for a while, and it didn't take Stan long to track them down when he returned from a timber-buying excursion. He joined them for tea and a muffin, promising to bring pastries to share tomorrow.

Lizzie was interested in Alice's former career and what had brought her to Halesmere. Alice explained about her passion for gardening and studying at college to gain her two qualifications. She'd started online and had soon switched to an in-person class, preferring the course content and being hands-on. Flexible working had been in place at the yard for some time, with drivers operational all hours, and she'd tried to let her staff be as adaptable as possible. She also tentatively explained that she had entered a triathlon in the summer, and Lizzie and Stan both offered encouragement. A small step but one in the right direction nevertheless, and she felt lighter for having shared it.

Stan wanted to know when Alice would give him a run out in a lorry, and she laughingly promised she would one day. But until then, he informed them cheerfully, despite what they thought, he couldn't sit around eating muffins with people who apparently had a lot less than him to do.

'Is that a hint, Stan?' Lizzie jumped up, scattering crumbs as she lobbed kitchen roll into a bin. 'Are you trying to get rid of us?'

'What makes you think that?' he questioned with a grin. 'Tell Cal I'll be round the cottage this afternoon to take a look at them doors.'

'I'll try but he's off up Haystacks with clients so there's not much chance of a message getting through now.' Stan was on his way to the door and Lizzie tugged his bobble hat as she darted past him. 'Besides, if you ever got a phone then you could tell him yourself.'

'An' what would I want with one o' them things? Not much use to me if it won't work with wood, make a decent brew or play *Test Match Special*.'

'Oh, it'll definitely play *Test Match Special*, Stan. One day you'll discover apps, I promise. I can't believe you haven't even looked at eBay. It'd be like having a giant, online workshop at your fingertips.'

'Pearl won't let me. Says it'd be dangerous unless I'm plannin' to sell stuff an' we haven't got room for any more tools. Or knittin' needles, now I come to think about it.'

Alice thanked Lizzie for lunch and her support, and said goodbye too. In the courtyard, milling around, was the film crew following Cal's reality TV star client and Max for a television series on the Lakes and the Dales, so Alice snuck back into the Flower Shed; she didn't want to pop up in the background on telly any time soon.

She only realised lunch had gone on later than planned when Arlo raced past in his school uniform, Max shouting something after him about getting changed and that the sheep could wait. Alice smiled as his words fell on deaf ears and Arlo took off through a gate. Ella appeared with Lily and Prim, who also disappeared after Arlo, and they came over to chat with Alice and check how she was settling in.

Lily was taking a keen interest in everything to do with the baby, although Arlo was more occupied with the care of his sheep. Ella and Max had decided not to discover the sex of the baby, which meant Lily was desperate for the new arrival to be born so she could find out. She also wanted to know why she wasn't entitled to sibling leave from school, like parents from work, and she was cross that half term had come and gone without any sign of the new baby. Arlo, cheeks pink with colour and muddy shoes, reappeared with Prim, and Ella gathered them up to take them home for tea.

It was dark when Alice locked up her studio later and she saw a light on in Zac's flat. Scooping up his hoodie, she crossed the courtyard and knocked at his door. Zac answered and she said hello to him and Neil, who was busy in the tiny kitchen.

'I thought you might be missing this, and I should return it.' She held out the hoodie. Such a simple gesture and one that drew them back to Zac's reason for lending it to her. 'I have washed it.'

'You weren't that dirty.' They shared a smile, and he shifted a shoulder, revealing more of the small room behind him. 'But thanks.'

'You're welcome.' The two-seater sofa was very snug, and she couldn't imagine Zac sleeping comfortably on that with those legs; he must be bent double.

'Would you like to come in?'

'No thanks, I'm on my way home for a shower.' She'd changed out of her waterproofs, and she was ready for something more presentable than her dungarees. 'Zac, I hope you don't mind my asking, but were you being serious when you offered to go cycling with me?'

Alice had thought about this on and off all day. If he'd meant it, then his proposition did make sense. He knew the landscape and where to cycle much better than she did. And it was only cycling – nothing more intimate, like a date or dinner.

'Totally serious.' His voice lowered. 'I'm no expert and I've never done a triathlon, but I know what it's like to train for something you need to do.'

'I think I could use the motivation of having someone alongside me, at least for now,' she said quietly. 'I'm not a huge fan of cycling, as you've probably guessed.'

'Is there anything about the triathlon that you actu-ally like?' His voice was teasing; his eyes told her he understood.

'I'm looking forward to trying the swimming,' she offered. She needed someone right now to push her, to make her carry on if she wanted to give up and remind her it was all worth it. He was smiling and she quickly held up a hand. 'Don't even think it,' Alice warned. 'Not before the spring. I'm not getting in a lake in November for anyone.'

'Point made. So have you got a date in mind?'

'A date?' She raised a brow.

'To go cycling, of course.'

'I can probably be more flexible with my hours than you at the moment. The weekend maybe, seeing as it's dark so early now?'

Zac was checking his phone. 'How about Wednesday afternoon? I was planning to take a look at the rest of the trees in your garden then and if I come earlier, we could take the bikes out first.'

'Are you sure you have the time?'

'I am.' He was tapping something on the screen, and she presumed it was their new plans. She liked that they were in each other's phones, linked by their messages, the banter they'd shared. She hoped there would be more.

'So, I'll see you Wednesday, then, about half one? It's a… No, it's not a date.' Alice corrected her mistake, loving that she could make him laugh. 'We don't do that, remember?'

'So what is it, then?' he asked, and she was also coming to really like how much he could say with so few words.

'A meeting.' She turned away, one hand on the railing. 'Just remember to go easy on me; I'm a novice.'

'I can't do that, Harvey,' Zac called. 'It's official, you're in training now.'

The food hygiene training was fine on Tuesday and Sandy was also one of the online participants who received a certificate at the end. Her aunt had mentioned to Alice that Ella and Max had offered the use of the barn for monthly community lunches, seeing as the church hall was out of action because of the state of the roof, and its survival wasn't guaranteed.

Other than the pub, which perfectly reasonably charged people for eating, there wasn't another suitable place for locals to gather except inside the church, which was large and expensive to heat with outdated and few facilities. The eight guests currently staying in Halesmere House on retreat were enjoying all the studios had to offer and Alice was thrilled when two of them signed up for a Valentine's Day flower-arranging course she was planning in February.

Lizzie had already suggested tying in the course to a romantic retreat package for couples in the house, and Alice loved the idea. Her new table for the Flower Shed was ready and Stan was putting it together in her studio as it was too big to manoeuvre in just one piece.

Later that evening, she caught up with Kelly online, purposefully not mentioning the planned cycle ride with Zac. Quite a lot had happened between them since Kelly's visit, and Alice didn't want to give her friend any more reason to badger her about dating him. Thankfully Kelly was too loved up with her new partner to remember that Alice had promised to review her online dating status in a month, which was creeping closer.

On a visit to town, Alice picked up a couple of books with local cycle trails and downloaded some maps, but other than that first ride after she'd built the bike, this was as far as her current cycling experience went. She was looking forward to going out with Zac, even if thoughts of the triathlon and all the training she needed to do were making her apprehensive. But as long as she could raise a decent amount of money for the charity, then every moment would be worth it. Her trepidation about the ride was tempered by the knowledge that she did actually trust him to take care of her, and she was ready when they met outside her studio on Wednesday afternoon, the bike propped against the wall.

'Hey. Time to get that thing dirty – it's far too shiny.' Zac had changed out of work clothes into all-black cycling kit, shorts over leggings with a tight-fitting T-shirt.

'Should I be worried?' Alice wheeled the bike across the cobbles, a small rucksack she'd packed over one shoulder. 'You're wearing a base layer as well as a T-shirt, which, knowing you, implies extreme weather and it does look like rain.'

'So? You won't actually melt if it does rain, I promise.' He opened the doors to his van and her bike did look decidedly different from his own mud-spattered one. 'You'll just get wet. That seems to happen a lot when you're around but even you can't ride in those waterproof trousers.'

'At least I have the sense to wear them.' She bit her lip. 'You will be gentle with me, won't you?'

'We'll take it slow, I promise.' He was the first to look away as he picked up her bike. 'Nice and light, carbon frame.'

'Does that matter? I know there's lots of different bikes, but they all need pedalling, which is the bit I'm not so keen on.'

'All the more reason to get started so you can smash that triathlon.' Zac followed her into the van once he'd loaded her bike and slammed his door. 'Yours is a gravel bike and it's a good choice, unless you're planning to ride some hard-core mountain trails.'

'Do I look like I'm crazy?' she retorted, and Zac laughed as the electric engine purred into life and he left the car park. 'A gentle pedal is all I require today. I've been on YouTube; you're not going to find me thundering downhill at thirty miles an hour on two wheels any time soon.'

'Good job I've planned some nice forest tracks that'll ease you in, then.'

'Will there be hills?' Nothing was level around here except the lakes, and she was seriously out of practice at any exercise other than walking and a bit of yoga right now.

'Alice, you're in Cumbria – take a look around you! We're not going up the side of a fell, but you can expect some climbing.'

Thirty minutes later, he pulled into a Forestry Commission car park and Alice insisted on paying as Zac unloaded the bikes. Her new helmet still felt strange as she adjusted the straps to make sure it was secure. She ignored a flare of anxiety when she noticed Zac packing a first aid kit and some biking essentials into a rucksack.

Even basic cycling technique seemed tricky when they set off, as though the simple rhythm of pedalling and keeping the handlebars steady had suddenly deserted her. They reached a courtyard with a café, which was surprisingly busy for a midweek afternoon in late autumn. They rode slowly past a grassy picnic area and onto a quiet lane beside a busy, narrow stream.

'Okay?' Zac, riding with one hand, angled his upper body to look at Alice and she envied him his ease.

'Fine,' she muttered grimly. 'How many months until August? I'm thinking maybe I should sign up for a 10k run instead? Less cycling involved.'

'Just think of how you'll feel when you cross that finish line next summer. It's the best thing. Do you want to go in front and set the pace?'

'I definitely don't.' That way she wouldn't suffer the ignominy of him having a perfect view if she did tumble to the ground. 'If I fall off, I give you full permission to carry on without me.'

'As if I'd do that. Quit moaning already and keep going.'

Alice seemed to be hitting every bump on the track as they went along, each little dip or bit of rock glancing off the bike's wheels reverberating straight through her. She pedalled carefully, and Zac eased back as the path widened to cycle alongside her.

'Don't look down – look where you're going. Try and feel the bike; you don't need to see it. It's right there, beneath you. It's not going anywhere.'

'If it is, it'll be taking me with it,' she said with a shudder as she steered around a puddle. 'You seriously do this for pleasure?'

'Just ride through the water; you can't avoid everything.'

'But I don't know how deep it is!'

'All part of the fun.'

She glared as Zac laughed, and gradually her balance improved as they carried on. Four other cyclists raced past them, and Alice put her pink face down to the steady climb and not the fact that two of them had been children, confident and capable, unafraid. The idea of hurtling downhill over some of the rough and narrow tracks they passed on the more challenging trails was enough to make her feel queasy.

At the top she was puffing in a very unattractive manner, her skin damp. 'You're absolutely mad,' she wheezed, sticking out a foot and tottering to an ungainly stop. She wouldn't mind taking her helmet off to do something with her hair, the breeze blowing loose bits across her face, but she could well imagine what state it was in if the heat on her face was anything to go by.

'Maybe but the adrenaline rush is something else. And check this out.'

Zac raised a hand to the landscape: a glorious view of shimmering copper, gold and amber as the forest eased towards winter. Bracken on the fells was turning too, and Alice recognised grazing sheep as the same Herdwicks that he'd helped her to gather that first time they'd met.

'If I had enough breath, I'd say something clever about how pretty it is.' She tugged a water bottle from her rucksack and slugged back a welcome, cold mouthful. Zac didn't even look like he'd broken sweat as he drank too, while she wiped her face on her sleeve. She was already filthy from the mud; she definitely hadn't factored in all this dirt when she'd been planning her new life. 'How much further?'

'Alice, we've done about three kilometres! If you get to the end without moaning again, I'll buy you a coffee in the café.'

'If you throw in a cake as well, you're on,' she muttered. 'I'm going to have aches in places I didn't even know I had muscles in the morning.'

'Still moaning. Do you want that coffee or not?'

'And the cake?'

'If that's what it takes to get you through, then yes, I'll buy you a cake.'

They set off again and even though her legs were still shaky, Alice found a rhythm that she started to enjoy. She tried to keep out of the way of faster riders passing them, and her balance had already improved as she navigated rough paths, rocks and standing water. They paused for another drink, and she found it easier to set off this time.

Back at the car park, she removed her helmet and scraped her damp hair into a ponytail after helping Zac load the bikes into the van.

'Would you still like that coffee?' He was leaning against the door, and she wasn't ready to end their time together yet. Did he feel the same?

'What about the cake? I swear, the thought of it is literally the only thing that kept me going. I'm going to be crawling like a crab out of bed tomorrow; my arms and legs feel like jelly.'

'I can't have you going home disappointed. Let's go.'

The café was quiet as closing time approached. Alice bagged a Bakewell slice covered in almonds and Zac went for a thick, gooey chocolate brownie to accompany their lattes. They found seats inside; the afternoon was cool, and a light drizzle was threatening to become heavy rain.

'So?' He pulled out a chair to sit opposite her. 'How's the cake?'

'Not bad. They were all out of Victoria sandwich and that's my favourite. It's a good thing this isn't a real date, or I would've marked you down for poor choice of cake.'

'Seriously?' The brownie was halfway to his mouth, one large bite already gone. 'Clearly, I need another chance to do better. You have very high standards, Alice Harvey. So if this was a real date, how would you score it so far?'

'So far?' She tilted her head. 'It's not over?'

'No. I've still got to check out those trees at the barn.'

'Oh yeah. Let's see, then.' Alice pursed her lips, pretending to think. 'I'd score this as a date at seven, maybe seven and a half.'

'Because?'

'Because it's not an eight.' She liked this new game; she was getting better at it, enjoying the smile lingering on his lips, the amusement in those deep brown eyes.

'So how do I get an eight? Better cake?'

'Maybe. That and not cycling on a date.'

'Oh, I wouldn't take you cycling. Not if we were going on a real date.'

'Oh?' Her pulse flared some more. 'What would you suggest instead?'

'I'm not telling you.' Zac shrugged. 'If I'm only a seven and a half, you're not finding out how I'd do better.'

'Then you can't improve your score.'

'Not without going on a real date.' The implication was obvious, and she held her breath. 'But we don't do that, you and me. Date people.'

She was wondering again why not, thinking of Neil telling her that Zac's fiancée had left him for someone else. 'You do everything so quickly.' She'd noticed that about him, reminded again now the brownie was gone. Eating, moving, driving: he did it all with haste.

'I can promise you I don't.' That lazy smile was back and her own was following as the teasing returned. 'So what would you have us do for a date?'

'You surely don't expect me to answer that after you refused?' Alice finished the Bakewell slice, pushing her plate away to linger over the latte. 'So I have passed the test, then? You'd come out with me on the bike again, even though I slowed you down and moaned?'

'You weren't that bad. And I'll make sure to include different cake next time.'

Chapter Ten

A family were passing their table and Alice noticed a child, an adorable little boy, toddling along with a toy dinosaur in his hand. She dropped her eyes, relieved that Zac had agreed to cycle with her again. Her own resolve to train might fade on the worst days and she was certain he'd push her when she wasn't sure yet how far she could push herself.

'If you're going to help me, Zac, then maybe you should know why I'm doing this,' she said quietly. She was aware of the family settling at a table further down and she brought her gaze back to him. 'I need to set up a fundraising page anyway to make sure entering the triathlon is worth it. You probably heard Kelly say that I'm doing it for a pregnancy charity who fund research and offer advice and support for those who need it, when things sometimes go wrong. I was one of them.'

'Alice...'

'No, it's okay, you don't have to say anything. Please just let me get it out there.' She tried to smile as she took a deep breath. 'I've been avoiding speaking about the triathlon because even though I want to do it, once people know, then my reason and therefore my own experience seems obvious. As though losing my baby is stamped on my forehead for everyone to see. But then I think of the difference more donations could make. I know mine won't be huge, but it'll be something, and I have to do it. I just can't not.'

Alice wasn't expecting his hand to cover hers on the table and she had to blink before carrying on. 'My pregnancy was a bit of an against-all-the-odds one after years of trying, until IVF worked on the final round. Last Saturday, when you found me that night, was the first anniversary of my due date and I couldn't help thinking of what might have been. Of course it doesn't mean that my circumstances are worse than anyone else's who has gone through a similar experience. But I have to do something, to acknowledge what the charity did for me and help those who'll come after me. My colleague Ray organised the bike after I mentioned the triathlon and I'm glad he did. I'm not very brave and I'd probably have kept putting it off to keep my secret safe.'

'Not brave?' Zac leaned forward, lowering his voice. 'How can you think that what you've achieved after everything you've been through isn't brave, Alice? Starting another business, creating a new home.' He swallowed. 'It's amazing, you have no idea. You're here, going to work each day, making friends, plans to support those who looked after you, caring for people. I think we could all be more Alice.'

'That's very kind.' A tear escaped to trail down her cheek. She hadn't got a tissue; their plates had been cleared and even the napkin had gone. She didn't want him to witness any more tears; there had been quite enough of those on Saturday night.

He removed his hand from hers, his fingers light under her chin to lift it gently. She held her breath as his thumb caught the tear before it landed on her lips, smoothing away her distress. She turned her face, letting him cup her cheek. She hadn't wanted anyone to hold her for months lest she shatter, and she resisted the temptation to place a kiss to his palm.

'I'm looking forward to shoving you and that bike up those hills you love so much.' There was a lightness in his tone, and Alice sensed he wasn't brushing past her confession, just easing them through it. 'I can't promise you cake every time, though.'

'Shame. This has been nice.' Better than that.

'Even though it was the wrong cake?'

'Even though it was the wrong cake.'

Staff were hovering, obviously ready to close up the café for the day. Zac slowly withdrew his hand, and they stood up, collecting the rucksacks at their feet. Even walking next to him was exhilarating. It was like having a panther at her side: unpredictable, lithe, beautiful; he was as different from her ex-husband as it was possible to be. Maybe that's why she was enjoying spending time with Zac so much.

'So can I really trust you to look after me?' It was a nonchalant, almost rhetorical question. He was the first new person she'd trusted since the end of her marriage, and a couple of weeks ago she'd have dismissed the notion as ridiculous. 'I do have a garden and a meadow to manage, and courses to run. I can't be sitting around in plaster with a broken arm.'

Alice liked how he'd teased his way through their ride, making her laugh and keeping her going when she'd rather have got off and pushed, or stopped altogether. She needed to be a whole lot fitter than this for the triathlon and summer would come soon enough. They'd reached the van and Zac unlocked it.

'You won't be. But luckily, I know the difference between a weed and a perennial so what's a few more hours' work if you need me to help out? Not sure about the courses, though; my idea of flower-arranging is ordering online and having something delivered.'

'You'd do that? For me?'

'Go online and order you flowers?' He grinned as he got in the van and she followed, grateful for the heat inside. 'Of course I wouldn't. I was talking about the meadow.'

'Zac?'

'What?'

'Thank you.'

'You're welcome.'

On the way back, Alice asked if he would drop her at the barn instead of Halesmere. 'I'm going to keep the bike at home and cycle to work instead of walking. Every bit helps, right?'

'Definitely. And that's fine.'

When they arrived, she opened the gate so Zac could park on the drive. He got out of the van and slid the door open to unload her bike.

'Would you like to stay for dinner, to say thank you for today?' she asked casually. It was a crazy thought that had been running through her mind for the last twenty minutes and she threw it out there before she decided she didn't dare. She took her bike from him and the sight of it all dirty made her proud. She'd started training; she was on her way to the triathlon. 'It won't be amazing, just pasta or something I can make quickly. Don't worry if you can't; it was only an idea.'

'No, I'd love to.' Zac glanced down at his muddy kit. 'I could probably use a shower, though.'

'That's okay. You can have one here if you like.' Alice hadn't really thought this through. She would also need to shower and change, and the picture in her mind of him doing that in the barn was a total distraction from wondering about what food she had in her fridge.

'Are you sure?' His eyes narrowed as they found hers.

'Of course.' She paused, still stuck on thoughts of him undressing in her house, getting wet under the shower. 'I can lend you a towel but not much else. Even my sloppiest T-shirts would be too tight for you.'

Oh, that sounded wrong! Like she was expecting him to sit around in his underwear or something, while she merrily cooked them a meal. 'I just meant that I haven't got…'

'It's okay, I keep a bag in the van for after the gym or taking the bike out.'

'That's great.' Alice found keys in her rucksack, and Zac locked the van and followed her inside. The barn was snug, the underfloor heating cosy beneath her feet when she took her trainers off in the utility room, aware of him doing the same. As she switched on lamps and drew the curtains against the day becoming dark, she couldn't help but note how the house felt more of a home.

'What about your dad? Won't he be expecting you to eat with him?'

'No, he said he was sorted. I think he's arranged something with Sandy.' Zac was leaning against the breakfast bar, a sports bag at his feet.

'Again? That's, what, the third time now?'

'Must be, and they're going to the pub as well. Do you think there's something we should know?'

'No. It's just lovely that they're enjoying themselves together.'

'Agreed. He seems in no rush to go home.'

'Does that mean you're still on the sofa?' She was picturing Zac hunched on it in that tiny flat, legs dangling over the end.

'It's fine, I've slept in far worse places.' He picked up the bag, glancing at the doors leading from the kitchen. 'So where do you want me to take that shower?'

'There's an en-suite in my bedroom,' Alice said calmly. She could, should, show Zac to the guest room instead, right behind him. 'It's just through here.'

She wasn't quite used to the layout of this upside-down house yet and a few seconds later she opened her door. Switching on a lamp, the soft light illuminated the patchwork quilt on her bed. She still slept on the left side, her book on mindfulness in nature sitting beside it. For months after she and Gareth had separated, she would wake and reach out, finding an unfamiliar, cool space on the other side. Opening the bathroom door, she chattered blithely about shower gel and hot water, that there was no rush and Zac should help himself to towels and anything else he needed.

'Wouldn't you prefer to go first?'

'What?' She turned, almost bumping into him right behind her, and they both apologised. 'No, it's fine, you go ahead. I'll have a think about dinner.'

She closed her bedroom door, leaving him on the other side, and returned to the kitchen, gathering glasses for drinks and unloading the dishwasher. She found her phone to put on a playlist – something cheerful, nothing too intimate or heavy with other meaning.

But Alice had a feeling she'd blown that notion out of the water the moment she'd shown him into her bedroom when she hadn't needed to. So much for not dating Zac;

right now she'd skip that stage altogether and jump in the shower with him. The thought made her splutter and she gave herself a very stern telling-off at the fridge door.

'Do you always talk to yourself?'

She whirled around, the atmosphere altering the moment her gaze met his. Zac's feet in socks were silent on the tiles, his hair still wet. He'd changed into a pair of worn Levi's and a white T-shirt, emphasising dark good looks she'd been trying for days not to keep on noticing. Desire was a dart across her skin, and she huffed out a laugh at the smile hovering on his lips.

'I wasn't. Peppers and courgettes have such a lot to say.'

'They do? It sounded more like you were muttering about showers and behaving yourself.'

'You must have misheard.' Her face was pink now and she very much appreciated the cool air escaping from the fridge as she stared inside it.

'Right.' She didn't need to see Zac to hear the amusement in that single word. 'Look, about dinner.'

'It's fine if you have to go.' Alice turned around, trying to balance relief with disappointment. 'It was only a thought.'

'I don't have to go, and I wasn't trying to cancel.' He removed his phone from a back pocket of his jeans. 'I was going to suggest a takeaway, so you don't have to cook. There's a nice Chinese just opened in the next village.'

'Oh!' So dinner was back on, and she appreciated his suggestion. 'Are you worried about my cooking?'

'Not in the least. You already made soup and I loved that, remember?'

'I do.'

'Plus next time I think it should be my turn to feed you, maybe after another training session?'

'I'd like that.' She swallowed, pinned by the intensity in his eyes even though her reply had been every bit as nonchalant as his invitation. It did sound a lot like a date but of course it wasn't. 'Do you have a menu for the takeaway?'

'On my phone.' Zac held it out. 'I've just downloaded it.'

'Thanks.'

They agreed on a couple of starters and two main courses, and Alice handed his phone back. It was busy with notifications constantly popping up and she made sure not to look.

'I could pick it up after you shower, if you like?'

'Perfect, thanks.' So it was her turn now and Alice retraced his steps across the kitchen to her bedroom. 'Help yourself to a drink and take it upstairs if you like.'

'Thanks. I've left my towel on the rail in the bathroom,' he called after her, and she nodded. 'I wasn't sure where you'd want it.'

Her bedroom looked exactly as it had when she'd left Zac in it earlier, but it felt so very different. He'd seen her bed now and would know which side she slept on, what she read before falling asleep each night. The shower was still wet too, the damp towel more evidence that he had been in here, had undressed and soaked himself as she was about to do.

The hot water felt wonderful on her body after the effort on the bike earlier and she didn't linger, drying herself quickly. Her towel looked strange sitting on the rail next to his, a matching pair. There was so little about her and Zac that matched, but that was a thought she didn't want to have right now.

Alice dressed in jeans with a green jumper over a vest, her hair dry and loose. She wore no make-up bar lip gloss, no perfume beyond the rose and almond shower gel she loved, nothing to suggest that this evening was anything more than a casual meal with a friend.

In the kitchen, Zac was sitting at the breakfast bar, one hand around a glass of water. 'Hey. Feel better?'

'Much, thank you.'

'Great.' He stood up, checking his phone. 'I'll go and pick the food up; it should be ready by the time I get there.'

'Perfect, thanks. Would you like something different to drink with dinner? I'm sorry, I don't have any beer that's non-alcoholic. I'm more of a wine person when I drink.'

'Water's fine.' He paused at the door to look back. 'I won't be long.'

Alice slid plates into the warming oven and poured herself a glass of white wine. She laid the stove upstairs but didn't light it. He might rush off the minute they'd eaten, and she wasn't going to presume he'd want to linger. She'd definitely be aching tomorrow after the bike ride, so an early night would probably be a good call. Alone.

Twenty-five minutes later, Zac was back, and she went to answer his rapid knock. His expression was so different, fraught with tension, that she wondered if he'd an accident, and she only realised her hand had caught his when they both glanced down.

'Are you okay? Has something happened?'

'It's my dad.' He followed Alice into the kitchen. 'Sandy's just called me from his phone; she tried you as well.'

'I didn't see it, I'm sorry. Is he okay?'

'I think so.' Some of Zac's tension was released in a sigh as he placed the takeaway on the breakfast bar. 'He fell while they were out walking and she's at A&E with him.'

'Is it serious?' Alice felt a tremor of fear run through her, too. Sandy wasn't one to panic in the slightest and if Neil had needed A&E, or she'd insisted, then it mustn't be great news.

'He's all right; it's his knee. Sandy thinks he might have twisted it when he fell. She had to call out mountain rescue because he was in a lot of pain, and she was worried it might be more than just a sprain. She couldn't support him down on her own and they stretchered him back. Apparently he wasn't very keen on going to hospital but between the volunteers and Sandy, they managed to persuade him.'

Zac glanced at the dining area: the table Alice had set for two, a pair of glasses sitting opposite one another. 'Alice, I'm really sorry but I have to go. He's my responsibility; I can't leave him with Sandy.'

'Of course, I understand.' She wondered about offering to keep the food warm for them but there was no point. Neil could be hours in A&E and that was assuming Zac would even want, or be able to, return. His dad was going to need some help and that came first.

'Shall I come with you?' Alice wasn't even sure why she'd offered, and she quickly tried to backtrack. 'It's not my place, of course, I was just suggesting it in case there's anything I can do.'

'You don't mind?' Zac looked surprised but he hadn't refused. Was that relief she read in his face now?

'Not at all. Just let me find my bag and grab a coat.'

He was already in the van by the time she locked up and she didn't offer to take the Porsche and follow him after her glass of wine earlier. Old habits die hard, and she'd drunk very rarely when she'd run the haulage business, always preferring to be fit to drive if she needed to. Zac was a great driver and even though he was very quick on narrow lanes in the dark, she felt completely safe, and they were in town in half an hour. After parking up at the hospital, they found Sandy waiting in A&E, still in her walking gear, without Neil.

'Zac, your dad's fine.' Sandy sprang to her feet and Alice heard the air rush out of him. If her aunt was surprised by her appearance, she didn't show it, and they shared a quick smile. 'It's his knee, the left one. It's looking like nothing more than a nasty sprain, but he's gone for an X-ray to make sure.'

'Thanks, Sandy.' Zac ran a hand through hair that had dried into something more untidy than usual. 'And for getting him here – I can imagine he wasn't the easiest to persuade.'

'You could say that; he didn't even want me to call you in case you were worried. But I'm well used to dealing with recalcitrant people who don't want to do what they need to, and your dad didn't stand a chance.' Sandy picked up a waterproof coat, pointing to her chair. 'Take a seat; he could be a while yet.'

'You're not staying?'

'No, I don't want to be in the way now you're here. I've got my car; I followed the mountain rescue ambulance so we could get back.' Sandy looked at Alice and she waited for her aunt to offer her a lift. Sandy must be wondering why Alice had turned up with Zac and she wasn't exactly needed here. 'The coffee in the vending machine isn't bad if you both fancy one.'

'I'll get them.' Zac was reaching into his pocket and Alice shook her head.

'No, let me, you sit down. You've had a bit of a shock; no one likes getting those calls out of the blue.'

Sandy gave his shoulder a squeeze. 'You'll let me know how your dad is? He's got his phone, but it died pretty much after I rang you.'

'Of course. Thank you, Sandy, I really appreciate it.'

'You're very welcome.' She shared a quick hug with Alice. 'I'm glad you're here,' she murmured. 'Look after him.'

She was striding down the corridor towards the exit before Alice could ask her which of the two men she'd meant. The doors slid shut behind her and Alice looked at Zac.

'Coffee, or would you rather risk the tea in that machine?'

'What?' His gaze was troubled when it found hers. 'Oh, the coffee for sure, I need it. Thanks.'

Hospitals were uncomfortable places at the best of times and at night there was a weird kind of lethargy as people waited to be seen, staring blankly at a television blaring out news that no one was really watching. One or two people left, yet more were arriving, and it wasn't even eight p.m. It looked as though it would be a long night for everyone trapped in the hospital's suspended stillness.

Alice wasn't sure she agreed with Sandy's verdict on the coffee being not bad as she sipped hers, thinking about tipping it down the toilet instead. Zac's elbows were resting on his knees, one finger tapping an anxious beat against the paper cup.

'I'm sorry about tonight, Alice.'

'It's fine; there's no need to apologise again. It was only a takeaway and it wasn't your fault. You needed to be here.'

'But you don't,' he replied quietly.

'You want me to go?' She leaped up. Sandy had left but she could call a taxi.

'No, sorry, that wasn't what I meant. Please.' Zac pointed to her seat, and she took it again. 'Just that you've given up your evening when you didn't have to.'

'I really don't mind.'

'We could try the Chinese again another time?'

Alice's impromptu invitation to stay for dinner, to let him use her shower and eat together had seemed a natural extension of the afternoon they'd already spent, the cajoling, the sensitivity he'd shown for why she'd entered the triathlon. There was no romance or fun to be found sitting in the glare of a hospital waiting room, but she wasn't done with this adventure quite yet. Nor would she think of him leaving in a couple of months.

'I'd like that.'

The minutes ticked away as the news on the screen looped itself around the same worrying stories in between the coughs and groans, and the hushed conversations, the occasional wail of a siren outside.

'You could end up in any hospital and it wouldn't matter which; they all look and feel the same. It's like the outside world doesn't exist apart from on that TV. Like time's been suspended and we've shifted into some other universe.' Zac's tone was wry as he glanced at his phone.

'Yeah. Not the nicest places to be.' Alice wasn't going to think of her own dash to hospital when she was losing the baby: the fright and the fear; the awful end. 'My brother and sister-in-law have two kids, so they've got more experience of A&E than me.'

'How old are they?' Zac took another mouthful of tepid coffee and pulled a face.

'Six and four, both utterly gorgeous.' There was a catch in her voice as she thought of the children, hugging them, holding them close. She was a good auntie, she knew that, but she missed them. Video calls were fun, but they couldn't make up for squishing the girls in her arms and making them laugh. At least they'd be together for a weekend soon and then for Christmas. 'What about yours? I remember your dad saying your sister has two children.'

'Also girls, eight and six. Total warriors and going to conquer the world.' The edge of Zac's mouth curled up, his gaze still fixed to the floor.

'They sound just like mine. Freya, the youngest, lives to dance while Lottie plans to be a footballer. The scale of their ambition is immense; I'm sure I wasn't that driven at their age. I certainly didn't want to dance. I wanted to race cars when I was little.'

'Have you ever driven a race car?' He gave up on the coffee and put the cup on the floor underneath his chair.

'Sadly not. My racing ambitions disappeared the day my dad took me out in a lorry, and I realised I wanted to drive those instead. I love it. Slower but so much fun.'

The moment of sorrow for her dad and their old business quickly fled. Alice couldn't keep on feeling guilty for selling every time she thought of it. There had been a lot of good years and she knew the company was still flourishing. Her dad would've told her to move on with her life and do what she wanted. He always fought for her, until she was old enough to fight for herself.

'What about you?' she asked, remembering that conversation over lunch at the barn with Sandy and Neil, his dad telling her how much Zac loved his cars. 'Ever raced a car?'

'Yeah.' His voice was so low Alice almost didn't catch it.

'One of those experience things with mates?'

'Not exactly.' Zac turned his head, eyes unfathomable, a trace of something wistful in his voice. 'It was my job.'

Chapter Eleven

'Zac! Sorry, what a bloody palaver! You didn't go and drag Alice out as well?' Neil was emerging through double doors, hopping awkwardly with crutches under his arms, a nurse just behind him.

'Dad! What's going on? What have you done?'

'It's my knee.' Neil grimaced. 'Just a sprain – the X-ray's confirmed nothing's broken so that's something. Ice, elevation and painkillers for a bit, that's all. Don't worry. Where's Sandy?'

'She didn't want to be in the way so she's gone home. She sends her love and asked me to let her know how you are as your phone's out of battery.' Alice had stood too, her mind still full of Zac and what he'd said right before Neil had appeared.

'Let's get out of here, then.' Zac was at Neil's side, an arm ready to support his dad. 'Do you need a hand?'

'Of course I don't; I'm fine.' Neil gave Zac a sympathetic look. 'Sorry, son, I know hospitals aren't your favourite places. If it's any consolation they're not mine either – all that time back and forward worrying about you after the accident. And this was not how I planned to end my evening.'

'I'm not sure that's something you should be sharing with us.' Zac glanced at Alice, and she smiled. It wasn't how she'd imagined ending their own evening too, although she couldn't quite pin down how that might actually have gone.

'We were going to eat at the pub after our walk, that's all.' Neil went to poke his son's leg with a crutch. He stumbled and Zac's hand shot out to grab him.

'Dad, watch it! If you fall again it might not be just a sprain this time.'

Alice was first through the doors into the night, the chill wrapping itself around her, and Neil was still grumbling at Zac as they followed.

'It's hardly a state secret and I know I don't have to tell you everything. It was Sandy's idea to go to the pub, only I went arse over whatsit on a rock, and now look at me.'

Slowly they reached Zac's van, and he unlocked the doors, ready to help Neil inside. 'Let's just get you home and your leg up.'

'Good luck with that,' Neil muttered. 'You go first, Alice, if you don't mind. Save me trying to crawl over to the middle seat. And I think you'll have to drag me backwards up to the flat, Zac. I'll be the one on the sofa now. I might manage to get up those stairs to the bedroom but right now I don't fancy my chances of coming down them again in one piece.'

'Well, you can't sleep on the sofa, Dad, not like that.' Zac jumped into the van; his thigh pressed against Alice's in the confined space, warming her. 'It won't do your knee any good if you can't support it properly. Maybe I should run you down to Hayley's instead and you can stay with them.'

'Your sister hasn't got time to look after me.' Neil barked out a laugh. 'Between work and the kids and all they've got going on, she barely has a minute. The last thing she needs is me laid up and they haven't got a spare bed anyway. I'm not turfing one of the girls out of theirs.'

'So what do you suggest?' Zac's mouth was set in a line as he left the car park. 'I could take you home and ask Brenda to keep an eye on you.'

'Not after last time.' Neil shuddered. 'She's a good neighbour, but her feet might get a little too firmly planted under the table for my liking.'

'You could stay with me, Neil.' The solution seemed perfectly obvious to Alice. 'All the bedrooms are on the ground floor, so you won't have to worry about stairs. The guest room is en suite too, with a walk-in shower.'

She'd barely finished her final sentence before two male voices rose in unison.

'Well, if you're sure, Alice? That's very kind of—'

'That's not going to work! He'll drive you mad and he's really not your problem.'

'Zac, it makes perfect sense. Your dad can get around in the kitchen and there's a TV in the bedroom, so he won't have to go up to the sitting room if he doesn't want to.'

'Look, you really don't have to do this. He'll get in your way, and he never stops talking. And he snores.'

'I am still sitting here, you cheeky bugger.' Neil couldn't nudge Zac from where he was sitting, and Alice laughed.

'I'd like to, and this way you can have your bedroom back, at least until your dad can manage the stairs again.'

'I think it'll be a good few days before I can do any stairs,' Neil said cheerfully. 'You're a star, Alice, thanks. I'll need some things fetching from the flat, Zac. Sorry.'

'Dad, it's not decided,' Zac muttered. 'Alice is busy too. She hasn't got time to wait on you hand and foot; she's got work to do.'

'Oh, I think it is decided, son. Alice has offered and I've accepted. I'm not sure you've got much say in the matter.'

At the barn, Zac helped Neil out of the van and they followed her into the house. The takeaway was still sitting on the breakfast bar, and it didn't smell quite so enticing now. Alice hated to waste it, but she wasn't sure it would heat up very well. The cake and coffee with Zac had been hours ago, and Neil looked pale and tired.

'Let me show you your room,' she said briskly, giving him a sympathetic smile. 'Then you can settle in, and I'll make us something to eat.'

'Thanks, Alice. Zac, could you make sure you bring my phone charger back with you as well? I'd like to text Sandy and let her know I'm okay. Say thanks, too.'

'I sent her a quick message before so she wouldn't be worrying but I'm sure she'd love to hear it from you.' Alice opened the guest bedroom door and Neil limped past her.

'This is very nice.' He was even more cheerful as he took in twin beds and cosy furnishings, the oak furniture. 'Thanks a million. I'm sure I'll be comfortable in here.'

'You're very welcome. Would you like a drink?'

'A cup of tea would hit the spot, thanks.'

'Dad, Alice is not here to run around after you!' Zac had joined her, and awareness flared on her skin as he stood beside her.

'Well, you make it then.' Neil grinned as he lowered himself onto the bed nearest the bathroom.

'I don't mind,' Alice assured Zac. 'Your dad needs to get his leg up and rest it as much as possible.'

'I do.' Neil nodded firmly and added a wince for good measure. 'Who knows how long it'll take? Could be a week, maybe more.'

'Yeah, well, don't get used to this,' Zac warned. 'A day or two at most and then you're going home or back to the flat.'

'I can't go home, not yet,' Neil informed him jauntily. 'I've signed up for Sandy's beginner's pottery class and the first one's next week.'

'What?' Zac ran a hand over his jaw and Alice stifled a smile when he sighed. 'When were you planning to ask me if you can stay on? It's not even my flat; it's up to Max and Ella who uses it.'

'Well, we can worry about that when my knee's right.' Neil leaned back. 'Ah, that's better. I should get my leg up, like Alice said, and keep out of your way. I don't want to be a nuisance. Could I just borrow a pillow from the other bed, please, Alice? Sorry.'

'I'll get it,' Zac muttered, and he squeezed past her. 'Sorry, Alice. You'll be regretting this before the morning.'

'Well, there is a solution.' Neil propped his crutches against the bed.

'You're right.' Zac grabbed a pillow and stuffed it none too gently under Neil's left leg. 'You can come back with me and make do with that sofa. And quit issuing orders.'

'Course, it depends if Alice doesn't mind?' Neil was looking at her and she would've sworn he was making a sad face on purpose as he readjusted his leg on the pillow.

'Mind what?' Zac glared at him.

'If Zac stays here too,' Neil said hopefully. 'That way he can look after me, and we won't have to trouble you too much.'

Alice's first dumbfounded response was a laugh that sounded more like a splutter. 'It does make sense,' she told Zac casually. 'It would save you coming back and forth to check up on your dad.'

'And there's two beds, ready made up.' Neil picked up a crutch and gave it a happy tap on the bed next to his.

Really, Neil's suggestion was bonkers, and Alice should have refuted it. She didn't regret offering him the guest room for a few days, even if he did talk all the time, but she definitely hadn't bargained on him attempting to include Zac in the invitation as well. And she couldn't retract it; she'd just said it made sense. Which, for Neil's sake, it did, having Zac around to help. What it might do to her, though, being so near to him night and day, was something else altogether.

'I'll make that tea and bring you some ice, Neil.' She backed away, putting the kettle on the Aga and checking the freezer.

'Alice?'

'Yes?' She straightened up, an ice pad in one hand.

'You don't have to do this.' Zac shrugged as he closed the bedroom door. 'My dad, me. We're not your problem.'

'I just thought I could help.'

'You really are, more than you know, and I appreciate it. Is that for him?'

Alice nodded and he accepted the ice pad she offered. 'Thanks.'

'You're welcome.' The kettle was whistling, and she took it off the Aga, pointing to a drawer and setting out three mugs. 'Tea towels are in there if you want to wrap one around it. Would you like some tea before you go back for his things?'

'Better not, I might as well do it now. He'll only want something he hasn't got if I don't get on with it.' Zac was at the breakfast bar, ice pad in hand. 'What would you like me to do, about my stuff?'

His voice was uncertain, and she understood at once. This was her call, and she could choose. But he wanted to stay; his eyes had told her that.

'Bring it back with you?' Slowly she poured hot water over two tea bags in mugs. Their bedrooms were on opposite sides of the house; she wouldn't see that much of him. They were both working, both busy. It would be fine.

'Sure?'

'Positive.' She'd been careful all her adult life where her emotions were concerned and look where that had got her. He nodded quickly and turned away. The front door closed after him, and Alice swiftly decided that not dating Zac was getting more exciting by the day.

She took the tea in to Neil and set it on his bedside table. He thanked her as she checked the bathroom for towels. The cupboard was empty, and she'd need to bring in some more from her room.

'Do you need any pain relief?'

'No, I'm fine, thanks. They gave me some at the hospital; that'll do me until bedtime.'

'Okay. I have paracetamol; I'll bring it through later and you can keep it.'

'Thanks, Alice, it's really good of you. I hope I can get the hang of these; I've never had to use them before.' Neil touched one of the crutches leaning against the bed. 'Zac was the one on crutches, after he did his leg and had all those weeks in hospital.'

'Hopefully you won't need them for long. So, how many Wainwrights have you bagged now?' Alice changed the subject on purpose and edged towards the door, thinking about dinner and what she could quickly put together for three. Neil was talking again, and she sidled into the kitchen, leaving his door open so she could get on and he wouldn't think she was ignoring him completely.

'I can't remember, think it's about fifty. I'm lucky it wasn't worse, like Zac when he smashed up his leg and had to have surgery. Then it was a cast, a boot for another six weeks and months of physio. Four months before he could walk again and even then he was limping. Not that he ever let it show; he pushed himself beyond what any of us thought was sensible, even his physio, to get himself right again.'

Neil had raised his voice and Alice was at the fridge. She couldn't have not heard, not without asking him to be quiet and that seemed too impolite for such a friendly man. She just wasn't convinced Zac would want his dad sharing all this, so she tried changing the subject again, calling loudly, 'It's looking like tuna and cheese on toast with peppers. Is that okay?'

'Lovely, thanks. And he did get himself right again, Zac. Sheer bloody willpower, most of it, I'm sure, especially when arthritis set in as well. Post-traumatic arthritis, they call it. Well, it was bloody traumatic, I can tell you. Never yet heard him complain about the pain but it was written all over his face.'

She opened a couple of cans of tuna, sliced some sourdough, then put the bread knife down, crumbs scattered on the worktop. Everyone had their own story and until Neil had burst through those doors at the hospital, it seemed that Zac might have been about to share some of his with Alice. She thought of Neil at lunch the other day after church, confessing that his children's mum had left them, and Zac had cried himself to sleep because of it. And the fiancée who had walked away. Why? When?

This wasn't a path she was meant to be treading but already her feet were on it. She swallowed back the rush of sadness for him, the things he had endured and of which she knew only the barest bones, thanks to Neil. Zac hadn't chosen to share his story with her. But when would he have been able to do so, among the teasing and the banter, the assurances they kept giving each other that they were on the same page and wouldn't be taking this attraction any further?

The en-suite door in the guest room clicked shut and Alice let out a sigh of relief. At least Neil couldn't shout from there. She grated cheese into a bowl, adding diced peppers, sweetcorn and the tuna. The sourdough slices went under the grill to part-toast, and she spread a layer of tomato puree on them once they were done, followed by the tuna mix. She put the loaded slices on a tray, ready for the oven when Zac returned. She was in her own bathroom finding towels when she saw the flash of light on her drive. She abandoned the search and went to answer his knock.

'Hey.' He had a bag in each hand and a rucksack over one shoulder. 'I hope he's not boring you senseless.'

'Of course not.' She didn't want to pretend that Neil had chatted about everyday things and not an episode in Zac's life that had clearly been so distressing. 'He said he hoped he'd be able to manage his crutches and that you had experience of them.'

'So he told you? About my accident?' Zac halted at the door of the guest room to face her.

'Not exactly, just that you had one.' Alice's hand found its way to his arm, resting lightly on it. 'I'm sorry, I did try and stop him but you're right, he's relentless.'

'Don't apologise; it's not your fault. I love him to bits, and I don't know where I'd be without him, but living together again is something else. And I am sorry too, about all of this. It's incredibly good of you.'

Alice let her hand slide away as Zac sighed. 'It's fine, really. You don't have to keep saying it.' She turned to pick up the tray of sourdough and slid it into the Aga. 'But you are helping me train for the triathlon, so you know, fair's fair.'

'I think you've got the rough end of the deal.' He glanced at the table still set for two from before the dash to hospital. 'Can I do anything?'

'It's almost ready. You could ask your dad what he'd like to drink.'

'Okay.' Zac was still holding the bags and he tapped on the door. 'I'll take these through and find out. Alice?'

'Yes?' She was collecting plates from the warming oven and stood up.

'Just so you know, I won't be sending you an invoice for the work I did. I really appreciate all of this, more than you know.'

'Oh, Zac, please don't do that. Having your dad staying for a few days is no trouble and I'd hate you to give up a day's earnings because of it. I'd never have offered if I thought you'd be out of pocket.'

'Decision made. I won't change my mind.'

He shook his head as Neil's muffled voice called, 'Come in.'

'We should be paying you. And I never got around to checking out those trees earlier.' He smiled as he opened the door. 'I'll do it tomorrow. I think I got distracted.'

'By what?' Alice lowered her voice and she seemed to be looking up at him through her lashes again.

'By racking my mind to come up with ways to improve my dating score,' Zac said casually.

Still smiling at that, she took the tray out of the oven and shared the tuna toasties between the three plates.

'Dad's going to eat in his room if that's okay, please? He wants to keep his knee elevated if he can. Just water to drink.'

'Of course, I'm sure there are some trays somewhere.' She rummaged in a cupboard, producing a tray covered in sheep, and passed it to Zac. 'Here you go. Glasses are just there if you'd like to help yourself, and there's some paracetamol for later.'

'Thanks. I won't be long.'

Alice refilled his own glass from earlier with water and took their plates to the table. She'd wondered what sitting down alone with him would be like. Different now, with Neil just through a door off the kitchen.

Zac reappeared, sinking onto a chair and running a weary hand over his face. 'Thank you.'

'It's okay, you don't have to keep saying it – once is enough. I know.'

'Not the evening I thought we'd have.' His gaze was level on hers as he picked up a thick slice of toast loaded with tuna and cheese.

'Don't say it, if you were going to apologise again. Also fine.' Alice had refilled her wine glass. With Zac here, there was a driver if Neil needed one. Although that was hopefully unlikely, with him comfortable in the guest room and the noise of the television quiet beneath her and Zac's conversation. 'What kind of evening were you expecting?'

'I'm not quite sure how to answer that.' He was halfway through a first piece of toast. 'Actually, I do. I was thinking we'd have a great time and I'd go home when it was over. How about you?'

'Same.' She waited a beat. 'Maybe a little more. Not planned, though,' she added hastily. She wasn't that good at this game, not yet.

'You didn't tell me your guest room had an en-suite.' That languid smile was back, and Alice swallowed as she put her wine glass down. 'Why didn't you make me shower in there instead of in your bedroom?'

'I knew there weren't any towels in the guest room,' she improvised quickly.

'Right.' The smile widened as his voice lowered. 'You couldn't have brought one in for me?'

'And disturbed you in the shower? Of course not.'

'For the record…' Zac's gaze caught on her mouth and her lips parted. 'If you ever need to bring me a towel again, just come on in. Disturb me some more.'

'More?' The word was forced out past the croak in her voice, needing to be certain of where they might be headed. A rush of desire came again, a new longing to touch and be touched, to wrap herself around him. The scent of her own rose and almond shower gel was fragrant on his skin, as fresh and sensuous as Zac himself.

'More than you already do.'

'I like that I can.' It was true and Alice felt lighter, less afraid of what she wanted and how it might end.

161

He reached across the table to brush her fingertips and she drew in a sharp breath. How would more with him feel if this simple gesture was a means of measure?

'I heard you before, at the fridge,' Zac said softly. 'Muttering out loud that you weren't going to let yourself misbehave with me.' He leaned over, smoothing loose hair from her face. 'Just so you know, you can misbehave with me as much as you like.'

'Your dad's here,' she whispered. Behind that door, a few feet away. 'We can't; he's expecting you to…'

'I didn't mean right now.' Still his eyes refused to let go of hers and she felt the disappointment rush back. 'But getting to know you is fast becoming the most fun I've ever had in my experience of dating. Or not dating.'

'And if we…' Alice paused, not certain quite how directly she wanted to frame her question. In truth she knew she'd changed the game the moment she invited Zac to stay for dinner. She just couldn't have imagined that Neil's accident would have upped it some more.

'What do you want, Alice? I know what we said the other night but…' Zac covered her hand and this time she was the one to raise them and brush his in a soft kiss. Her confidence soared as his eyes darkened, breath trapped in his throat. His hands weren't smooth, the skin worn by working outdoors and she let her lips trail across his fingers. This was her reply, and his voice was hoarse. 'I have to leave. We can't forget that.'

'I won't,' she whispered. 'And it's okay.' Right now, it was. She'd barely touched her food, and she didn't want any more. She stood up, holding out her arm. This evening couldn't be over yet.

'Do you want to go upstairs? I'll light the fire.'

Zac pushed his chair back and accepted her hand. 'In a different house that would be a very different question,' he said wryly.

Chapter Twelve

The fire in the sitting room didn't take long to catch and Alice chose the sofa, leaving space for Zac beside her, but he settled on an armchair to her left. She supposed talking would be easier if they weren't touching – this swerve in their relationship was still very new and for all her burgeoning flirting skills and apparent confidence at what might come next, she was still nervous about how it would be between them.

'You look miles away.' Zac's voice jolted her out of the apprehension, and she sipped the wine she'd refilled.

'Just lost in thought.'

'Nice ones?'

'I was thinking about you and me. How lovely this is.' She couldn't help it, her thoughts were bound up in his leaving, too. She was going into it with the facts of his situation clear. But still, a part of her already knew it wouldn't be easy when he left. 'Tell me about your new job.'

Alice hadn't thought to google him and learn what was available online. She was fairly sure he didn't do social media and she liked finding out more about him as they went along, uncovering their layers little by little.

'I'll be leading a team of foresters in the High-lands. It's quite a diverse role, overseeing harvesting and marketing timber, restocking, establishing new wood-lands, managing the lands sustainably.'

'It sounds great. And the Highlands, too. Beautiful.'

'It is. I'm heading up in a couple of weeks to have a look at some properties to rent.'

'Not buying?' As if it would matter to her.

'Not yet. I'll need some time to settle in but that's the long-term plan. My base is a small village at the southern end of Loch Ness. It'll be me, some locals and loads of tourists searching for Nessie.'

'Your dad will miss you,' she said wistfully. Neil and Zac shared a closeness that reminded Alice of her own father.

'Yeah, I'll miss him too.' Zac stretched out his legs, crossing one ankle over the other. 'But I can't keep living in his house for much longer.'

'Because you'll drive each other mad?' She could well imagine it. They were both strong characters who knew their own minds, and then there was Neil's love of chat.

'Because it's too easy. He likes having me there, still tries to take care of me. At thirty-two I'm long past needing to let him know when I'll be home and who I'm with. He's a worrier, at least about me.'

Thirty-two? Six years younger than her, if another reason was needed to remind her they were only temporary. Neither of them wanted to settle but maybe for different reasons, and one day Zac perhaps would. With a woman who could give him a family, if that was what he wanted. Not one like Alice: divorced and nearly broken by the loss of a baby she'd never held, yet had loved and longed for all the same.

'Because he loves you.' A simple and truthful reply. At least her own dad had been spared the emotional upheaval and sweeping changes in her life. He'd have been devastated by them, too, bereft over a grandchild he'd never know.

'Yeah. I'm sure keeping a close eye is one reason why he wanted to work with me. But it is good, having that time together. It was different when I was racing. He was working and he came to everything he could. I was busier then too, travelling, practising, sponsors, all that stuff. Living life a bit faster. I like the pace of this one better.'

'What cars did you race?' Alice was imagining Zac behind the wheel, pushing a highly tuned machine to the max, and that was a thrill. 'My dad and I went occasionally and the roar of the engines is something else.'

'It really is. I was with a Formula Ford team before I switched to F4.'

'Did you come up through karting? I don't know much about it, to be honest.'

'No, I had a very untraditional start. I came to it late, just lucky really. I had a mate who was a mechanic for a race team. I went to a test day with him and between us we somehow managed to blag them into letting me have a go. It would never happen now; I still don't know how we did it. We were lucky I didn't wreck the car or kill myself. I wasn't the best at school, bunked off, got into trouble, things that don't seem quite so clever when you look back. All I had to my name was a painting and decorating apprenticeship because my dad said he wasn't going to carry me, and I had to learn a trade. He's probably already told you that my mum left when I was seven.' Zac's resigned smile faded. 'It took me a long time to get past the idea that it must have been my fault somehow.'

'Oh, Zac.' Alice wanted to wrap her arms around him, and he sighed.

'I know. I got it, eventually. She and my dad, they wanted different lives, and he didn't want to leave us, so she did. Then it turned out that I was quite good in the car and the team were interested enough to offer me a place, subject to me getting a motorsport licence and making some changes in my life. Training, discipline, responsibility. Dad said it was the making of me and doesn't know how I'd have turned out in the end without it. Racing gave me an outlet for my anger, and I pushed me and the car as hard as I could. I was racing myself half the time and I hated anyone getting in my way.'

'I'm sorry for what you went through, with your mum.' Alice was trying to imagine it. For all that she and her mum weren't as close as she had been to her dad, she couldn't picture what her life might have been like as a child without her mum around.

'Thanks, Alice.' Zac's gaze seemed bruised as unwanted memories slipped back in. 'Even though it was such a long time ago it never quite goes away. I don't think stuff like that ever does.'

'No.' The chasm between them was shrinking and she was falling into Zac's life, his history, her heart aching for what he'd gone through and the man he'd become because of it. Everyone had a story and somehow theirs were becoming a thread binding them both. 'You just find a way to learn to live with the sadness.' She hesitated. 'Was the accident the reason you gave up racing? I understand if you'd rather not say.'

'I'm surprised my dad hasn't already told you.'

'I don't think he's quite had the chance. But there's time yet; he doesn't seem in any hurry to leave. And he's obviously so proud of you.'

Zac raised a shoulder. 'I'm glad I gave him something to be proud of, eventually. It was touch and go for a while. He threatened to have me arrested twice.'

Alice's gasp was one of shock edged with laughter. 'What did you do?'

'Not my finest hour,' Zac said wryly. 'I took Hayley's car once for a day out with mates when she needed it for work and he went ballistic; I thought he was going to lock me up himself when he found out. The second time it was a fight between a load of lads, and he threatened to haul me into the station until I managed to prove I wasn't actually there.

'I did my leg in when I was leading the championship, pushing to the limit as usual. The team were on at me to play it safe for a podium finish because then I couldn't lose the championship; the points from a top three would be enough. But I hated settling for second best and the car flipped out when I was trying to overtake, and nearly took my leg with it.'

Zac reached down and Alice wondered if he was touching his leg subconsciously, making sure it had healed and he was whole again. Or as whole as anyone ever got with a fractured family history and a high-pressure career that could have killed him.

'That was it. My season was over, I lost the championship and it was all my fault. The team were livid, among all the concern. That was the first time I finally realised I wasn't racing just for me, that we were all in it together and they'd wanted to win too.'

'But you came back?' Alice was thinking of his recovery, the trauma that Neil had shared and how hard Zac had worked to return.

'I had to. It was unfinished business, and I still had a year left on my contract. I won the championship the following season.' His lips curved in a half smile. 'And announced my retirement on the podium, soaked in champagne. Hadn't told a soul, not even my dad, but I knew I was going to do it. The team weren't happy, and my agent was furious; he'd already started renegotiating my contract and bigger sponsors were interested.'

'So why did you give up?' This was the question, and she wondered if Zac would tell her.

He drew in a long breath, staring into the flames flickering around the wood. 'After the accident I had some counselling, for flashbacks, that kind of thing. But inside I was terrified of it happening again, losing control like that, and my dad was the only one who guessed. He tried to talk me into giving up and I wasn't having any of it. I knew if I admitted it out loud then it would be game over and I'd never go back. It was like living in a house of cards. One wrong move, one word in the wrong ear, and I'd bring the lot down. And I hadn't put my life back on the line to walk away a failed champion.'

Alice couldn't stay on the sofa after that. She kneeled in front of him and took his hands. 'That was incredibly brave,' she whispered.

'And stupid.' Zac eased off the chair until he was beside her, shoulders, arms and thighs touching in front of the fire. The glow made it easier to see his face, the thoughtful, deep brown eyes loaded with memories, not all of them good. 'I was lucky to get out in one piece. I wouldn't do it now. I'd ask for more help.'

'It's quite a leap to becoming a tree surgeon.'

'I needed it,' he said simply, shifting his head to look at her. 'Like you, I have to be outside. When I was in hospital, I watched patients and visitors, and staff, coming and going from a garden and it wasn't long before I wanted to explore it, to see what they were seeing. It was like an oasis of calm among all of the crazy, and I had the idea that I could find something similar once I retired from racing. I went to college, managed to qualify, and found some work. I lived in London then and eventually I met Max through a mutual client. He's become a really good friend and I have a lot to thank him for.'

'I'm glad he was there for you. And so do I.' Alice wasn't sure who was leaning into who, and her head found its way to Zac's shoulder. 'It was very good of him to give a newbie like me a chance. He's been incredibly generous with his time and advice. I try not to bother him unless it's really important, not with the baby so close.'

'Yeah, they're very excited; there's a lot going on for them right now.' Zac hesitated. 'Are you okay, seeing Ella and everything? It can't be easy.'

'I'm fine, really, and I appreciate you asking. It's wonderful for them and I wouldn't begrudge them a second of it. I can't escape normal life, and I don't want to live on the fringes because I had something awful happen to me. Everyone does.'

'So do you think I'll make a decent godparent, now you know what a bad boy I was?'

She shuffled round to face him. 'Zac, that's wonderful! You'll be brilliant and they wouldn't have asked you if they didn't think so.' She paused. 'I've never dated a bad boy before.'

He huffed out a small laugh. 'So it's a good thing you're not dating me, then. I might ruin you for the good ones.'

'I could live with that,' she whispered.

His phone on the floor lit up with a notification and they glanced it at. Alice realised the time and her smile was rueful.

'It's late and we've both got work tomorrow.' She almost bumped heads with him as they stood, and they laughed, easy and awkward all at once. The fire had burned itself out and Zac turned off the lamp and followed her downstairs. In the kitchen she didn't quite know how to say good night to a man who was staying over but not where she wanted him to be.

'See you in the morning.' But that was still a thrill and sharing breakfast if he had time would certainly be a different start to her day. 'If you have to leave before me, just help yourself to whatever you want.'

'I don't think I can, not yet,' he said softly. 'Sleep well.'

Zac dropped a kiss on the top of her head and Alice was the first one to reluctantly turn away. In bed a bit later, unable to drift into sleep, her phone lit up and she reached for it.

Zac had messaged, followed by an emoji pulling a face:

> Sorry about the snoring. I swear it's not me.

Alice was already composing a reply:

> I only have your word for it

> Only one of us in this room is asleep and it's not me.

> Why aren't you asleep?

> Thinking about you. You?

> Same. Got to try, though. Night

This time Zac added a kiss, and she sent one straight back.

In the morning, the house was silent as she walked into the kitchen and filled the kettle. Alice loved having a regular milk delivery from the local dairy who supplied the shop and three mornings a week she collected it from her gate before she did anything else. It was another wake-up call, stepping outside and feeling the new day on her face, whether it was wind, rain or sharp cold air. Another opportunity to feel part of the landscape and observe it changing day by day, readying itself for winter.

She was setting out everything she had for breakfast, hoping it would be enough for Neil and Zac, when the guest room door opened.

'Morning.' Zac gave her a smile, running a hand through his hair. She only needed a second to notice he was in shorts and a T-shirt, not the work clothes she'd been expecting, and her breath caught. The flutter in her stomach since she'd woken had let her know how much she'd been looking forward to seeing him first thing, but this was a whole other view. Her eyes drifted down and she noticed the faded scar running along his left leg and around to his ankle: another chapter of his story, and her heart softened in a most inconvenient manner.

'Hi.' She cleared her throat and looked at the bread in her hand, trying to remember what she'd been planning to do with it. Her mornings were never usually this exhilarating. 'How did you sleep?'

'Not bad, given the din my dad was making. It's even worse close up than in the flat.'

Alice was still trying to work out quite what terms they were on now. She'd really like to kiss Zac good morning but seeing as they'd barely even touched, that thought was a bit far-fetched.

'How is he?'

'Okay thanks, slept like the dead apparently. At least one of us did.'

'Well, it's good the pain isn't bothering him too much.'

'Yeah. Alice, sorry, there aren't any bath towels in the en suite.' Zac's smile was more of a grin now. 'I did wonder if you'd confiscated them on purpose, so I'd have to come and ask.'

'I might have.' She hadn't, she'd just forgotten to go back for them last night after Zac had returned but she preferred the more flirtatious reply. She put the bread down. The flutter in her stomach had been joined by a warmth on her face after that look he'd given her. 'Sorry, I'll bring you some. Is that why you underdressed on purpose, to ask me?'

'I didn't. I usually sleep naked so...'

'Oh! Right,' she muttered. Alice made herself stroll nonchalantly into her bedroom and re-emerged with four bath towels. Zac thanked her as he accepted them and she held his gaze, wondering if that same thought about kissing was in his mind too.

'You really don't have to sort breakfast for Dad and me.' He dragged his gaze away to take in the preparations she'd been making. 'I'm happy to do it, if you're okay with me in your kitchen?'

'I'm fine with you in my kitchen.' Especially dressed like that. 'Especially if you can cook as well.'

'I could do that tonight, if you want? Dad's knee is still pretty swollen; I don't think I'm going to get him out of here any time soon.'

'That's okay, there's no rush. There's more ice packs in the freezer too. And tonight sounds great.'

'Morning, Alice. The front door wasn't locked; I did knock. Oh, sorry!'

Alice whirled around to see Sandy hovering behind her and Zac, and a bit more colour erupted on her cheeks. 'Sandy, hi! We were just, er, Zac's just…' She must have forgotten to lock the door when she collected the milk.

Sandy held up a hand. 'No explanations necessary – I'm sorry I burst in. I thought I'd call and ask how your dad's doing, Zac. He messaged me to say he was staying with Alice and I'm on my way to a meeting at nine.'

'He's fine, thanks, making the most of all the attention. He'll be up soon; I'll tell him you're here. Right,' Zac said briskly. 'I'll go and get that shower.'

He disappeared and Alice quickly put the radio on, filling the kettle and setting out mugs.

'How are you?' Sandy pulled out a stool at the breakfast bar. 'Is everything all right?'

'Absolutely.' For once the glow on Alice's skin hadn't come from the fresh air. 'Neil suggested that Zac should

174

stay too and they're sharing the room. Just so I don't have to look after Neil on my own. It's not what you might be thinking.'

'I'm not thinking anything, I promise. Your private life is your own, my love. My only concern is being sure you are okay.' Sandy hesitated. 'Zac seems like a lovely man, but you do know he's leaving at Christmas? I'd hate for you to get hurt again.'

'I won't, I promise.' Alice slid bread into a toaster. The possibility of a second heartbreak felt a million miles away from the exhilarating attraction she was sharing with Zac. 'I'm not going to do anything silly, like fall in love with him. I like him and he likes me. That feels pretty amazing right now.'

'Look after you, that's all I'm saying.' Sandy got up and Alice appreciated her aunt's arms around her, the extra squeeze on her shoulder, all of it letting her know how much Sandy cared.

'Did you and Neil have a nice time yesterday? Before he fell over, of course.' They separated and Alice was curious too. Sandy was pragmatic and not given to wild flights of fancy. She'd divorced many years ago and had been single for a lot of them.

'We did; his stumble was just one of those things that happen.' Sandy thanked Alice for the mug of tea she placed in front of her. 'But he really loves the area and he's thinking he might move up here. His house is already for sale, and he'd like something between Hayley and where Zac's going to be. He's all about the family; he dotes on those grandchildren. I really like that about him.'

'Wow. How lovely.' If Neil were living here, then Zac would have another connection to Halesmere, a reason to return. Alice wasn't sure if that made her feelings for him more complicated or a whole lot clearer. She was thinking about last night, sitting beside him as he shared his story: the career he'd walked away from after the accident that had stolen his nerve and made him afraid. Was he happy now, living without the adrenaline rush of racing, the total need for speed? Was life here, or the new one he was planning in the Highlands, fast enough for him? 'And you'd see more of Neil, Sandy. If you both want to.'

'I think we would.'

Sandy's laugh was a quick one as Zac emerged from the bedroom with Neil on crutches behind him. He greeted everyone cheerfully and went off to rest his leg on a dining room chair that Sandy moved for him. Alice knew that Sandy spent much of her time visiting people in her parishes and seeing Neil wasn't something unusual, but she hadn't missed the glimmer in her aunt's eye and the comfortable way they chatted together. For all he was a talker, he listened too, and they were already making plans for another walk just as soon as he was fit enough.

Sandy refused Alice's offer of breakfast as she'd eaten at home, so Alice took hers to the table and left Zac to sort out his and Neil's. It was both easy and strange, having him moving around in her home, helping himself, offering more drinks when the two women had finished theirs. She mustn't get to like this too much, she reminded herself sternly. Zac was temporary, in every sense.

Sandy had to leave for her meeting and Zac needed to go too. Neil limped back to the bedroom, ready to rest his leg and watch a bit of TV. Alice was planning to cycle down to Halesmere and work in the Flower Shed, getting it ready for her first courses in a couple of weeks. In the utility room to collect her coat and a hat, Zac gently caught her hand.

'I'm hoping to call around lunchtime and check on my dad. Will you be back by then?'

'Maybe, depends on the weather. I'm not going to be planting more bulbs if it rains and the ground's saturated again, but there's a few things I can do in the polytunnel. Why?'

'I thought I'd bring us some lunch if you were going to be here.'

'That's a lovely idea.' She was enjoying this, whatever it was. What did you call not dating someone you wanted to sleep with? Kelly would know. Though Alice was certain she couldn't simply drop it into their next messages without Kelly guessing exactly what was going on. 'But I'll say no, just in case. I still have four hundred tulips to get in now it's colder.'

'Okay, I'll see you tonight, then. Any preferences for dinner?'

'Not really, I don't mind most things. Except fennel, I can't stand that. Tastes foul.'

'I'll make sure not to include it.' Zac's phone was ringing so he let go of her hand to check it, swiping the call away.

'We should invite Sandy tonight, don't you think?' Alice tugged on her hat, pulling a face at Zac for the grin he gave her. 'She and your dad seem to be loving the time they're spending together.'

'They really do – I'm sure Dad would like that too.'

'Shall I ask her, or will he?'

'I'll get him to suggest it.'

'See you later, then.' She eased past Zac, and they said goodbye.

At Halesmere, her final order of supplies for the studio had been delivered and Alice spent a happy couple of hours arranging everything. She wanted the Flower Shed to be a practical space where people felt comfortable working, but also welcoming and homely, with some second-hand books on crafts and the local area, which she placed on the coffee table Stan had also restored.

Stan always arrived early to make himself useful, and it wasn't long before Alice spotted the film crew again, capturing him as he strolled in and out of his workshop, a beloved brew in his hand. He'd told Alice the other day he was quite chuffed at the thought of being on telly. His portrait, painted last year by Max's mother, Noelle, already hung in a London gallery, pleasing him no end.

After a morning indoors, Alice was ready for some exercise, and she layered up to plant the tulip bulbs and clear the last of the weeds in the meadow. She was so excited to see the meadow in spring once all these bulbs had come up, but as she worked, with that thought came the unwelcome reminder of Zac leaving at Christmas. Afterwards she was chilled, ready for a hot drink, and she retreated to the studio to get out of the cold.

Stan stuck his head around the door, apparently able to smell a fresh mug of tea at a thousand paces. 'Are we 'avin' a brew, lass? Pearl's popped down with some flapjacks an' they're still warm. Film crew's 'ad enough of me an' gone off after Cal an' that daft lad 'e's workin' with. Good luck to 'em.'

Alice had to laugh at Stan's description of the famous and very popular reality television star, who was apparently still trying to live off-grid even though he'd refused to give up his phone.

'I can do better than just a brew, Stan. How do you fancy toasted marshmallows? I saw them in the shop and thought of you. It seems just the right sort of day and you can save the flapjacks for later.'

'Now you're talkin'.' The rest of Stan appeared around the door, and he closed it behind him. A yellow and green bobble hat was today's accompaniment to his usual donkey jacket. 'There's no one else around 'cept you an' me.'

They spent a pleasant half an hour drinking tea and toasting marshmallows on long forks until they were hot, sticky and caramelised. Stan headed home and Alice was thinking wryly that she'd have to give up eating treats like this and add a lot more miles on the bike to get fit enough for the triathlon. But like the reality of long hot summer days that right now felt so far away, so too did the demands of the triathlon.

Zac had messaged her, and she read the text before she cleared up. His dad was comfortable and had already received a few visitors. Pearl had dropped in some flapjacks and Rachael, who was a physiotherapist, had called to leave some information on exercises Neil could do to help his knee when the swelling had improved, having heard from Ana through the Halesmere grapevine about his accident.

Stan had also told Alice to let Neil know that he was welcome to stick Stan's leg up in his workshop any time he liked and watch *The Repair Shop* with him. The programme was a sacred hour in Stan's week, and he caught up on repeats in spare moments at Halesmere. Alice knew this was a generous invitation as Stan didn't appreciate being disturbed while it was on and even Pearl had to do her knitting in another room.

Alice replied to Zac, ready to lock up and take care of a few inescapable admin tasks at home. Suddenly, her door was flung back, and she leaped of the way as Max burst in.

Alarm was written all over his face and she felt a tremor of anxiety. He didn't usually look like this; he was one of the most composed people she knew.

'Alice, sorry! I was looking for Stan.' Max's anxious gaze was darting between her and his phone. 'He doesn't have a mobile and I can't find him; there's no one else here.'

'He's gone home; one of their daughters is on her way up and they're going out for a meal. Are you all right? What is it?'

'It's Ella.' Max's breath escaped in a rush and Alice's heart squeezed in worry. He was pacing the floor, unable to stand still. 'She's gone for an appointment with the midwife, and she's just called to say they're sending her to hospital for monitoring, something to do with the baby's heartbeat. They might decide to deliver the baby because she's already over her due date. I'm going to get her now and I wanted to ask Stan to pick Lily and Arlo up from school.'

'I'll do it.' Alice took a steadying breath, trying to quell the sudden dread running through her. It would be fine. Ella and the baby would be fine; they had to be.

'Are you sure? Thanks, Alice.' Max was already removing a key from the bunch in his hands. 'Please don't say too much to them, other than she's having a check-up because the baby's late and it could be a long time until there's more news. It might be nothing and they might send Ella home again. Don't tell them that; let's wait and see.'

'Of course.' Alice knew the primary school was right next door to Sandy's church. 'Shall I bring them home to yours?'

'Please.' He passed her the key. 'I don't want to concern them unduly and they've still got school tomorrow so they should go to bed as normal. Prim's there; she'll help keep them calm and Arlo will want to see the sheep before dark. Ella's mum and dad are moving over at the weekend, so they'll be here soon. Thanks so much, Alice, I really appreciate it. I'll call the school and let them know to expect you.'

'Max?' He was halfway out the door and looked back. 'I'm sure everything will be fine. We'll all be thinking of you and if there's anything else…'

'I know. Thanks.'

And he was gone. She heard his feet racing across the cobbles and the roar of an engine before his pickup tore off down the drive.

Chapter Thirteen

Alice let herself into Max and Ella's cottage to collect Prim, who greeted her happily and didn't seem to mind the change in personnel. She knew that Ella usually took Prim to meet the children and thought it would be a good idea to do the same to help distract them from the sudden swerve in Ella and Max's day.

At school, the children's first concerned questions were for Ella and why she wasn't here, and Alice reassured them as much as she could without alarming them. She explained that more check-ups and hospital visits were normal this close to a baby arriving. She'd already messaged Zac on the way to school to let him know she probably wouldn't be back for the dinner he'd promised to cook. He'd replied to say that he'd join her with the children if she wanted and would pick up something to eat on the way, and she accepted at once. Lily and Arlo knew Zac better than they did her, and they might prefer his company.

Back at the cottage, the family's four chickens needed putting to bed and afterwards they checked on the guinea pigs and fed them too. Lily was less interested in seeing the sheep than Arlo, who, in wellies and holding the shepherd's crook made for him by Stan, strode confidently into the field to check on them. He informed Alice proudly that they were all expected to be in lamb and should give birth in the spring. For such a small boy, she thought he was very knowledgeable, even though he was barely bigger than the grey ewes, who came trotting to meet him, eyeing her warily.

After their walk, as Alice was unlocking the cottage – while surreptitiously checking her phone for word from Max, even though she thought it would be too soon – Zac pulled up on the drive.

'Zac!' Arlo ran across, still clutching his shepherd's crook, to share a merry high five.

'Hey, buddy. How are the girls? All looking good?'

Arlo assured Zac the sheep were all fine and Zac smiled at Alice. She was happy to see him, more for the children than for herself as Arlo chattered on. Lily wanted a hug and Zac obliged, bending down to scoop her off her feet, making her giggle. Prim sat obediently until Alice opened the front door and she trotted inside. The children ran in after her, and Alice hung back to speak with Zac.

'Any news?'

'No.' He'd returned from the van holding pizza boxes. 'Doesn't mean it's a bad sign; it'll probably be hours before we know any more. There might not be much to say yet.'

'I know.' She still couldn't ease the niggling worry; she desperately didn't want anything to go wrong for Ella and Max.

'Come on, let's get the pizzas in the oven and keep these two happy.' The touch of Zac's hand on her back was brief. 'Ella's mum is on a train on her way; she didn't want to wait for the move, not now the baby might be born any day. I told Max I'd collect her from the station.'

'So she'll be here to look after the children?'

'Yeah, but I'm happy to stay with them until then.'

'Me too.' Alice nodded firmly; she wasn't going anywhere until she wasn't needed. 'What about a meal for your dad?'

'Guess.'

'Sandy?'

'Yep. She'd heard the news about Ella and knew you were here, so she said she'd pop in and sort something out for him.'

'That's very kind of her.'

'Well, he's already promised to reciprocate when he can.'

The combined kitchen and family room in the cottage was cosy, and Lily set the table while Alice poured drinks and Zac put the pizzas in the oven. The children had a bit of homework to finish, so she went through spellings with Lily and helped Arlo with his reading. It wasn't anything she hadn't done before with her own nieces, and it felt both strange and very ordinary.

Zac was checking his phone as often as she was hers, and after they'd eaten, he drew Alice to one side so the children couldn't overhear. 'Max has just messaged to say Ella and the baby are okay but she's being induced so it could be ages yet. Her mum's due at the station in forty minutes so I'll head off now. Back soon as I can.'

'Okay. Thanks for letting me know.'

She followed him to the door to lock up, recognising the red pickup tearing up the drive in the opposite direction. Stan was scattering gravel as he pulled up and clambered out as fast as his stocky legs could carry him.

'I've just 'eard about Ella; we was on our way back an' Pearl's phone lit up like a bloody beacon once she got signal,' he shouted. ''Ow is she? What's goin' on?'

'Ella's okay; her labour's being induced but that's all we know, Stan.' Alice couldn't help her smile; he was practically hopping from foot to agitated foot and it was the first time she'd ever seen him without a hat. She'd heard he loved his ties as well and tonight this one was covered in galloping fairground horses. 'Why don't you go home? Pearl will probably know something as soon as we do.'

'I won't be able to settle.' He let out a long sigh and scratched his head. 'I 'ave to be 'ere; I want to know what's 'appenin' soon as I can. An' there's somethin' I need to do.'

'Stan!' Lily flew out of the cottage past Alice, and he swung her up, spinning her around until she shrieked. 'My mum's in hospital getting ready to have our new baby sister.' He put her down and she pulled a face. 'Or brother.'

'Don't you want a new brother, Lily?' Stan questioned.

'I don't mind really, as long as they love animals. Dad's promised we can rescue another chicken as soon as the baby's born. I think we should call it Stan.'

'What, the baby or the chicken?' Stan coughed and Alice laughed. 'I think your mum an' dad might 'ave somethin' to say about the baby's name, Lily, an' I can't see it bein' Stan. I can 'elp you find another chicken, soon as there's some news to share.' He tapped his nose. 'I know someone.'

'Dad said you know everyone.' Lily was staring up at him, and he grinned.

'Everyone that matters, aye, I do. Like you an' Arlo an' this baby, when it comes.'

'Do you know anyone who has donkeys?'

'I might.' Stan's eyes narrowed suspiciously. 'Why?'

'I thought Arlo's sheep might like some company.'

Stan roared. 'I'd keep quiet about donkeys for now; your mum an' dad will 'ave enough to think about. An' Arlo's sheep 'ave probably 'ad all the company they need; they're goin' to lamb in the spring. Isn't it your bedtime anyway?'

Lily looked at Alice pleadingly. 'Do we have to go yet? Nana will be here soon and I want to wait up in case the baby's born. Mamie's in London; she's supposed to be coming back at the weekend. If the baby comes tomorrow, she'll want to come home sooner, won't she?'

'I'm sure she will,' Alice confirmed. She knew about bedtime routines from weekends with Jenna, Steven and their girls, but at times like these, 'normal' often went out of the window. 'The baby might not come for a day or two yet, Lily,' she said gently. 'But I think it's fine to stay up and see your nana first, and then maybe she can read you a story? You've still got school tomorrow.'

'Okay.' Lily went back inside, and Alice looked at Stan. 'Are you coming in?'

'Nah, thanks all the same.' He shrugged out of his smart jacket and reached inside the pickup for the old donkey one, and a hat. 'I'll be in me workshop; I need to keep busy till there's any news.'

Back in the cottage, Alice put a movie on for the children and the three of them snuggled on the sofa to watch it. Arlo was falling asleep, and she didn't want to disturb him. Zac was due any time with Ella's mum and Alice was certain she'd want to see both children. He arrived fifteen minutes later, and Ella's mum thanked Alice for looking after them. Arlo woke up and she was watching from the door as he and Lily tried to throw themselves onto their nana's lap at the same time, both talking excitedly as she hugged them tightly.

'Ready for home? Yours, I mean.' Zac's quick laugh was self-conscious. 'Max will let us know any news when he can.'

Alice nodded. She'd pretty much forgotten about Neil and Zac staying at the barn while she'd been here. They hugged the children good night too, and Lily asked if they would look after them again and read the story Zac had promised. He assured them he would, and Lily wasn't happy until Alice agreed to join him.

Sandy had already left when they returned to the barn and Alice heard the quiet hum of the television in the guest room, meaning Neil was probably still awake. It wasn't that late, and Zac stuck his head around the door to ask if there was anything his dad wanted. It had felt strange but nice all the same, coming home with Zac, as though they did this all the time.

'I'm going to shower and then I'll light the fire. Not that you have to sit up there with me,' she added hastily. 'You must have your own plans.'

'What?' Zac had been staring at his phone and he rammed it into a pocket. A muscle was flickering in his cheek and tension was evident in the lines around his mouth. 'Sorry, Alice, I just need to make a call.'

'It's not Ella?' Alice knew Stan wasn't the only one who wouldn't settle until the baby was safely here and doing fine with Ella. She didn't even realise she was clutching Zac's arm until he glanced down, and she snatched it away.

'No.' He was already making for the door. 'I'll let you know if it is. I won't be long, sorry.'

After her shower, Alice could hear he'd returned from the low voices muttering in the guest room. Both men sounded strained, and she heard Zac exhale as he told Neil sharply that he'd sorted it, whatever it was. She escaped upstairs, unwilling to overhear any more. She'd made herself some tea and left the extra two mugs ready so they would know she hadn't excluded them on purpose. She'd thought about finishing off the wine she'd opened last night but just didn't feel like it.

She lit the fire, phone nearby, but there were no more messages about Ella. News travelled quickly around here, despite the remoteness of the valley, and Alice knew she'd just have to wait. She didn't often draw the curtains and kept a cosy throw handy for stepping out onto the terrace. Wrapping it around her shoulders, she went out, appreciating the bite of air on her face.

'Alice?'

'What is it?' She spun around and Zac held up a hand.

'There's no more on Ella.' He hesitated. 'I think I'm going to shower and have an early night. Sorry.'

'Zac, it really isn't a problem.' Alice hid her disappointment, but she had spoken the truth. 'You don't have to explain anything to me. I just hope you're okay, that's all.'

'I'm fine.' He didn't quite sound it. His usual teasing grin had been replaced by a tautness in his expression as he glanced at the fire, the empty mug on a coffee table. 'The swelling in Dad's knee has improved so hopefully we'll be out of your way in a day or two.'

'Please don't rush for my sake,' she told him quietly. 'Whenever is best for both of you.' She returned to the sitting room and slid the throw from her shoulders. 'Too cold out there now.' She added a quick smile, hoping Zac wouldn't think she was coming back in to persuade him to join her.

'Night.' He turned away and Alice let the fire burn out once he'd gone, staring into the flames without really seeing anything. Something had upset him this evening, but it wasn't her place to ask what, or why. For all that they were having fun, flirting and enjoying this game they were playing, tonight had been a glimpse into their reality and how little they really knew one another. Better to keep it that way; better to keep things simple.

In bed later she couldn't help checking her phone again. She didn't expect to be high up on the list of those Max would inform once the baby had arrived, but Zac would let her know as soon as he could, and Pearl and Sandy were definitely in the loop. Alice was restless and she couldn't relax into her book, despite how soothing she normally found it.

All was silent, still, and she realised she must have eventually dozed off when she startled awake at what sounded like a tap on her door. She thought she'd dreamed it and eased down again. But the tap came a second time, and Zac's voice was a whisper.

'Alice? Sorry to disturb you. It's Ella – I thought you'd want to know.'

'What is it?' She shot up in bed, heart clattering.

'Can I come in?'

'Yes!' Alice just needed to know.

Zac's phone was in his hand as he hovered in the open door. He was smiling, and she leaned back with a rush of relief. 'Ella's had the baby?'

'She has, and everything's fine. Want to see?'

'Absolutely!'

'May I?' He took a hesitant step into her room.

'Of course.' Alice pointed to the bed and Zac sat down at the end. She shuffled across until she was beside him, half out of the duvet, and he turned the phone so she could see. She was staring at the most adorable little bundle, small pink face all round and peaceful, pale lashes sweeping onto cheeks.

'A boy, seven pounds nine ounces, mother and baby doing fine.' Zac let out a breath. 'They did a caesarean as Ella's labour didn't progress and they were a bit concerned about the baby. They're both ecstatic.'

'Oh, Zac, he's gorgeous! And I'm sure they are absolutely thrilled. I hope Stan's heard the news; he's probably still in his workshop.'

'He will – Max or Pearl will have seen to that. He's going to be over the moon too; he thinks the world of the family.'

'He's adorable. The baby, not Stan! Although Stan's pretty awesome too.' Alice looked at Zac, eyes shimmering. 'Your beautiful godson. Congratulations.'

'Thank you.' His smile was full of wonder. A new arrival in his world, one who would help hold him to Halesmere. 'I hope I can do him justice.'

'You will.' She let her shoulder bump against his arm. 'I have no doubts. I've seen you with Lily and Arlo and you're brilliant.'

'Well, they are amazing kids. They're gonna be so excited about this one. Max was worried about moving on from his wife when he and Ella met, but they're so great together and she adores Lily and Arlo.'

'I'm so pleased for them all. Have they chosen a name yet?'

'I think so but they're going to share it tomorrow.' Zac glanced at the book by her bed, the half-drunk glass of water. 'I'm sorry for waking you this late.'

'Please don't be – I'm glad you did. I feel better now I know they're okay.'

A few seconds ticked by as Alice waited for Zac to stand up and say good night. He'd shared the news about the baby and now he could leave.

'I'm sorry about before too; I was a bit terse.' He touched his phone, and the screen went dark.

'There's no need to apologise.' Alice was conscious then of her pyjamas, Zac in shorts and a T-shirt. They were both very similarly and decently dressed, and yet having him sitting on her bed suddenly didn't feel like it. 'As long as you're all right. I was probably being presumptuous, thinking we'd spend the evening together.'

'You weren't, because I was thinking it too.' He sighed. 'Someone sent me a message, just after we got back here. One I didn't want, and it needed sorting out.'

'I'm sorry. Is everything okay?'

'I think it is.' He nodded slowly. 'In fact, I know it is. I blocked them, something I should have done a long time ago. It was Serena, my ex-fiancée, still trying to play her games.'

'Games?'

Zac unlocked the phone again and held it up. 'That's her.'

A young woman, probably around Zac's age, was staring adoringly at the equally stunning man standing next to her, arms wrapped around one another. Whip-thin, she wore a white dress with a plunging neckline and slit nearly to one hip, gorgeous blonde hair drawn back from her face.

Serena was one of the most striking women Alice had ever seen and she was very clearly loved up with someone else. No wonder Zac was hurt, hiding out at Halesmere if he'd lost her. And she was as different from Alice as it was possible to be. Alice, with her wind-blown hair, skin exposed to the weather and the waterproofs she wore nearly every day. And she'd never have legs that long, even in killer heels. Her curves didn't feel quite so luscious now she'd been presented with this vision.

'She's very beautiful.'

'Yes. On the outside, at least. Not so much on the inside.'

'I'm sorry.' Alice touched his arm, dark hairs soft beneath her fingers. 'I know how it feels to be blindsided by something you're not expecting.' There were still occasional moments when she'd remember the sight of Gareth stumbling out of their bed, another woman smirking next to him.

'Thanks.' Zac placed the phone face down on the duvet, as though that would be enough to delete the image from the device, his mind, his memories. 'She messaged to say there was an online interview coming up and to let me know they were going to run an old picture of me and her. The interview's not why she messaged me, though. She likes to touch base every now and then, make sure I'm thinking about her.'

'Zac, that's awful.' At least Gareth had never tried to make a nuisance of himself when they'd split; he simply hadn't wanted to know once their shared lives had been divided.

'Serena's kind of the reason I'm here. We met at a race, and she completely bowled me over; I thought she was incredible. She ran her own marketing company, and worked for another team. We were together from that first weekend, and it seemed like we wanted the same things. A home, a family one day – we even got a puppy and I asked her to marry me six months after we met. I thought it was perfect, that I'd found my soulmate.'

Alice couldn't begin to compare her own steady marriage to Zac's life lived quite literally in the fast lane with a woman like Serena. Worlds apart, and somehow theirs had come together for now.

'We'd set a date for the wedding; it was going to be in Barbados once the season was over. Then I had my accident. Me with my leg in a cast and smashed up, while Serena told everyone how wonderful I was and that I was going to come back even stronger and win next time. At first I tried to tell her how nervous I was about racing again, but she shut me down. I played along, worried I would lose her too if she knew I was thinking of quitting. We postponed the wedding for a year because she said I needed to focus on winning the championship and that was more important. She was all about the future, only it just felt like it was getting further and further away from me.'

Zac tilted his head and Alice rested her cheek against his arm, trying to let him know she was sorry for what had happened, that the relationship he'd thought was forever and his accident had nearly crushed him too.

'Serena was livid when I announced my retirement after that last race, absolutely appalled, once she'd stopped smiling for the cameras. I realised then that I had no idea who we actually were outside of racing, and she left me that night. Six months later she married another driver and tagged me in her wedding photos.'

'I'm so sorry.' No wonder Neil had looked disgusted when he'd mentioned Serena's name that day after church. Was this why Zac didn't date, because he'd been so broken by the woman he'd loved and who'd left him for someone who could offer the success and attention she clearly craved?

'It's okay.' He sighed, running a hand through his hair. 'It's been over for a long time. Eventually she wanted her half of the house we'd bought and I had to sell it and move in with my dad. There wasn't much left when I quit racing and I couldn't afford to buy her out on my own. Not very clever – my dad was always telling me to wise up, in everything. He never much liked Serena.'

'I'm sorry for what you went through.' Alice shifted until she was behind him and wrapped both arms around his shoulders. 'I think you're pretty amazing, for what it's worth. And I'm saying that to you as a tree surgeon who drives an electric van, not some hotshot, sexy racing driver.'

'Thanks, Alice.' Zac covered her hands with his and she felt him relax as a long breath left his chest. 'So are you saying you think I'm sexy, but my van isn't? Or is it the other way around?'

'Right now you're leaning against me and letting me hold you,' she whispered. 'Which one do you think I meant?'

'Definitely the van.'

She smiled against his neck. 'Wrong answer. What happened to the puppy?' Alice was bristling again at the thought of his heart being broken twice over.

'She took that too.' His laugh was brief. 'It's okay, I didn't much like it. I'm not into dressing dogs up in clothes and carrying them around. It didn't like me either. Barked every time I got within two feet.'

'Silly dog,' Alice murmured. 'Who would want to chase you away?'

'You did, as I recall. That night in the pub when you said you didn't want to date anyone.'

'You said the same thing,' she reminded him. 'I understand why not.'

'Yeah.' Zac picked up her hand to brush it with his lips. 'I'm sorry about tonight. The past has a knack of turning up at the wrong moments.'

'It does. A few months after Gareth and I broke up we were tagged in a post by a charity we'd both supported. An easy mistake, just one of those things. Only he was at the event with his new partner, standing next to her and her two children.'

At the time it had nearly crushed Alice. He'd ended their marriage for another relationship, but not only that, a relationship with a woman who already had children. Gareth had skipped straight past the anguish of their own loss and launched himself into another family, a ready-made one, all beaming for the camera like their own marriage had never existed.

'It was weird, like seeing a stranger and yet one who I knew hated leaving dirty washing on the floor and snored when he slept on his back.' Alice huffed out a laugh. 'It sounds funnier when I say it out loud.'

'But it's not funny, not in the least.' Zac's voice was a low rumble against her hands resting against his chest.

'No. But it's over and I'm done with looking back.'

'Me too. Serena won't contact me again. I pointed out a few truths about our relationship and why they might not sound so great if I ever decided to talk about my career. There were rumours she was seeing her husband before we split and I didn't want to believe it at the time. I needed a different perspective to see our history for what it was, and I've found that here. Life's a bit simpler. That's why you're here too, isn't it? Because you're healing as well.'

'Yes.' Alice loved that he understood without needing her to explain every detail. That he knew what Halesmere and making a new life meant to her. Her fingers found the tag on his necklace, and she picked it up. 'Is this a date that's important to you?'

'It's the day I qualified as a tree surgeon, the start of my life after racing. I've done more courses since then, on woodland management and tree health. I was never a good kid at school, but I want to keep learning.' She sensed, rather than saw, his smile. 'I'm not just into cutting trees down.'

'That's good, because I'm all about the planting.' Alice couldn't hold back a quick yawn. 'Sorry. It's been such an emotional day.' Her arms around Zac slipped away and she eased herself back into bed.

'Do you want me to go? I know I should but I...' Zac was staring down at her and she saw the reply he wanted. She pulled the duvet back and he slid beneath it.

'Can I hold you?' she whispered, and he nodded. He turned over and she snuggled against his back, wrapping an arm around him. He felt so unfamiliar, his chest broad and firm, and she caught the moment when his breathing slipped into sleep, his hand over hers on his heart.

Chapter Fourteen

Alice opened her eyes, barely awake until she realised an arm was around her waist and Zac's chest against her back. He was still asleep, and she held her breath, loath to wake him up. Carefully, she reached for her phone to check the time. It was six thirty and he was due at work around eight. She didn't need to rush out this morning and planned to catch up on the admin she'd missed yesterday.

'Morning.'

The single word was a breath on her neck, and she whispered back, 'Morning. We should get up.'

'Should we?' The arm around her waist tightened and she slowly turned around. A smile lingered on those full lips, dark curls tousled by sleep, brown eyes somehow tender and teasing. She curled a palm against his cheek.

'I didn't realise your nose was freckled.'

'So's yours.' He touched his lips to it. 'And your shoulder. Both of them, in fact. How far do those freckles go?' His smoothed her top out of his way, mouth following, and she closed her eyes.

'Zac, your dad…'

'I know, I'm sorry.' He raised himself on an elbow. 'I didn't mean to make my staying here awkward for you.'

'It's okay, you haven't. It's my house and I'm glad you didn't leave last night.' Alice's smile was wistful. 'And Ella and the baby, it's so wonderful.'

'It is; I bet Stan didn't go home until he'd heard.' Zac paused. 'Alice, I'm not going to say anything to my dad, not unless you want me to?'

'I don't. This is just between us.'

'Agreed. He can think what he thinks.'

Her gaze wandered to the tattoo on Zac's arm, and she traced its outline with a finger. 'It's beautiful.'

'I love it. The symbolism of the leaves, the different colours changing through the seasons. A reminder that life keeps turning, spring follows winter. Light after dark.'

'You got it after you'd finished racing?'

'Yeah.' He tucked the hair falling to her face behind one ear. 'I knew you'd get it.'

'You don't mind?'

'You're asking me that? Now, in your bed, after what we talked about last night and I fell asleep next to you?' He laughed. 'No. It's too late for that.'

'So who's getting up first?'

'Me. I've got to get to work.'

Alice eased away from him and sat up, unwinding her arms to raise them in a languorous stretch.

'Alice,' he muttered hoarsely. 'Are you doing that on purpose?'

'No, I really did need to move. I thought you were getting up anyway.'

'I am; I have to.' He yanked the duvet back and swung his legs out of bed. 'Can we catch up tonight, maybe not here?'

'I've got an idea. Meet me at the studio around six?'

'Does it include dinner?'

'Only if you're going to cook it.'

'Either that or we'll go out.'

Halesmere was buzzing when Alice arrived later. She and Zac had shared a quick breakfast and Neil had tactfully eaten his in his room, but she'd decided to do her admin in the studio instead; she wasn't sure she could face a cheery conversation with Neil after Zac had spent the night in her bed. Stan was holding court in his workshop to celebrate the arrival of Ella and Max's baby son, and he and Pearl had pulled out all the stops. Pastries and bacon butties from the community shop were aplenty, and he'd even borrowed a coffee machine for those who didn't like tea or hot Bovril, so everyone knew it was a momentous occasion.

Ella's mum was staying in the cottage and Lily and Arlo had reluctantly gone off to school, with a promise from Max, who'd apparently seen them this morning after returning at six, that they could visit the baby and Ella this afternoon. All being well, she and new-born Isaac might be home in a couple of days and Stan, as the unofficial welcome party, was on it.

He'd tracked down a fifth chicken and was collecting it after lunch so it would be here when Lily and Arlo returned. Pearl said that Ella had suggested Isaac as the baby's name because it meant laughter, and Max loved it.

Sandy was at the workshop too, and when no one could put off tasks any longer, she followed Alice into her studio.

'Are you okay?' Sandy hovered in the doorway. 'I can't stay, I'm sorry, I'm off to visit someone in hospital but I just wanted to make sure you're all right. I know you're thrilled for them, but all this baby joy can't be easy.'

'I'm fine, Sandy, thank you.' Alice set her laptop down and flipped it open. 'I'm not so broken that I can't share in someone else's happiness.'

'I know. And you're doing brilliantly. You're settling in so well and Stan can't do enough for you.'

'He's so sweet.' Alice didn't mind changing the subject. 'Do you know what he's planning for Ella and Isaac when they come home?'

'No, but it could be anything from a marching band to a flypast. Who knows?' Sandy's phone was ringing, but she let it go to voicemail. 'And you and Zac, you seem to be getting on well.'

'Is that a question or a statement?' Did Sandy know he'd slept in her bed last night? Had Neil told her already, voiced his own concerns about how close Zac and Alice were becoming?

'Maybe a bit of both. Darling Alice, please don't forget he's leaving. I know he's got a job all set up.'

Alice gave her aunt a level stare. 'And that's why this is so much fun. Because it's not forever and there's nothing on the line, for either of us. Sometimes I feel like I've spent my whole life being sensible.'

'Right.' Sandy's voice was kind. 'That's good, then. Just remember a little bit of sense goes a long way. As long as you're both okay.'

'We are, thank you.' Alice logged herself into the laptop. 'Actually, I was going to ask if I can borrow your studio, please?'

'When do you want it?'

'Tonight? Would you mind?'

'Not at all.' Sandy found keys in her pocket and separated one. 'Just clear up and lock up is all I'm saying.'

'Promise.' They said goodbye and Alice got to work with her laptop, thinking about this evening with Zac as she replied to emails. She'd brought a change of clothes from home and later she went into the pottery studio at five to prepare. She saw him running up to the flat and twenty minutes later he emerged, changed into jeans and a shirt. He was crossing the courtyard and she opened the door to meet him.

'Hello.'

'Hey.' He paused, giving her a grin. 'Aren't you in the wrong place?'

'Not for what I've got planned.'

'Oh?' He quickly changed direction. 'That sound interesting.'

'I hope it will be fun as well.' Alice leaned past him to close the door.

Part work area, part shop, Sandy's studio was welcoming and comfortable: walls painted white with all shelving in natural oak. She specialised in porcelain and everything she made reflected her simple and elegant brand, from the narrow bud vases to pretty espresso cups and matching latte mugs. Alice had a full dinner service at home that Sandy had made for her, and she adored it. Her aunt often tried to persuade her to use it more often, but Alice only brought it out for special occasions, knowing it couldn't be easily replaced if a piece was lost.

'How are your centring skills?' She pointed to the wheel at the back of the workshop.

'Probably non-existent but I'm looking forward to finding out.' Zac took her hand. 'I was just thinking I'm not sure how we say hello, after last night. What do we do now, seeing as I fell asleep in your bed with you holding me the way you did? Maybe like this...'

He lowered his head to skim his mouth against her cheek.

'Or this?' Alice said softly. It might have been years since there'd been anyone else, but she trusted Zac, and that was both a reassuring and thrilling thought. She stood on tiptoe to let her lips touch the corner of his mouth. She heard Zac's breath catch, and a rush of longing and desire was swift, leaving every part of her body tingling.

'I'm so out of practice,' she whispered, trying to laugh away her inexperience.

'I don't think you need any,' he muttered. 'And you're not the only one.'

'Seriously?' Her head jerked back; she hadn't been expecting that.

'Yep.' His smile was wry. 'There hasn't been anyone since Serena. I'm not into meaningless flings or hook-ups, Alice. I don't understand the language and I can't be bothered to try. I gave up social media a while ago; I have a history and when people think they know it, sometimes they're more interested in that than me.'

'So we take this slowly, then?' Despite the desire, that was something of a relief. She didn't intend to change her mind but being with someone else after so long was still a leap.

'I think that's a nice idea. We'll take care of each other.' He let go of her hand to glance at the pottery wheel, the stool sitting next to it, the clay Alice had already divided into pieces. 'So where do you want me?'

'Ideally with you sitting on the stool so I can give you some guidance. You'd better put this on.' She handed him an apron, larger than hers, to cover his clothes.

'You know what you're doing, then?' Zac sat on the stool, which suddenly looked much smaller.

'I know more than you, anyway.'

'So I'm in your hands. This already looks fun.'

Alice swallowed. 'I thought you said you were out of practice too?'

'Are we still talking about pottery or something else?'

'Here.' She laughed as she placed a piece of clay into his hand. 'I've already wedged this, so it should be easier to work with and centre on the wheel.'

'Wedged?' He raised a brow.

'Precisely. The idea is to remove any air pockets, so the clay is more of an even texture. And the bottom is slightly rounded, see, so that it won't trap any air between it and the wheel while you're centring it.'

'So what do I do? Just whack it down?' His hand was poised.

'Sort of. But it needs to be in the centre. Try it.'

Zac's hand came down and despite the thud, his clay just missed the centre ring on the wheel.

'Try again. That's better, you're nearly there. Once more.'

This time the clay landed more evenly and in the right place on the wheel. 'Good. Now you need to get your body in the right position. May I?'

He nodded and she moved behind him, taking his left arm. 'Lean your elbow against your waist, like this, so your weight is also leaning into that side of your body. Good, now rest your forearm on the tray. You should roll up your sleeves. That's a nice shirt; it would be a shame to spoil it.'

'I can't.' He turned his head, a smile playing on his lips, inches from hers. 'My hands are covered in clay. You'll have to do it.'

Alice wiped her own hands and carefully rolled back his sleeves to his elbows, revealing the muscular arms she'd woken to find around her this morning. That thought was a distraction from clay and pottery and wheels.

'So now you can start centring the clay. Do you want me to show you how?'

'I think you'll have to.'

Alice was on Zac's left side, and she took his hand. 'Use your palm to hold it steady; curve it with your fingers around the clay, with some pressure, like this.'

'What about the pedal? Shouldn't the wheel be moving?' His voice was low, and that same quiver darted across her skin, hair brushing his face.

'Not quite yet.' She slid her fingers over his. 'Now bring your right hand down, in a fist, right in the centre and use the same pressure in both.'

She leaned across to flip some water over the clay. 'Press the wheel, gently, otherwise the clay will probably fly off. That's good, no faster.' She let go of his hands.

'Where are you going?' His were on the clay and it shot sideways, crashing into a heap on the edge of the wheel. 'Look what happens when you leave me alone.'

'So what are you suggesting?' She knew it and he'd already stopped the wheel and pushed the stool back to stand up.

'I think you're going to have to show me how to do it.'

Alice took his place, pulling the stool closer to the wheel; her legs were simply not as long as his. The wheel was wet, and she dried it; the clay wouldn't stick to the surface otherwise. She took another piece of clay and slapped it down onto the wheel, tried again when the first didn't land dead centre. She was utterly aware of Zac right behind her, and she inched forward on the stool.

'Maybe there's room for you to sit down too, then you can follow my hands, feel the pressure I'm using.'

She felt the stool sink under his weight, uncaring that she was pressed between him and the tray surrounding the wheel. His chest was firm against her back as his arms came around her, conscious of his hands covering hers around the clay, thumbs stroking them absently. He dropped a single word into her ear, breath light on her skin.

'Better?'

'Not for my concentration. I really am trying to teach you, but I don't think us sitting like this is helping much with your lesson.'

'Sorry.' His lips caught on her earlobe, and she gasped. Her head tilted onto his shoulder, and he accepted her silent invitation to let his mouth trail across her neck.

'I don't think you are sorry.' Her own voice was husky, and she had no idea what was happening with the clay. She looked down. It was still in her hands, just. 'We should try again.'

Zac shifted so Alice could tuck her left elbow against her waist and his forearm was beside hers on the tray. She flipped a little water over the clay again, his left hand around hers.

'See how I'm leaning to my left, using my weight to apply pressure through my hand?' She brought her right hand down on the clay in a fist. 'This is the same pressure. We want the clay to be fixed and firm on the wheel, so it doesn't slide off.'

Aware of Zac's nod, she was almost past caring about the supposed lesson, the clay slipping across the wheel, with him so very close. She tried again, keeping the wheel steadily turning with the pedal beneath her foot, fixing her concentration on that as best she could and not him at her back, pressed against her, hands wet and messy around hers. A minute later, just when Alice thought they were improving, her hand slipped and the clay shot off the wheel, splattering them both.

'I think we should give up.' She had to laugh. 'We're not exactly making progress and I've got to clean up the studio before we leave.'

'It was a lot of fun. I wouldn't mind doing this with you again.'

'Sure? Even though your shirt's in a bit of a mess?'

'I can change it. And you're not much better.' Zac offered a hand to pull her upright. 'Those dungarees are covered.'

'I've brought something else with me. Do you have any suggestions on where to eat?'

'I know a nice pub a few miles away. Would you like to try it?'

'What about your dad?' Alice bit her lip. 'I feel like we've abandoned him.'

'I dropped in something earlier he can just stick in the microwave. He doesn't mind and he can't sit on the bed all day; he needs to move.'

'As long as you're sure he's all right?'

'I am.' Zac looked around the studio. 'Let's clear up and then we can go.'

They had a lovely dinner in the pub, one Alice had never visited before. A roaring fire and Christmas decorations were cheery, although they were a reminder, as if she needed another one, that she and Zac would be going their separate ways when the holidays came. Would he miss her too? Single by choice, she was certain he wouldn't be for long if he decided to date again. He was temporary in every sense, and she would only think of now.

Conversation came easily and Alice shared her plans and hopes for the future of the Flower Shed. Zac offered nothing more about his new job and she didn't ask, wondering if she was the only one who didn't want to mention it. When they returned to the barn, Neil's bedroom door was open and he was watching television with his leg propped up, another ice pack underneath it. He greeted them cheerfully, telling them about his latest visitors, including Pearl again, who'd brought him a cake from the shop.

'Zac, I'm off to Hayley's tomorrow.' Neil cleared his throat. 'She said it wasn't fair on you, having to look after me, so I'm going to have a few days with them.'

'Dad, you don't need to do that.' Zac glanced at Alice, and she flushed. Was this their fault? Had they been too obvious, made it seem like he was in their way? 'Alice has been very generous, and I know you're comfortable here.'

'She has.' Neil gave her a smile and the glimpse of understanding in his gaze made the colour on her cheeks a little brighter. 'But I was meant to go back to my place tomorrow anyway, and Hayley said it's not a problem. I'll have the weekend with them and then I'll go home. It's another chance to see the kids as well.'

'I thought you said Hayley didn't have a spare bed?'

Neil coughed. 'Well, apparently that new sofa in their living room is a bed as well so I'll be fine.'

'Was this your idea?' Zac's eyes narrowed. 'Or did Hayley just come up with it out of the blue?'

'Does it matter? Sandy's going to drive me down. You two need some time to yourselves and she'll keep my place on the pottery course for another visit.'

'Dad, look...' Zac tailed off. 'It's not...'

'Life changes, Zac, just remember that. Even when you've made all your plans and you think you're sorted. Sometimes you just have to go with it. Thanks for everything, Alice – you'll never know how much I appreciate it. Time I went to bed.'

Neil closed the door quietly and she looked at Zac. 'Are you staying tonight?' Her voice was a breathy whisper and he nodded.

'If you're okay with it? But I was thinking I'd be back in there with Dad,' he murmured, hooking an arm around her. 'Next time you and I share a bed, I'd prefer us to be alone.'

'So would I.' Alice knew where they were headed as well, and she didn't want to be skulking around her own home. 'Because then we could eat breakfast naked or stay in bed all day.'

She didn't know where these words or the startling new assurance was coming from. Understanding Zac's history and his reticence to have another relationship after throwing himself into his previous one made them on some level the same. It had been a while for him, too.

The groan he uttered had her confidence leaping another level, his voice a murmur on her neck. 'That's assuming I'll be able to let you get out of bed at all. You feel incredible to hold and I don't want to let you go.' His hands tightened on her waist, and she leaned into him. She wouldn't be able to sleep for thinking about him beside her, wanting him. 'Alice, you can trust me with this, I promise.'

'I know. I do.'

'I want it to be wonderful for you.'

She had to gulp back the emotion his words produced. 'Wonderful for us.' She needed to make her own promise, to let him know that he could trust her too.

Chapter Fifteen

Before they'd reluctantly gone their separate ways last night, Zac had asked Alice if she'd like to spend a couple of hours with him, Lily and Arlo today, and she'd quickly said yes. He'd promised to look after the children while Max went to the hospital to see Ella and Isaac, giving them a run around, and Ella's mum a break for a bit. Zac had a plan and he'd told Alice to wrap up. She dressed accordingly and when she met him at Halesmere, he was wearing an unzipped coat over a T-shirt and walking trousers. They'd already said goodbye to Neil, who'd packed up his things and set off with Sandy down to his daughter's house.

'I'm worried now.' Alice made a point of looking to the skies. 'You've brought a hat. Are you expecting extreme weather?'

'I thought you might need two, that's all.'

She grabbed his hand, tugging him close. 'I feel much warmer these days,' she murmured. 'Can't think why.'

He'd already sorted a packed lunch and Stan was bustling around, almost beside himself with excitement at the thought of seeing Ella and baby Isaac, hopefully coming home on Monday. The other inhabitants of the courtyard were also busy, with Ana opening her jewellery studio after an early morning yoga session in the barn for the guests staying in the house. Marta was in her studio too, pouring candles ready for her spring collection. Ella's dad was on his way down from Scotland to join the family, ahead of a removal lorry so they could settle into their new house.

At the cottage, Alice shared a celebratory hug with Max before he left, delighted to be able to congratulate him and the children in person. Lily and Arlo's disappointment over not going to visit again until this afternoon with Ella's mum was tempered by the promise of a woodland adventure with Zac, and Alice loved that they didn't question her inclusion in the outing as well. Lily collected Prim and they set off, stopping to check on Arlo's sheep and feed the chickens and the guinea pigs on the way.

Lily and Arlo knew the wood well and they raced on ahead with Prim as Alice and Zac strolled behind them. The air was crisp, the ground carpeted with faded leaves still falling. Alice had learned to take her time in nature these past eighteen months, and they halted when a rare red squirrel shot across a branch in front of the children, making Arlo squeal with delight before Lily shushed him.

The wood was readying itself for winter, hawthorn saplings thin among the more established silver birch, narrow trunks glistening white against the brown of alder and rowan, and glossy green holly leaves sharp with spikes. Alice and Zac watched as the children leaped with Prim across a shallow steam, the water burbling busily over uneven, slippery stones beside a crumbling stone wall smothered in soft green moss.

'It's a perfect day to be day out, Zac. Thank you for asking me to join you.' Much as Alice liked Ella, Max and the children, Zac was their friend, part of their family too, especially with Isaac's birth and his new role as godfather. He hadn't needed to include her in this walk.

She bumped into him on purpose as they walked, stepping over twisting tree roots poking up from the ground.

'I'm glad you came.' Zac slung an arm around her shoulders. 'Two lively kids and an energetic dog notwithstanding, I wanted to have the time with you as well.'

'I've never been down this path before.' She'd spent more time in the meadow and her longer walks were snatched in between work and the weather. 'How far does the wood go?'

'We passed the boundary of Halesmere at the stream; this land is in different ownership. It's about another six acres and the footpath runs all the way through it.'

'So it's the Halesmere wood you're going to be working in, before you leave?' Sometimes Alice felt as though all roads were leading to that point now, and her life would change again.

'Yes.' Prim had bounded up, tongue lolling, and Zac reached down to pat her before she took off again, racing after the children. 'There's a lot of rhododendrons to come out and Max wants to plant more native species. The conifers aren't native, but they support wildlife with shelter and food, so they aren't going anywhere.'

'That's not what you said about mine.'

Zac laughed, and her arm went across his back, keeping him close too.

'Would it reflect very badly on my professional skills if I said they weren't as urgent as all that? I wanted to see you again.'

'Not in the least; I think you're an excellent tree surgeon. Had you not insisted on removing them so promptly, I might have been tempted to push one over and call you out anyway.'

'I won't get all the work Max wants done before I leave; it's a long-term project.' Zac halted, letting his arm drop as he faced her. Lily and Arlo were investigating a burrow with Prim, who was far too large to think about going down it.

'Does that mean you'll be coming back?' she asked lightly. His connections to Halesmere were growing and each was another thread, tying him to this place. Might she be one of them? She didn't dare presume or hope; it was against everything they'd promised each other about his moving on.

'I'm sure I will,' he replied just as casually. 'But it's a twelve-hour round trip so I won't be nipping down every weekend.'

'I understand.' If he'd meant that as a warning, then she'd got it. Have fun, enjoy this time, but it wasn't going to last. Alice took a deep breath; every minute together was starting to count. But next year wasn't here yet and Zac was. 'Are we still taking the bikes out later? I could do with the practice.'

'I'm game if you are.'

'As long as you promise to go easy and feed me cake afterwards.'

'I'm promising no such thing.' He went to grab her, and she darted out of his way. 'You need those miles now, Harvey, not more cake. But if you'd like to come home with me, I will arrange dinner.'

His eyes were understanding when they caught hers, letting her know he wasn't making light of her reason for entering. But the triathlon was months away and she would get there; she could feel it. Every day she was stronger – physically and mentally – and every day she was making progress and contentment was returning. She just couldn't allow too much of it to be bound up in Zac and the time they were spending together.

'I'd love to. Have you ever done a triathlon, or a road race?' She'd wondered about an outlet for the competitiveness that had dominated his racing career, when he'd hated other drivers getting in his way, and her question was a distraction from thoughts of going back to the flat with him later. 'You're obviously fit enough, and I can imagine you battling to the finish to cross the line in front.'

'No, my competition days are over.' Prim was racing towards them with Arlo in hot pursuit and they stepped aside as she crashed past. Lily blew her dog whistle and Prim turned and took off, skidding to a halt to sit in front of her, waiting expectantly for a treat.

'I don't want to go there, Alice. I know myself and I'd push too hard. I hate the thought of having another accident, maybe surgery again, hospitals, physio, recovery, all that. I was very, very competitive and it cost me my career. Racing for fun, when there's nothing on the line but finishing first, isn't worth it now. I need to be able to work.'

'But you ride those mountain trails! Surely you're taking just as much of a risk when you do that. You could crash at any moment.'

'I know my limits now.' He shrugged and she took his hand to squeeze it. 'I can get off any time I like, slow down and take it easy. There's a reason I ride alone.'

'So no one can see, if you...' Alice wasn't sure if her guess was correct, or that he would want her saying it out loud.

'Yeah.' He forced out a laugh as he looked away. 'Even my dad thinks I ride hard, when I don't. I just let everyone

213

assume. But I have to keep trying otherwise I'd never get out there and that's not how I want to live.'

'I understand.' Alice put her arms around Zac, holding him tightly. 'I'm sorry you won't be here in the summer to see me finish the race.'

'Who says I won't?' He tilted his head to look at her. 'I'll be there, dangling cake to get you over the line.'

'You will?' That was an unexpected pleasure. 'I won't need the cake; just the sight of you will be enough.' She hesitated. 'And I'd love you to be there, but please don't make a promise you might not want to keep, Zac. I know I'm going to be okay, more than that, and it's ages away. Things might have changed for both of us by then.'

'I know. But I also know what it means to you.'

He dropped a kiss onto her hair, and they separated as the children reached them, pink-faced and breathless. Lily and Arlo were ready to eat, so they turned around, heading back towards Halesmere to find a perfect spot the children knew well. Alice had never seen this lovely glade before, the tree canopy above them bare without its leaves. She helped them spread out a picnic blanket and Arlo was the first to flop down onto it.

Lily shared the crusts from her sandwiches with Prim, who was hoovering them up gratefully as she leaned against Lily, head on one of Lily's legs. Alice had made hot chocolate and she shared four cups between them, so welcome on such a brisk winter's day. The children didn't sit still for long, and Zac suggested a game, splitting into pairs of one older and one younger. Lily immediately wanted girls versus boys and Alice was happy to oblige.

One person would be blindfolded, and their partner would lead them to a tree to explore it using touch and smell. Then the blindfolded person would be returned to their starting point via a different route, the blindfold removed so they could try to recognise their tree from their sensory exploration. Alice gave up her hat to Lily and Zac did the same with the spare he'd brought, pulling it low over Arlo's eyes. They chose a tree and led the children out of their glade. Lily was convinced she had a silver birch from the single narrow trunk and thin stems, while Zac had guided Arlo to a beech, its trunk rippled and ancient.

After touching, sniffing and trying to describe everything they'd discovered, Lily and Arlo were led back to their starting point and Alice and Zac removed the blindfolds. Both children managed to find their trees again, which delighted them no end. The adults needed a turn too, and Alice and Zac obliged, pulling the hats over their own eyes, and laughing as they tried not to stumble over uneven ground.

It didn't take Zac long to identify the holly Arlo had him touch when he caught a finger on a spiky leaf and he threatened to dunk his young partner in the stream as a punishment. Alice found her tree trickier, and it was Zac who identified it as ash when her blindfold was removed, its lateral black buds in opposite pairs making it easy for him. The children begged Zac to bring them again for more games another day, and he promised to show them how to light a fire and bake apples.

Back at the cottage, the children rushed to get changed for the hospital and Ella's mum pointed to the gifts Stan had made. He'd wanted to keep Lily and Arlo firmly in the centre of all the excitement now they were three. There was no marching band, flypast or dressing up, as Sandy had wondered the other day.

Instead, he'd brought over three wooden boxes for Ella and Max to give to the children once Isaac was home, and Alice had to cling on very firmly to tears when she saw them. Each was a tiny wooden trunk in miniature, with thin strips of wood carved to represent straps, and a beautifully crafted and clever lock. The boxes were big enough for keepsakes and small enough to hold in two little hands. But it was the decoration that had her gulping.

Lily, Arlo and Isaac's names were carved and varnished into the wood, along with an oak leaf and their dates of birth. Underneath the leaf Stan had inscribed: *Fill with dreams to take you travelling and memories to bring you home.* They were so simple, beautiful and heartfelt, and Alice guessed he must have been waiting for the baby's name to be revealed so he could carve it the minute he found out.

Ella's mum was desperate to meet the baby later, and Alice slipped away with Zac. Stan was in the courtyard and on impulse she ran over and gave him a hug. He told her he had better things to do than stand around being popular all day, and Christmas trees didn't tend to decorate themselves, he'd found. But she'd seen the glint in his eye as she turned away and he coughed.

—

'Did you pick this route on purpose?' Alice halted to stare warily at the hill rising in front of them. 'I do not like that look of that.'

'You'd better get used to it because it's part of the triathlon course.' Zac was sitting on his own bike, one foot on the ground. 'Don't forget there might be cake at the end.'

'Might?' She raised a hopeful brow. 'It had better be a good one. Victoria sponge or a scone with jam and proper clotted cream, not that airy stuff that dissolves before you can eat it.'

'Alice, there's only one café for miles; you'll have to take what you can get.' He adjusted the strap on his helmet and swallowed some water.

'That's very bad planning on your part,' she grumbled. 'I'm going to need some kind of incentive to get me up that bloody hill on two wheels.'

'Will this do, for starters?' He leaned over, bending his head so their helmets didn't bump together, touching his lips to hers in a brief kiss.

'I was thinking more like a long hot bath afterwards but seeing as I currently don't have one, that will definitely do. As a starter.' Alice caught hold of his jacket, keeping him close.

'You can have a long hot bath later. At the flat, before I make you dinner.'

'You have a bath in that tiny space?'

'A very big one. In my bedroom.'

'I like the sound of it even more now. Will you run my bath for me?' She lowered her voice on purpose and he laughed.

'Don't push it, Harvey; this hill's not that steep.'

They'd parked in a hamlet and had already ridden a couple of miles before the ground started to climb, stopping for a drink. Alice was trying to distract herself with the view. Woodland on their right rose to meet a high fell, clouds skidding over the top, trees bare and bony without their leaves.

A lake lay below them, glistening blue, and a group of hardy paddle boarders in wetsuits were braving the chill of the water. She shuddered, thinking of swimming in there next year. But her resolve to complete the triathlon came straight back the moment she thought of why she was entering this race, and for whom.

At the top of the hill, she yelled in triumph when Zac told her it was the highest climb in the triathlon cycle. Her thighs might be screaming and shaky, and her face scarlet, but she'd done it. After a quick breather, they carried on until they arrived in a small village and sat outside the local pub to enjoy a drink.

'I've decided that triathlons would be an awful lot more fun if there were café stops along the way.' Alice produced a couple of energy bars from her rucksack and passed one to Zac. 'I bet there'd be loads of takers.'

'You think?' He unwrapped the bar and chucked the paper in a bin. 'That's a whole other race.'

'Exactly. Every time I set foot in a café, there's always a group of cyclists tucking into cake so there must be something in it.'

'Nice try but we're not finished for today. Let's go.'

'I'm not bothered about cake; I'm looking forward to my bath. It's been weeks and I've missed them.'

It wasn't even really that keeping her going; it was the thought of spending more time with Zac, in his flat, his home for now. They left the village to follow a track that would eventually lead them back to their starting point and the van. Alice was focussed on her own path as they cycled, only vaguely aware of him in front, so when his bike suddenly jerked and sent him crashing to the ground, she fought to control her own, managing to rebalance as she shot past and hauled on the brakes.

'Zac!' She flung her bike aside to run back. He was already sitting up, a trickle of blood running from his cheek. 'Don't move; are you all right? I'm going to need the first aid kit from your rucksack. I'll be careful, I promise.'

'I'm fine.' He groaned as he gingerly touched each shoulder in turn. 'It's just a scratch.'

'Maybe it is, and you are, but there's blood and it needs cleaning up.' She was working hard to keep her voice steady and not betray her shock that he'd come off. Her phone was in her own rucksack if they needed any help, and she eased the bag from his back.

'Are you in pain?' If he was hurt then it might have to be mountain rescue; she doubted she'd be able to help him walk if he needed support. Phone signal would likely be non-existent out here but she'd already registered her number with mountain rescue so she could text for help, and that should make it through.

'No. My pride's dented, that's all.' Pale, with a tremble in the fingers resting on his thigh, Zac smiled nonetheless in an obvious effort to calm her. 'It's only a cut. Let's just carry on and get back. It's not far.'

'In a minute, when we catch our breath. We've both had a shock and it's probably not a good idea to move until you're certain you're okay.'

'I know when I'm hurt and when I'm not, Alice, and I'm all right.'

'I'm sure you do but I'm cleaning that wound up, whatever you say.' It would delay him for the time she wanted him to take, at least.

Alice tore open a packet of antiseptic wipes and carefully removed the blood from his face. He was utterly still, beyond a muscle twitching in his cheek and the fingers trembling on his thigh. The cut needed a couple more wipes and she finished with antiseptic cream she also found in his kit. The cold was rising from the ground, the chill already seeping into her legs and back, and it was damp. She wondered if he'd even noticed.

'Ready to go?' He grimaced as he went to stand up.

'If you are?' She was watching him as well as she packed everything away, stuffing the rubbish into a small plastic bag, which went in her pocket.

'I'm fine, thanks. We'll stiffen up if we stay here too long and we shouldn't get cold.'

They set off and she followed, trying to keep an eye on Zac as she rode. They made it safely back to the van and she refused to let him lift the bikes into it in case he was more injured than he'd let on.

'Would you like me to drive us home? You can put your head back, just chill.' She slammed the door on the bikes, turning to face him.

'What? No.' He laughed off her suggestion, already heading around to the driver's side.

'You're quite sure?' Alice put out an arm to halt him, recognising the hint of steel in his expression. She'd seen it often enough before in her old career, when someone wanted to drive and probably shouldn't.

'Totally.'

'Zac, if there's something wrong here then say so. I don't want you to drive if you don't feel comfortable doing it. If your head hurts or you feel dizzy.' She wasn't sure how far she was prepared to push this point. 'It's not fair on you or me, or anyone else on the road, if you were to have an accident because you're not feeling right. I'm an excellent driver, as the saying goes, and I've driven way bigger lorries than your van. I'll be careful.'

'It's not that I don't trust you, in theory.' His voice was hollow, empty of his usual confidence.

'Then what is it?' She had a feeling she knew and didn't want to second-guess him. 'This is just between us, I promise.'

'I don't really trust anybody to drive me.' Zac's breath escaped in a long sigh as he leaned against the van. 'It's a control thing. I worry about someone else losing it behind the wheel and me having another accident. I know it's stupid, pointless, all those things, and I'm still trying to get past it.' He shrugged. 'I don't even drink so I can always drive when I need to. I'm always the mate giving the lifts, picking people up.'

'It's okay, I understand why you'd feel that way.' Alice raised a hand to his face, his smile brief against her palm. She also liked to be in the driving seat; never again would she be a passenger in her own life. 'I'm sorry if I triggered something.'

'You didn't; it's not your fault. It makes sense to offer – anyone would do the same.'

She was thinking of Zac's care for her that night in her studio, when she'd been bereft over the date of a birthday that never was. The career he'd loved and lost, the fears he still lived with and refused to reveal. How had they penetrated each other's layers the way they had, both seeing behind all they presented to the world? She was done with fear and the worries it brought about what was next. What might land in her lap tomorrow and shock her all over again. And she trusted him.

'Promise me your head isn't hurting, you feel dizzy or anything like that? Because if you do and you drive me back, then…'

'I'm not, I swear. I wouldn't risk you, Alice. I'd be calling a taxi or even Stan to come and get you. I didn't hit my head; my cheek caught on a rock when I went down. I was lucky. I'll probably be aching and sore tomorrow, that's all.'

'Okay.' She got into the passenger seat, and he started the engine. She had no reason to doubt his awareness as he drove, no need to doubt his word. He was as quick, efficient and careful as ever and they were soon back at Halesmere. The courtyard was quiet now the visitors and all the artists had finished for the day, and the chickens in the gardens were squawking, about to go to bed.

'Would you still like that bath?' Zac shifted to face her in the van.

Alice didn't want to go home yet, not alone, and there was no bath in the barn. And no Zac, unless she invited him to join her. 'Yes please. I think I've earned it after that climb.'

He went ahead up the steps and unlocked the door. Inside the flat, he switched on a lamp, the afternoon easing into evening already, revealing pale grey walls and a compact white kitchen. He drew the curtains and her anxious gaze flickered up to a roll-top bath behind oak spindles on the mezzanine floor, the glimpse of a bed further back.

Her heart was racing as she clutched her bag in front of her like a barrier. What might it be like, this first time with someone else? Why had all her confidence suddenly fled when they'd already spent the night in the same bed? But this was different, oh so different, and still she wanted this, him, with every part of her body and soul.

'Would you like me to take that?'

Zac held out a hand and her voice cracked as she gave him the bag. 'Please.' Adrenaline was quivering in her limbs. 'I'm a bit nervous. Sorry.'

'Hey, don't apologise. You're not the only one.' He ran a gentle finger down her cheek. 'There's no pressure here, no expectation, okay? This is whatever you want it to be.

You can have a long hot bath and I'll make us some dinner if you like.'

'What about you?' she croaked. 'What do you want?'

'I want you, Alice,' he said softly. 'But we can talk about that when you're ready. Why don't you give me five minutes to run you that bath and then come up?'

Chapter Sixteen

Alice couldn't stop trembling as Zac moved around upstairs, the rushing of the water filling the bath matching the pulse pounding in her neck. She took off her trainers, leaving them beside the front door, as though she might flee into the night at any moment.

'Ready?'

He was leaning over the spindles, and she placed a hand on the banister, one cautious foot following the other up the stairs. His bedroom was small, tidy, the bed neatly made with a laptop on one bedside table and oak wardrobes built into the eaves. The roll-top bath looked incredibly inviting, with foaming bubbles and rising steam, and she kept her eyes on it and not him.

'I didn't know if you'd brought anything with you, so I've put some stuff in.' Zac pointed to a bottle on the floor. 'Lizzie gave it to me as a housewarming present.'

'That's nice.' Alice was still in the yoga kit she'd worn for cycling, hair scraped back, pink face, palms clammy. 'Are you going to go downstairs, or...'

'Tell me what you want me to do.'

'Stay,' she whispered. She had to lean against the end of his bed to steady herself when he cupped her face with both hands, deep brown irises darkening some more. Her breath caught as he placed a kiss on her forehead. His lips had barely skimmed her skin and still she felt his touch in every part of her body as desire raced through her. He kissed each eyelid in turn, the tip of her nose and her cheeks.

'You're still shaking.' Zac gathered her into his arms, smoothing his hands over her back. 'Does that help?'

'Yes.' She held him too, her cheek against his chest, his own racing heart giving her confidence. Was that her voice, so full of longing? Had she ever wanted someone quite so much as she did him in these moments? 'Zac, it's been so long and I'm…'

'Perfect.' His hands went to her shoulders so he could look at her. 'Alice, I've thought of you every single day since we met. I'm not even sure you know how strong and incredibly sexy you are.'

'Sexy? Looking like this?' Why hadn't she planned a candlelit dinner at the barn, when she'd be wearing a dress, not this practical black kit? It didn't even feel breathable right now.

'I think you look hot in everything you wear, even those waterproof trousers. Especially with the dungarees. It's quite a unique look, entirely yours.'

'Now you're teasing me.'

'Maybe a little, but it's also true.' The laughter disappeared from his eyes. 'Are you sure about this, us? We're not a next step you have to make yourself take if you don't want to.'

'I'm absolutely certain,' she whispered. 'When you hold me it's almost too much and somehow not enough. I want more. I want everything with you, if you want me too?'

Alice had to ask the question as she sought his own certainty, already lost in his unspoken promise that he would take care of her this first time since the end of her marriage. She wanted to take care of him too and never had anyone looked at her with such desire and longing, as if they had all the time in the world to make this last and every moment would never be enough.

His reply was to capture her mouth with his and they were kissing as though trying to banish the memory of anyone who'd come before. Nerve endings in her body felt on fire as she clung to him, kissing him back with the same frantic desire. Every step they'd taken since the beginning had put them on this path and now Alice was ready to run.

She dragged down the zip on her jacket and he slipped it from her shoulders and tossed it aside. Her confidence surged again at the stifled groan he uttered as his hands began to explore curves outlined by the tight base layer. She could barely wait another minute and her fingers covered his, inviting him to remove her top, and he raised her arms to pull it over her head.

'Alice,' Zac muttered roughly. He dragged in a breath at the sight of her pink satin bra edged with black lace roses. 'You're wearing that under those layers?'

'A sports bra would have been more practical, but this is prettier,' she whispered. 'Cycling kit isn't the most attractive thing to wear so I needed something nice to make up for it.'

'Nice?' His hands were around her waist, thumbs smoothing her skin in a rhythm she found entirely too distracting as they edged higher. 'You look incredible. How am I ever going to train with you again after this?'

'You'll just have to try.' Alice was impatient as he kneeled to roll down tight leggings and he took his time, placing soft kisses on the body he was uncovering until she whispered his name, unsteady on her own feet. He stood up, gathering her in his arms as he murmured against her ear.

'They match.'

'Yes. I want to see you too.' Her own voice was husky as she reached for his top and tugged it over his head, letting it follow her clothes to the floor. He helped her remove the rest until he was left in tight grey shorts edged with green. He took her hands, placing them on his chest, covered with dark hair running to his stomach, so she could explore as he had done.

'Zac, you're beautiful,' she whispered. 'Inside and out.' Her two hands didn't seem enough to discover his muscled body, and she followed a path down his chest with her mouth until he was clutching her shoulders, his eyes burning and desperate on hers.

'Are you getting in that bath or I am taking you to bed right now?' he muttered, tugging her upright.

'I think I should have my bath. You took the trouble to make it lovely for me.'

'Alone?' Zac trailed a finger across her shoulder, letting it slide beneath her bra strap until it slipped down to her elbow.

'Isn't there room for both of us?' She watched his gaze following the second strap along the same path and his hands went around her back to the clasp.

'Okay?' he whispered, dropping a kiss on her neck, and she nodded frantically, uncertain whether her legs would actually hold her up for much longer.

'More than okay. Are you?'

'Same.'

Their underwear followed their clothes and she'd never felt sexier or more confident in her own body; Zac's eyes were telling her everything she needed to know about how she looked and what he felt. The water was still hot when she got in the bath and he followed, drawing her gently against him. Her head was on his shoulder as his hands began to explore, every sense blazing in anticipation of his touch. His knees were bent to accommodate his legs and she felt his own reaction as her toes teased his calves, tracing his scar with her foot.

'Would you like me to wash your hair?' he murmured against her neck.

'I'd love you to.' Never had Alice shared a bath with anyone before now and he took his time to return his hands to her head, gently tilting it until her hair was soaked. Utterly weightless in the water, she couldn't hold back a tiny moan of desire and pleasure as he slowly massaged shampoo through her hair and carefully rinsed it off.

Alice had no more words to tell him how she felt as she wriggled around. Only her body could continue this conversation they'd started. He cupped her jaw to hold her as they kissed, and she wanted only him.

–

Neither of them could be bothered to cook and when they did get hungry, Zac left his bed to disappear downstairs, returning with pitta bread stuffed with chicken and salad, and bottles of beer. He'd bought red wine for her, and she hoped it didn't sound presumptuous when she asked him to save it for another time.

'You're making breakfast, just so you know.' He left their empty plates on the floor after they'd eaten and Alice curled an arm across his stomach.

'Oh, am I?' She ran a teasing finger up to his chest, across it, his hand tightening on her hip. 'Does that mean I'm staying?'

'If you want to? I'll drive you home if not.'

'Please don't.' She wanted to banish the uncertainty in his gaze, and she inched higher to kiss his shoulder. 'I don't want to be anywhere but here, with you.'

'Same.' He took hold of the duvet, a lazy smile on his lips. 'Are you warm enough?'

'Very.' Alice eased away from him to stretch unhurriedly.

'Good, because then you don't need this.' He slid the duvet away to lean over her, kissing her collarbone before letting his mouth trail a little lower.

'I might. I get cold in the night.' She laughed as he gave her a look that was somehow loaded with desire and mischief all at once. 'Can you lend me something to sleep in?'

'I already am. My bed.'

–

When Alice woke in the morning, it took her a moment to remember where she was. Zac's flat, in his bed. In his arms as well, one curled around her, and she smiled when he murmured a greeting, smoothing her hair from her face to kiss it.

'Hello.' She kissed him back; his mouth was the only part of him she could easily reach, and she was too comfortable to move. He'd warmed her so thoroughly she wasn't sure she would ever feel cold again, except perhaps in her heart. He'd begun to thaw that too, and she was trying not to dread what the new year would look like without him. 'Did you sleep well?'

'Very. I fell asleep with you in my arms, lying next to me, so… How about you?'

'I feel extremely well rested, which is surprising considering we were so late and every time I was about to fall asleep you woke me up.'

'Not on purpose. You feel wonderful and I wasn't the only one. If you hadn't…' He laughed as Alice changed her mind about moving and leaned over him, silencing him with another kiss. The first was followed by another on his jaw and then his chest, and she looked up.

'I'm hungry,' she murmured. 'I never usually sleep this late.'

'Maybe that's because you don't usually make love the way we did last night.' He was sliding down the bed to join her. 'And this morning.'

'That was hours ago.'

'Exactly. So I think maybe we should do that again. Start the day as we mean to go on.'

'What about breakfast?'

'You can get up and make it any time you like. I'm not going to stop you.'

'Okay. Shall I do it now?'

'Please.' Zac dropped a kiss behind her ear. Another landed on her shoulder and then her neck. 'I thought you were getting up?'

'And I thought you weren't going to stop me?'

'I'm not,' he murmured, inching lower. 'I'm not doing a thing. I'm not even touching you.'

'I think your mouth right there definitely counts as touching. I thought you were hungry as well?'

'Let me show you just how much.'

Alice closed her eyes, and all thoughts of breakfast were abandoned. It was another forty minutes before she dragged herself out of his bed, searching for her bag. She found it behind the bath, where he'd left it last night. Zac propped a hand beneath his head, watching as she lifted out an ivory silk robe she'd never worn. She slipped it on and tied the belt.

'You're wearing that to bring me breakfast?'

'I am. I didn't bring much else with me and I'm not putting that cycling kit back on now.' She looked at him over her shoulder at the top of the stairs and very nearly turned around. He was sitting up in bed, the duvet around his waist, and she was wondering again if breakfast could wait.

'Please don't be long.'

'I'll try.'

Downstairs, it only took a couple of minutes to explore the cupboards in the tiny kitchen, and ten minutes later she returned to the bedroom with a tray.

'Tea and toast. There isn't any cereal and anything else would take too long. I hope you don't mind crumbs in the bed.'

'Not if you're joining them. Come here.'

Alice set the tray down beside him and he took her hand, sliding her onto his lap. 'Do you have any plans for today?'

'No plans, just an idea.' Last night was already over and she'd made sure to keep today free, just in case. 'Do you?'

'No.' The teasing laughter from before disappeared. 'Alice, just say if this is too much and it's not what you want but I was wondering how you felt about spending the day together?'

'Really? I'd love that.' She curled an arm around his neck, pulling him in for a kiss.

'Perfect. So what's your idea?'

'Didn't you say you wanted to see my car?'

'I did. I've been wondering when you were going to suggest it.' Zac hooked a finger through the belt on her robe.

'Then how do you fancy a drive up the coast?'

'I can't think of anything else I'd rather do.' He undid the belt and slid the robe from her shoulders. 'Later.'

Alice showered and changed at the barn and when they were ready, she opened the garage, starting her Porsche with the usual thrill as the engine roared into life. Everything inside it, from the steering wheel beneath her fingers, the view of the three dials on the dashboard and the seat snug around her, were all so familiar as she eased the car onto the drive, winter sunlight streaming off it.

'Wow. That's some colour.'

'Are you being rude about my car already?' A breeze was catching at her hair as she got out and gave him an indignant look. 'I know she's bright, but I love her.'

'So this isn't the right moment to say something about bananas?'

'You'd better not,' she warned, one arm leaning on the open door. She turned the engine off and flicked the keys at him. 'Not if you're going to drive.'

'Me?' The grin faded as Zac came around to her side of the car. 'Alice, are you sure? You don't have to do this, not if you don't want to.' He hesitated. 'I'll be okay. I trust you.'

'You do? That's so lovely.' She raised a hand to his face. 'But you've never seen me drive.'

'Well, how fast can you really go in a lorry, and this?' He ran a hand along the door. 'It's practically an antique.'

'Do you want to take her out or not?' Not all of Alice's outrage was pretend now, and he laughed as he kissed her.

'I definitely do. But only if you promise to drive us back.'

'Deal.'

Zac drove north, keeping to the coastal route as they passed through small villages and Georgian towns with pretty, pastel-coloured properties. Alice had barely ever sat in the passenger seat of her own car, and it was a completely different and exhilarating experience to driving it herself. He handled the car so brilliantly, barely wasting an inch of tarmac, and the car, old though it was, responded. They didn't pull over until they reached a seaside town with spectacular views of the Solway Coast a couple of hours later.

'You're an incredible driver.' Alice tucked her arm through Zac's as they wandered along a path beside the beach, hugging him close. 'Loved every second.'

'Thank you. And thanks for trusting me with your...'

'Don't you dare say "banana"! Because that will be your first and last drive if you do!'

'I wasn't going to,' he protested as she wriggled free and poked him in the ribs. 'Okay, maybe I was.' He caught her up, wrapping an arm around her shoulders.

'Oh, smell that!' She loved the cold, biting air on her face, a beanie holding her hair back. 'Fish and chips? I'm buying. It's compulsory when you're by the sea.'

They had to queue; even out of season, the little town was busy with visitors, and they huddled on a bench facing the beach, eating the food straight from the trays. The light was flawless, the horizon so clear they could see the

Isle of Man in the distance, rising like a serene blue whale out the water.

'I've never been this far north in Cumbria before,' Zac remarked. 'It's beautiful and so different.'

'Me neither.' Alice stared straight ahead, trying not to let thoughts of him moving even further north in a few weeks spoil these hours together. For all the promises she'd made to herself, and even to him, that they were just having fun and could walk away whenever they wanted, it didn't feel quite so easy right now.

Zac looked at her as though he was the only person who'd ever really seen her and he'd made their first time together the most wonderful experience of her life. He'd awakened senses she'd never known she possessed, and she'd found confidence and strength in his desire for her.

He'd shared with her the most vulnerable and distressing time in his life and she knew how hurt he'd been by a woman who'd loved what he represented rather than who he was. Alice had held him that night in her bed as he'd fallen asleep, knowing she would always feel something for him. He had so swiftly become a part of her life that she was coming to dread giving him up. But she wouldn't tell him any of this; she had to make it easier and not let him suspect that she was beginning to wish things were different, that there wasn't a lovely new job waiting for him six hours north of Halesmere, and her.

'Ready to go? You were hungry again.' Zac stood and took her empty tray, pausing for a kiss.

'It must be the cold.' She blinked away the sadness, smiling up at him. 'Let's go and explore the beach before we freeze on this bench; I can see rock pools.'

They lingered over coffee in a café after messing around in the sand, poking through pools in search of crabs and miniature sea creatures. The afternoon was disappearing into evening when they set off for home. Alice drove, not quite so quickly, and after an hour she realised that Zac had fallen asleep, and the sight made her heart clench. He trusted her and she trusted him. It was all very simple and yet so hopelessly complicated. She drove them back to Halesmere, holding him tightly for a final kiss good night.

'Would you like to come back to the flat with me?'

'I don't think so. We've both got work in the morning and all that sea air has definitely made me sleepy.'

'That, and being awake for a lot of last night.'

'Yes.' She'd thought of it all day: being in his arms, holding him, making love the way they had and taking care of each other. 'Maybe we could grab a drink or dinner one night, if you're around?'

'That sounds a bit like one of those "I'll call you" messages,' Zac said lightly. 'Only they never do call.'

'I didn't mean it to be. I just think we should be careful, that's all. We've spent quite a lot of time together and today has been wonderful.'

'Are you saying it's a mistake?' He sighed as he let go of her hand. 'Because I know it's not straightforward, but it doesn't feel like a mistake to me. Right now I can't think past you and me, together.'

'Zac, you're leaving,' she said quietly. 'We can't keep this going, whatever it is. Six hours is a long way and neither of us needs a complication like that in a new relationship.'

'I know, I get it. And I wasn't looking for commitment, for anything while I'm here. My life is going to be somewhere else. But what do we do, Alice, between now and then? I want to see you and I know it won't be easy to walk away after what we've shared. But if you need this to be over now, then I understand.'

'Let's just sleep on it and see how we feel tomorrow,' she said softly. 'I want to see you too.'

Chapter Seventeen

On Monday, Halesmere was excitedly gearing up for Ella and Isaac's homecoming. Alice arrived early, half hoping to catch a glimpse of Zac before he left for work. But his van was already gone and most of the landscaping team with him. With Max on paternity leave, Will had taken over as project lead at the hotel and the team were trying to keep ahead of the weather if they could. Ana was working and doing her best to ignore Stan, who kept popping in to pass the time until Isaac arrived. In the end Alice heard her tell him if he didn't let her get on with Christmas orders, she'd go online and sign him up for spin classes at the nearest gym. That did the trick and he shot off back to his workshop before Ana could carry out her threat.

It was dark by four and Alice was ready for home. Despite what she'd said to Zac last night, she didn't feel any differently about him today. He was still in her thoughts, she still wanted to see him and the idea of letting go of any time they might have together before he left was an uncomfortable niggle that just wouldn't go away. A light was on in his flat and after a moment's hesitation, she went over and knocked.

'Hey.' Zac's grin lit up his face and she knew hers was telling the same tale. 'I was about to call you.' He stepped back. 'Do you want to come in?'

'Tell me why you were going to call me first.' If he'd decided to err on the side of caution then it wouldn't help her resolve if she was in his space, close to him.

'It's maybe not what you're expecting. Ella and Isaac are home, and Max wondered if we'd like to see them.'

'We? You and me?'

'It's not such a strange thought. He knows we've been spending time together – everyone does; we haven't exactly been keeping things a secret. Stan saw us leaving the flat yesterday and I think us kissing before we even got in the van might have given something away. But I understand if you'd rather not go.'

'Oh Zac, I'd love to see Isaac, of course I would.'

'Sure?'

'Certain.' She swallowed. 'He's your godson, and I'm thrilled for all of you. They must be expecting loads of visitors; it's very good of them to think of me.'

'Shall I say we'll come over now?' Zac's hand found hers to squeeze it firmly. 'If they're okay with it?'

'Absolutely.'

–

At the cottage, Alice took a deep breath as Max opened the door to Zac's knock and Lily was right behind him, bouncing excitedly with Prim. Zac was holding Alice's hand and she knew she could've made him let go, but she appreciated his support and his understanding that this might be a happy occasion tinged with some sadness for her. More than anything, more than whatever hormones or emotions might do to her now, she was going to celebrate with others and delight as they did in their children and families. Life would be too hard otherwise.

Arlo was busy with his toy sheep as it was too dark to do anything more with the real ones tonight. Ella was tucked up on a sofa in the family room, a Moses basket beside her. Lily and Prim trotted in first, followed by Alice and the two men. Alice gave Ella a hug, congratulating her before she peeped in the basket at the tiny baby. He was asleep, his head dusted with fine dark blonde hair, miniature fists pink and scrunched.

'Oh, Ella, he's beautiful,' Alice gulped. 'Absolutely exquisite.'

'Thank you.' Ella's blonde hair was longer than her usual pixie cut, falling towards eyes shadowed with tired-ness, and she smoothed a gentle hand over Isaac's head. 'We definitely think so and he's got Stan entranced already.'

'Congratulations, Max.' Zac hugged him and kissed Ella after taking a peek. 'He's not got his dad's nose so that's something.'

'It really is.' Max's look at Ella was adoring. 'Who wants a hold?'

'Please don't disturb him if he's sleeping,' Alice said quickly. 'I'm sure you need to make the most of every peaceful moment.'

'No, really, it's fine, cuddle away.' Ella leaned gingerly towards the basket and Max was quicker.

'Let me.' He lifted Isaac and the baby whimpered as Max held him. 'Alice?'

'Oh no, let Zac go first as he's Isaac's godfather.'

Alice wasn't expecting the blast of emotions charging through her as Zac held Isaac over his shoulder, patting his back gently as the baby grumbled. 'I've had some practice with Hayley's girls,' he said, his smile for Alice understanding.

Max disappeared to answer another knock at the door and Lily and Arlo were engrossed at the breakfast bar with iPads, Prim curled near Ella's feet.

'We ought to go,' Alice said at the sound of more voices in the hall. 'You must have so many visitors wanting to pop round and meet Isaac. He's gorgeous.'

'There's no rush, Alice.' Ella was smiling. 'Not if you'd like a cuddle before you go.'

'I'd love one,' Alice said wistfully. She held out her arms, clinging on to another gulp as Zac transferred Isaac across, and she stared at his tiny round face. She hadn't held a new-born since her nieces, and back then she'd still thought she might one day hold her own. She couldn't quite process the wonder, the tenderness and still a little hurt, the never-ending shadow of sadness she lived with. But holding this precious and so very loved child was a gift, and she tried to soothe him as he wriggled, a grizzle threatening to become more, rocking him in her arms in the age-old way.

'I think he might be ready for another feed,' Ella said. Max's mother, Noelle, had appeared, and she'd brought gifts for the children to celebrate their new brother, exclaiming over the beauty of the baby and how clever Ella was as Alice returned him to Ella.

'Thank you for including me,' Alice said quietly. 'I wouldn't have missed it for the world. I'm so happy for you all.'

'Thanks, Alice, that's very kind.' Max followed her and Zac to the door, and she hugged him after Zac had done the same. Max was saying something about holding a christening in the spring and she must come, but her thoughts were still with the baby. The warmth and feel of him in her arms, the wonder on Ella and Max's faces.

Outside, Zac looked at her as they strolled through the arch towards the courtyard. 'Are you all right? I know it can't have been easy.'

'I'm fine. Thank you for asking. He's utterly adorable; no wonder they're besotted.'

They drifted to a halt outside her studio, and Alice's mind was spinning. Last night she'd made a decision, one rooted in sense, practicalities. Now, after seeing the baby and wanting to grasp at all the happiness she could, she landed on another.

'Zac, if you're okay with it, then I want to see you too.' She shrugged helplessly. 'Life's just too short to pass up on something wonderful, even if it's not forever, don't you think?'

'I do. And we'll deal with Christmas when it comes. We've got time before then.'

Zac came home with her that night and over the next week she couldn't pin a description to the relationship developing between them. 'Inseparable' wasn't quite right, not really, but they both went out of their way to make time for the other. Sometimes she'd catch sight of him at Halesmere, passing through for work, and one day he'd found her in the studio, alone. She'd caught his intent the moment he was through the door and had locked it after him. It was too dark to cycle in the evenings and she'd decided to put training for the triathlon on hold until the new year. She and Zac had a limit on their time together and they were making the most of every spare moment.

They went to the pub for dinner on Friday night, bumping into Ana and Rachael, as well as Marta and Luke from the farm. Rachael, who balanced her physiotherapy work with mindfulness coaching, had just accepted a full-time job with a rugby team and everyone was in a celebratory mood. At one point, Alice had been about to put an arm around Zac, and hesitated, not certain he would want for them to be quite so publicly affectionate. He'd noticed and raised her hand to his lips to kiss it. The six of them hung out together until closing time, and as he'd left his van at the barn, he walked the short trip back with Alice.

'Would you like to stay?' She opened the front door, making sure her question was a casual one. Her feelings for him were becoming more complicated by the day. She enjoyed his company; they made each other laugh and he was keen to support her burgeoning new business if he could. But all of that was difficult to balance against the space he'd leave when he moved away to begin a new job six hours' drive further north.

'Very much.' Zac caught her for a kiss that had her bag falling to the floor and Alice leaning against the wall for balance. 'What time are the girls arriving tomorrow?'

'Ten thirty. I'm going to take them on a tour of Halesmere and have lunch before Steven and Jenna leave.' Alice's brother, sister-in-law and two nieces were making the journey up from Cambridge. The girls were staying with Alice until Sunday so her brother and sister-in-law could have an evening away in a luxury hotel to celebrate their wedding anniversary. 'Then me and the girls are going to the aquarium before a sail on the lake and tea out somewhere nice.'

'Would you like some company?' Zac framed his question just as simply as Alice had asked her own about him staying over a few minutes ago. Her arms were still around his neck, and one hand went to his face, loving the feel of his short beard against her palm.

'Seriously?' She was trying to measure the ramifications in her mind. 'I'd love to spend the time with you as well, but I haven't told Steven and Jenna about us.'

Us. It sounded very intimate, much less casual, and far more meaningful spoken out loud.

'Would you like them to know?'

'What would we say? You're moving in a few weeks and however wonderful this is, I have no idea what to call it. But you could still stay and leave before they get here.'

'Okay.' His nod was accepting. 'I understand and the offer's there. If your nieces are anything like Hayley's girls, they'll be relentless.'

'They definitely are. It's "Auntie Alice this", "Auntie Alice that" from the moment we're together,' she said wistfully. 'And I love it.'

–

In the morning, Zac helped her prepare a leisurely breakfast and they'd nearly finished eating when a car pulled up on the drive. Alice's hand flew to her mouth, and she grabbed her phone. She'd barely looked at it all morning and had therefore missed the message from Jenna informing her they'd left early and hoped it would be okay to arrive an hour ahead of schedule.

'So best-laid plans and all that. Are you ready for this?'

Alice took a deep breath as she answered the front door and seconds later the girls had thrown themselves into her arms. She was on her knees to hug them back, squeezing them tightly, breathing in the fresh smell of shampoo on their hair, their little faces smooth against hers.

'Oh you gorgeous people, I've missed you all!' The girls raced into the kitchen, and she hugged Jenna and

Steven too, laden down with luggage for the one-night stay, and relieved them of some of it.

Her brother looked more like their dad with every year that passed. His hair was already turning gunmetal grey, and he was tall but without their dad's booming voice that always carried across the haulage yard or the workshop. Jenna was slightly taller than Alice, with light brunette hair almost always in a ponytail and today was no different. She and Alice hugged the longest, then Alice led them nervously into the kitchen. Zac was sitting at the breakfast bar with a mug in front of him, and he stood up as she made the introductions, shaking hands with everyone, including the girls, who were staring at him in bemusement.

'But who is he, Auntie Alice?' Lottie was clutching a musical jewellery box decorated with fairies that she'd just had to bring with her. Alice was searching for the right reply to her eldest niece and Zac was quicker.

'I'm a friend of your auntie's; we work together at Halesmere. I've got two nieces who are about the same age as you, and Alice thought it might be nice for me to say hello because I miss them, just like she misses you.'

'Okay.' Lottie accepted that and she turned to Alice, who offered a smile of thanks to Zac over Lottie's head. Alice knew the explanation she was going to have to find for Jenna wouldn't be quite so simple.

'Can we see our bedroom, please, Auntie Alice?' Lottie took a firm hold of Freya's hand. 'We've brought our unicorn pillowcases to go on our beds.'

'Absolutely you can – it's this way.' Alice held out her hands and the girls tucked theirs into them. 'Who else would like a tour of the house?'

Zac caught her eye and the corners of his lips flickered as he stood up. 'Would you like me to make some drinks, Alice?' he said. 'If you don't mind? You showed me where you keep everything, that time I was here to remove the conifers.'

'That's very nice of you, Zac. Yes please.' Such politeness and formality when last night they'd wrapped up to sit on out the terrace and watch the dark skies before tumbling into her bed. 'There's juice in the fridge for the girls, or hot chocolate. What would you like?' She addressed this to the girls and they both wanted hot chocolate with marshmallows, so Zac set to work.

After a quick house tour, Steven sat at the breakfast bar to chat with Zac and while the girls were racing from their bedroom to the kitchen, excited by this upside-down house, Jenna drew Alice aside.

'Alice Harvey, all those messages and you never once mentioned that gorgeous man,' Jenna murmured. 'Nice cover story, by the way, about him wanting to meet the girls. I think it was only me that spotted the two of you having breakfast at the table when we arrived.'

'I don't really know what to say,' Alice offered quietly, and her smile was suddenly sad. 'He's a tree surgeon working temporarily for Max and he's leaving to start a job in the Highlands after Christmas.'

'So those are the facts.' Jenna was searching Alice's face. 'But what about how you feel? And you obviously feel something for each other; you seem very easy together.'

'It's…'

'Complicated,' Jenna finished. 'So can't you find a way to make it less complicated? I mean, I know I've barely even met him but anyone who can be nice to a stranger's children like he was to mine and smooth things over for you at the same time has got to be worth something.'

'Neither of us are looking for a relationship or anything permanent. We've both been hurt before and right now we're just enjoying each other's company. And it's wonderful but I can't think any further ahead.'

Alice was telling the truth, but her resolve was weakening. If Zac wasn't leaving, she would be hoping that this, whatever it was, might continue. That maybe they'd both learn to trust again and build the foundations of a relationship. But he was leaving, planning to make a new life six hours away and settle into the job he'd chosen. He'd make friends, connections, and eventually she was certain he'd meet someone with whom he would want to start a family. Someone who wouldn't be her, and she needed to remember that. It would be all she had to shield her heart when he left.

'Auntie Alice, we asked Zac if he was coming on the boat with us and he said we had to ask you if it would be all right! Can he come with us? Please?'

Alice whipped around at Lottie's voice and her gaze went from her niece to Zac, sitting at the breakfast bar with her brother, and back to Lottie. Zac had already met the girls now; they lived far away, and he wasn't going to be a permanent feature in their lives. What would one day matter? They'd forget him soon enough, just like she'd have to try to do.

'Why not,' Alice replied, and Lottie ran to Zac to high five him. He had to bend down to reach her hand and Alice was smiling as Lottie whacked it cheerfully.

Steven and Jenna loved the Flower Shed at Halesmere. Lily and Arlo were outside playing with their guinea pigs, and Lottie and Freya soon joined them, with Stan keeping a watchful eye, delighted to have two more children to entertain. Zac went across to the flat and when the girls realised it was where he lived, they wanted to see that too. He showed them around, which didn't take long, before delivering them back to Stan's workshop for the hot chocolate Stan kept solely for Lily and Arlo, and any other young people who might visit.

Alice had booked a table at the Hart for lunch with Sandy and the family, and Zac thanked the girls when they tried to invite him too. He said he'd see them afterwards for the aquarium and promised to meet them there. Alice, who still had to sort out a more practical vehicle for work than her Porsche, asked Steven to drop her to collect the car she'd hired for the weekend to ferry the girls around, as her beloved two-seater simply wasn't up to the job.

Steven and Jenna set off excitedly for their precious anniversary evening away and Alice drove the girls to the aquarium, Zac already waiting for them when they arrived. The girls adored their journey around the aquatic world, from the Lake District through to Asia, Africa and the Americas via the rainforest. Freya wanted to know why leafcutter ants were always so busy and Lottie couldn't quite see why a poison dart frog wouldn't make a suitable pet as she liked the golden colour.

The four of them had a lovely day, which finished off with pizza in the Jetty Museum beside Windermere. After a long journey and a busy time, the girls were getting grumpy and tired. Alice scooped them into the car for home, but not before they'd elicited a promise from Zac to explore the wood with him at Halesmere tomorrow.

The next morning, the girls were up and racing around early, still excited about the different house, and Zac had messaged Alice to suggest bringing Lily and Arlo on their woodland adventure to give them a run in the fresh air, and maybe Ella and Max some sleep as well if Isaac was settled. Of course Prim was part of the expedition and with hot chocolate in flasks that Alice brought, and brownies from the community shop picked up on the way, they had a fabulous couple of hours exploring the woods and playing games. Lily and Arlo showed the younger ones all their favourite places, and only Arlo came back filthy after tumbling over in the shallow stream, making him laugh and Prim shoot back to check he was okay.

Zac stayed behind when Alice returned to the barn with the girls, and Steven and Jenna arrived to collect them at three. Loaded with snacks, toys and tablets for the journey home, the four of them were ready for the off. Alice held the girls very tightly and promised they could come and stay whenever they wanted. She hugged her brother too, who started loading the car and muttering it was unbelievable how much stuff two adults and two kids needed for one blinking night away.

'So, all the girls can talk about is how much fun they've had, and that they've made friends with Lily and Arlo, who want them to come back and meet the new lambs.' Jenna wrapped her arms around Alice, continuing after they'd embraced. 'Oh, and a certain person called Zac and how cool he is and how he showed them how to tie a knot, Lottie couldn't remember which one, and that they're going to play acorn hide-and-seek next time they see him. Or was it mud faces? I could barely keep up! Anyway, they've had a blast and will hopefully sleep all the way home, so thank you. Both of you.'

'You're very welcome – we did have a brilliant time.'

'And?'

'And what?' Alice shrugged. 'Nothing's changed.' Except how much she liked Zac and enjoyed his company more each day. 'Safe journey home, love you all.'

'We love you too. And it's perfectly obvious how much he likes you too, Al. All those secret smiles and shared glances. Fabulous though you were with the kids, you both definitely looked like you couldn't wait to be alone.' Jenna smiled wryly. 'I can barely even remember those days. I hope you're going to be okay; you really don't deserve to get your heart broken again.'

'Neither does Zac, Jenna. And I'm trying, I promise. That's the last thing either of us set out to do.'

Chapter Eighteen

The days and weeks eased towards Christmas as December arrived with a blast of freezing weather. Talk of next year was something Alice and Zac barely ever touched on. Stan had set up a huge Christmas tree in the courtyard and everyone was gearing up for the Artisan Open Day next weekend. Decorations were popping up all over the place and Alice ordered a few new ones for the barn, as she'd only kept those that had come from her mum and dad's old house.

Last year had been Max and Ella's first at Halesmere and they'd swum in the tarn on New Year's Day to raise money for charity, which Stan had gone on to declare as the first inaugural Halesmere swim, and this year Ella had asked him to choose a charity for the occasion. Stan had decided on a local hospice in town and Max, not the biggest fan of wild swimming in winter, plus Lizzie and Cal, who were, had so far signed up.

Alice's first wreath-making workshops went really well, the guests all delighted with their creations at the end of the day, giving her further confidence in her future. She was thinking ahead, searching for ways to make the Flower Shed more interesting. It was the largest and most homely of the studios and everyone naturally congregated there when they weren't crammed into Stan's workshop. She was exploring the possibility of mindfulness training in the new year, as Rachael wouldn't have the time with her new job. Ana had been very encouraging, and they joined Alice and Zac to chat about it over dinner one night at the barn.

Neil, his knee much improved, had arrived for another visit, though both Alice and Zac suspected it was as much to do with seeing Sandy as it was Zac. Alice suggested that Zac stay with her rather than sleep on the sofa in the flat as Neil wasn't planning to leave until Christmas. The four of them ate at the pub each week and Sunday lunch at the rectory after church was becoming Neil's domain as much as Sandy's as he helped in the kitchen.

Alice spent every spare moment with Zac, neither of them wanting to miss a minute. They were living together in the barn, although neither of them ever quite referred to it in those terms. They had a takeaway with Ella and Max one evening, taking turns to soothe baby Isaac in between feeds.

Alice was still adapting to the physical demands of her new job and Zac would give her massages when she was tired and ensure she slept very thoroughly by making wonderful love to her. Wise words about being sensible with her heart were no use when she woke before him and saw his face peaceful in sleep, the short curls she loved on the pillow beside her. Resolve not to miss him when he left would disintegrate every time she caught his grin across the courtyard and he would run over for a kiss, or message to say he'd pick up something for dinner so they could relax after work and not cook.

Halesmere was evolving again, and Sandy held the first community lunch in the barn, assisted by Neil, who had also gained a food hygiene certificate and wanted to make himself useful. The Artisan Open Day was a huge success, following on from last year, and Alice had enquiries for more courses as well as a couple of private events. Max, a gifted classical musician himself, had arranged for a young cellist from Cumbria to stay in the flat from January to begin her career as a professional musician. Even Stan had been seen to wipe away a tear when he'd heard Maura playing, although he'd insisted it was a bit of sawdust in his eye.

One studio was changing, and from February beautiful and scented natural soap handmade from Jersey milk would be on offer, and Lizzie planned to use it for guests in the house. Ella's parents were settling in, and her mum was often out with the children and the pram, giving Ella a chance to sleep in between feeding Isaac. Alice knew she had found her home here, and it was a comforting thought helping to keep away the chill of Zac's leaving.

The day before Christmas Eve was an opportunity for everyone at Halesmere to celebrate together if they could. Stan was in charge of entertainment, and he found a local brass band who played carols after a sumptuous meal cooked by a couple of students from the catering college in town. Everyone was there, except Ana and Rachael, who'd already left to visit Rachael's family in Wales. Alice and Zac sat together throughout, hands linked whenever they could. Each smile they shared was sadder than the last, each touch more meaningful than their first.

He and Neil were leaving the following day, heading south to spend Christmas with Hayley and her family in Chester. And Alice, too, was joining Steven, Jenna, the girls and her mum at Center Parcs. Much as she was excited about seeing her family again, she was utterly dreading this full stop on her time with Zac. Tonight was their last evening together and she wanted to treasure every moment. He was already packed, and she hated seeing his belongings gathered in her bedroom, an irrefutable reminder of their parting.

Zac had shown her online images of the neat, one-bedroomed cottage he was renting, near the banks of the Caledonian Canal. It seemed alien to Alice, some far-off realm that had no place in their lives here. She knew he was looking forward to getting started with the job and making a career in forestry.

Alone in the evening, there were no more words after they'd made love. Before either of them were ready for it, Christmas Eve had arrived when they woke. Alice got up first and disappeared into the shower, trying to make it easier for both of them. Zac made breakfast and she stopped dead at the familiar sight of him in her kitchen. How much less of a home it would feel, without him in it. She was packed for Center Parcs too, and they loaded their vehicles in silence. Snow was forecast in Cumbria and there was no point in lingering before it held them back.

'Will you be okay, in that?' Outside, only goodbye was left, and Zac glanced at her Porsche. 'Sorry. I know you've driven in everything. You've probably got more miles on the clock than me.'

'Don't be.' She touched his face; she couldn't help it. 'You were being concerned and I appreciate it. But I will be fine. Message me when you arrive?'

'In Chester? Or up north?'

'Both, if that's okay,' she replied. 'Send me some images of the cottage if you want; it'll be so pretty in winter.'

'Yeah. And I want to see that meadow.' Zac held out his arms and she walked into them. 'So. This is me, not saying goodbye. I'll see you sometime.'

'You will.' Alice made herself smile. 'You've got a gorgeous godson to keep an eye on and a christening to look forward to.'

'That seems ages off. You could come up, if you want to?'

'It's a long way, and we're both going to be busy.' She had to let him go; holding him was making goodbye even harder. 'And then what, if I do come for a visit? I don't want some on–off, friends with benefits thing. We both need the space to move on. Don't you think?'

'I suppose.' Zac sighed as he ran a hand through his hair. 'Doesn't feel that way right now, though.'

'I know.' Alice swallowed. 'It's been wonderful, truly, but we were never going to make a future together when you're not going to be living here.'

'I'll never regret it, Alice.' He caught her hand, raising it to kiss her fingers.

'Neither will I.' She kissed him once again, the man who'd slept beside her these past weeks. The one she'd held when he'd been contacted by his ex-fiancée, and it had brought back a painful time in his life he'd tried to move on from. The man whom she'd let drive her beloved car because he hadn't quite come to terms with letting someone else take control. He trusted her now and that thought almost made her weep.

He'd cared for her too, had looked after her that night when she'd been broken all over again from the loss of her baby. He'd understood what it meant when she'd held Isaac and marvelled over his birth when she hadn't been able to do the same with her own. So many layers they'd revealed, and Alice would only ever be glad they'd let each other in for the time they'd had together.

'Make sure to give your girls a big hug when you see them. And you know I wish you all the luck in the world with your job.' Alice threw her bag into the car, aware that each movement was a step away from Zac, back to a life without him.

'Merry Christmas, Alice.' He kissed her cheek quickly and she wasn't sure he'd even heard her whisper 'Happy New Year' as he got into the van and took off first.

Chapter Nineteen

To Alice, Christmas at Center Parcs was like landing in another universe after Halesmere. Even with the comfort of a woodland lodge and her family there, bikes outside the door and so much to enjoy, she felt flat. Despite her efforts to make sure no one else noticed, Jenna did, and she was often at Alice's side with a kind word or an understanding look.

Alice missed Zac horribly and even the wretched trees reminded her of him. They messaged a couple of times, sharing images of their families and the children's excitement over Christmas. But there was a stiltedness already becoming evident in their chat as they tried to navigate a friendship that had been so much more.

She threw herself into all the activities on offer with the girls – meeting Santa, swimming, archery – and she and Jenna managed one luxurious afternoon at the spa. Despite missing the girls the moment they left when the break was over, Alice was very glad to be returning to Halesmere and her own home. To her surprise, her mum had asked if she could come back with her, and she'd agreed.

They returned in time for the New Year's Day swim in the tarn, which was made even more exciting after Max, Lizzie and Cal had all taken their icy dip and Max announced that he and Ella had got engaged that morning. Max's mother, Noelle, was there, along with Lily and Arlo's other two sets of grandparents, all cooing over Isaac wrapped up against the chill, and champagne was opened back in the barn at Halesmere. Stan was ecstatic about the news, until he inadvertently swallowed a mouthful of champagne, which he hated, making Noelle roar. Neil, his own family Christmas with Zac over too, gave Alice an understanding hug and said he'd missed her, making her smile through a sniff.

Alice enjoyed having her mum stay, even though it felt strange to be sharing a house with her after so long apart. They'd never been in the habit of taking holidays together and it was only once Steven and Jenna had had the girls that they'd started. Her mum loved Halesmere, the barn and the studios, and they had a happy time driving round antiques shops and choosing more vintage items to furnish the Flower Shed.

Alice felt tired and even her mindfulness wintering exercises each day weren't really lifting her mood the way they usually did. She missed Zac and the barn seemed so empty when her mum left too, taking the train back down to Cambridge. She was cycling every day when the weather allowed, so uplifted to see the gradual return of light when she came home after work. A sign, surely, that spring was slowly on its way.

Weeks soon became a month, and she shared a couple more messages with Zac, careful to keep things light and not reveal how she still felt about him. He'd sent images of his cottage and a view of the nearby canal at first light, and she reciprocated with a shot of the meadow in the mist one morning and another of her muddy bike propped against a wall out on a ride.

Her workshops were starting up again and she had three booked for the weekend before Valentine's Day. She'd devised a planting plan for the meadow and most of the seeds overwintering in the polytunnel were doing well. She'd lost a few to the cold and still had hundreds more annuals to sow once the weather improved. The polytunnel was great and provided shelter, but it wasn't warm, and she didn't usually linger inside it.

Towards the end of January, she was still feeling weary and trying to throw off a bug she'd caught. Nausea had added itself to her symptoms and it wasn't until the fifth morning in a row Alice woke feeling the same way that a shocking thought landed in her mind, and she sat bolt upright in bed.

No! It couldn't be!

She couldn't face breakfast once the idea had planted itself and after a shower she jumped straight into the car and raced to a supermarket thirty-five minutes away. She paid for the pregnancy test and locked herself in the toilets. This couldn't wait for another thirty-five-minute journey home.

Alice took a deep breath, trying to calm herself. It wouldn't be. It was beyond all hope that she might be pregnant, and she mustn't wish for it. The box promised the test was 99% accurate and she read the instructions three times before she dared try. She laid the test flat and waited. A digital countdown appeared, flashing before her eyes and she felt lightheaded. Her periods had always been erratic, and she was trying to think back to the date of the last one. Only once before had anything ever mattered so much.

Three minutes later, the countdown stopped flashing and the result appeared. In writing, no faint line or squinting required to read it. *Pregnant.* That one single word stared right back at her, and she thought her pounding heart might leap straight out of her chest. Her palms were clammy, and Alice felt dizzy with delirium, delight and disbelief. Hot, fat tears were already splashing down her cheeks and her hand went instinctively to her stomach.

'Hey, you,' she whispered, trembling from head to foot with adrenaline and a new joy threatening to overwhelm her. 'This is a surprise. But hang on, okay? Just hang on. I love you.'

How many weeks pregnant was she? She tried to drag her mind back to November, that first time she and Zac had made love, and all the times since. How, when, had this happened? And then she remembered how, and her laugh was shocked and happy all at once. Every possible emotion seemed to be tumbling in so fast she couldn't process it before another one followed. Hope, fear, joy, worry, uncertainty. And love. A huge, great whoosh of love for the tiny little bean nestled in her womb.

Zac! His name hit her again, this time like a punch, and she gasped. How had she managed to conceive their baby when all hope and expectation was against her? And how was she going to find a way to tell him he was going to be a father when they were over? He might be brilliant with Lily and Arlo, their respective nieces, and a loving godfather to Isaac, but this was a whole other level of involvement, and she had no idea how he might take it. Would he even believe that she hadn't done this on purpose in some way, to fulfil her dream of being a mother, holding her child?

He was as different from her ex-husband as it was possible to be. On paper, Gareth was the safe choice, the steady one who'd wanted a family, at least at the start, as much as she had. Zac's life had mostly been lived in the fast lane and he was only thirty-two. He'd only ever wanted a future with Serena, and he'd been shattered when she'd left him because he wasn't able to provide the one she'd demanded.

How was Alice going to deliver this news? The adrenaline rush in her limbs came again and she blinked back the tears. Maybe this time she would actually hold her own child, hers and Zac's, in her arms. She'd told him when he'd left that she wouldn't ever regret their time together and she didn't. Wouldn't, couldn't, because he'd given her this.

August was nine months after November. But summer seemed very far away right now and the last time she'd been pregnant her baby had been lost. But maybe this one would be different. She gathered her things, dried her eyes and walked outside to ring the doctor's surgery to make her first appointment. She wasn't going to be taking any chances.

–

'Oh, Alice! Congratulations!' Sandy threw her arms around Alice, and they hugged tightly as she sniffed into her aunt's shoulder. 'I'm so pleased for you. It's wonderful news.'

'Thanks, Sandy. It is for me.' Alice let go and caught the kettle on the Aga just as it began to whistle. 'I hope I'm not putting you in a difficult position with Neil. You're the only person I've told so far. Not even my mum knows, not until I've worked out how to tell Zac. I don't want anything slipping out.'

'I understand.' Sandy settled at the breakfast bar as Alice made their tea. 'And family comes first. It's perfectly reasonable for you to take some time to get used to it and make plans before you speak with Zac. He's not here and you'll probably be the one… Well…' Sandy tailed off and Alice thought she knew what might have been coming next.

'Left to manage,' she said lightly. 'On my own?'

'We don't know that, not yet. And I'll support you totally; you know I will.'

'Thank you, I appreciate it more than you know.' A smile lit up Alice's face and her hand was on her stomach again. 'I still can hardly believe it. I worry it's a dream and I'll wake up one day.'

'It is a little miracle. So how many weeks are you now?'

'Thirteen.'

'Thirteen! What about your dating scan, when are you having that?'

'I had it yesterday.' Alice couldn't stop staring at the tiny black and white shape on the image the sonographer had given her. Doing well, growing as it should, heart beating steadily. Joy of joys.

'You went on your own?'

'Yes. I really couldn't face telling anyone until I knew everything was okay with the baby.' Would she ever get used to saying, thinking, that? A baby, safely cocooned inside her. Her baby, their baby, hers and Zac's. 'And my bloods all checked out fine too. I hadn't had any miscarriage symptoms and I was already about nine weeks when I found out.' She hesitated. 'I'm still not going to say anything, other than to Jenna. I want to make sure I'm the one who tells Zac. I don't want Max mentioning it in a message by mistake.'

'Mum's the word.' Sandy tapped her lips and they both laughed. 'Have you heard from Zac?'

'Now and then,' Alice said, trying to keep the sadness from her reply. She didn't want Sandy to realise how much she missed him. 'We've messaged a few times and he's sent me photos of the cottage and the work he's doing. He's leading a team working in sustainable forest management and there's a lot going on.'

'Are you planning to travel up to share the news?'

'No. I don't think I could do six hours right now without throwing up, no matter how many times I stop.' Alice took a sip of ginger tea; it was still the only hot drink she could manage. 'It's Isaac's christening next month; I thought I'd speak to him then.'

'Sounds like a plan.' Sandy's gaze drifted to Alice's stomach. 'You'll probably be showing as well.'

'Yes.' The thought was a thrill and she laughed. 'I won't be able to keep it quiet and I'll have had time to make more plans.'

Jenna was overjoyed when Alice shared her startling news, and she offered all the help she could from miles away. Alice did feel a bit guilty about not telling her mum, who might want to hasten straight to Halesmere and cart her off to the nearest parent and baby shop. They'd had a lovely time when her mum had stayed at New Year, but the timing of Zac hearing Alice's news was more important for now.

She still felt nauseous every morning and it began to ease as the weeks passed. It was difficult to avoid Stan's builders' tea and if he saw her drinking the ginger tea that he'd mentioned was all Ella had wanted when she'd been pregnant with Isaac, Alice knew it would be very difficult to pretend around him.

The first time she felt the baby move she was at home, curled up on the sofa watching a movie, when a strange new flutter came into her stomach. Her fingers raced to follow it and the baby moved again, and tears were following. Another first, another milestone. Another signal that together they were moving in the right direction.

Feeling horribly guilty about the charity challenge she'd planned, she had given up cycling and withdrawn from the triathlon. It wasn't as though she could ride the bike in a race or run with a nearly nine-month bump in August. She'd have another attempt when the baby was older, and she could put in the necessary training. Alice instead decided to donate a regular amount from Flower Shed earnings to the charity for now.

There were more changes she'd have to make in her life. Managing the gardens at Halesmere and the work required to keep the meadow in shape would be a challenge as her pregnancy moved on, and she would have to speak with Max as soon as she'd delivered the news to Zac. A new Cumbrian School of Horticulture was opening soon, and she wondered about finding someone part time to take on the most physical tasks for now. Max had been approached with a view to lecturing at the school and he'd turned it down as he simply didn't have the time.

–

During the week leading up to Isaac's christening, Alice felt more anxious about telling Zac about their baby with every day that passed. His moving away had been difficult for both of them but it simply wasn't possible to maintain a relationship with three hundred miles between them.

Online messages and calls were fine, and they still caught up now and then. And on Sunday she was going to give him an almighty shock and bind their lives together in some way through their child.

Ella and Max were holding a gathering after the church service in the barn at Halesmere and the house had been made available for family and friends to stay for the weekend and this, Alice knew, included Zac. He'd casually dropped in that he was travelling down on Saturday, and she'd put him off before he suggested that they get together. Much as she couldn't wait to see him and had missed him every day, she didn't want him at the barn and discovering her news before the christening. She wanted that safely out of the way before he heard what she had to share.

On Sunday, Alice arrived at church almost at the last minute, hoping to avoid bumping into Zac until afterwards. But he was standing beside the porch as she walked up the path, the lovely spring sunshine keeping others outside too. He looked wonderful and she had to gulp back the worry blended with a blast of joy at seeing him. Her hand was resting on her new little bump, reassuring them as much as herself that they would be fine, however this day turned out. She'd never seen him in a suit, and the navy blue worn with a white shirt suited his colouring beautifully. His hair was a little longer than she remembered, the dark curls tamed, beard the same.

He turned around and his wide grin had her swallowing again. All these weeks without him and she wanted to rush over, tell him how much she'd missed him and wished he could come home. But she would say none of that; it wasn't how their lives would be. All she needed was for him to accept the baby in some way and play a role in their future so that their little one had a father they knew.

'Alice!' He was jogging down the path and her own smile was an uncertain one. 'You look amazing; I've missed you!'

'Hi, Zac.' She wasn't expecting his arms around her, and she had to force herself not to melt. He felt so familiar and yet strange, as though he was a song she'd played over and over, and now she couldn't quite remember the lyrics.

Would he feel the bump in her stomach and notice she felt different? Did she have that pregnancy glow she'd heard about? When, really, she felt tired more often and sometimes still sick, too. Was it written all over her face, this secret she couldn't keep for much longer and needed to share with him?

'You look great too. The Highlands obviously suits you.' Alice eased herself free. She had to protect herself as well as the baby, and emotions, hormones, whatever it was racing through her mind, weren't helping her cling to the reality of six hours between them. Distance didn't seem to matter when she was looking up in the face of the man who'd teased her, laughed with her and supported her into this new life.

What if he'd met someone else and not told her? Why would he? It wasn't necessary; it was none of her business. But still she glanced around in a moment of panic in case he'd brought a guest who was waiting for him.

'You think?' Zac huffed out a laugh, checking over his shoulder as someone called his name. 'I've got to go; they're about to start.' He took her hand. 'Can I see you afterwards? I'd love to catch up so we can talk.'

'Of course.' That helped – she wouldn't have to make a point of trying to waylay him alone now he'd asked first. 'After the christening, back at Halesmere?'

'Sounds great, see you then. I'm driving back tonight so I can't be too late leaving.'

And he was gone, running into the church to take his place as Isaac's godfather. The baby also had two more: Jamie, Ella's brother, here with his husband; and Stan, who'd apparently been silent for ten whole minutes together when Ella and Max had asked him. He'd stumped off to his workshop without replying to gather himself, and knowing him as well as they did, they'd taken that for a resounding yes.

Lizzie was Isaac's sole godmother, and the whole group looked wonderful as they made their solemn promises of care in front of Sandy and a packed congregation. Prim had been allowed to join them and she sat very quietly at Lily's side, only barking once at the end of a hymn, and frightening a pair of elderly ladies who squawked in alarm.

The service was over in less than an hour and most of the guests were making their way outside for photographs. Neil was walking down the aisle with Zac and Alice suddenly felt lightheaded at the sight. This wasn't just her baby she held. This little one already had grandparents, aunties and uncles, and four fierce little cousins. The baby connected all of them now, and Zac was their father.

Her legs trembled as a wave of nausea hit her and she gripped the back of the pew in front. She just needed some fresh air. She turned, swaying. But the ground suddenly seemed an awful lot closer, and she heard a roar.

'Get out of me way! She's expectin'!'

Alice's bemused glance was on Stan, trying to guess at the focus of his attention as he shoved his way through the throng. She swayed again and his arms caught her before she fell.

'How did you know?' she said faintly.

'I lived in an 'ouseful o' women an' I'm surrounded by 'em. I wasn't born yesterday, lass; I know you've stopped drinkin' tea. I've got you – sit down. Take a breath.'

Alice eased back onto her pew, mortified by the fuss she'd caused and very thankful that Ella and Max had tact-fully gone outside and taken most of the guests with them, leaving her with Stan, Sandy and Neil. And Zac, who was standing, white-faced and frozen, a few feet away.

'You all right now?' Stan stepped back. 'Sorry if I blurted out summat I shouldn't, lass. You looked like you were about to keel over.'

'I'm fine.' She was still quivering, with nausea or anxiety, she wasn't sure which, terrified of what Zac might, must be thinking. 'Thank you for catching me.'

'You're very welcome.' Stan patted her shoulder. 'I'll be outside if you need anythin' else.'

'I'm sure I won't.' Alice carried ginger biscuits every-where and she took one from her bag to nibble on. She breathed in and out, closed her eyes. Maybe when she opened them again Zac would be gone, and they wouldn't need a conversation to talk about the future. Then she would understand his response to the news Stan had blurted out to save her from falling.

'Do you want me to stay?' Sandy hunched down in front of her and Alice shook her head.

'Thank you but no.' Her smile was a weak one. 'I'll see you back at Halesmere.'

'Okay. Here if you need me.' Sandy stood up and Neil came over.

'Alice,' he said quietly, glancing at Zac, who still hadn't moved. 'Oh, love. It's lovely news, it really is.'

The old door clicking shut behind him and Sandy seemed to reverberate around the church, bouncing through the silence. Alice took a deep breath. What would she say now, when all her carefully rehearsed words had bolted?

'Are you sure you're okay?' Zac's gaze dropped to her stomach, and he shoved his hands into his pockets. 'And the, er, baby?'

'I'm fine, thank you,' she replied quietly. Her hand covered her neat little bump, and she felt the baby flutter, filling her with relief. Every day was a new experience; every day their baby grew bigger. Silently she promised their child she loved them, and they'd be fine, no matter what. Whatever role Zac might or might not play in their lives, this baby was her future, and she was going to create the best one for them she possibly could. 'I'm so sorry about how you found out, Zac.'

'Shit, Alice!' He didn't seem to know what to do with his hands now and he ran both over his face. 'I mean, how the hell? I thought this couldn't happen, that you couldn't…?'

'So did I,' she said calmly, making herself take slow, steady breaths. 'I tried everything for years to get pregnant and nothing worked, beyond the final round of IVF. And you know what happened after that.'

'When's it due?'

She wondered if he was asking because he wanted to know when his life might change. Hers already had. 'On the thirtieth of August.' It felt like years from now, but it came closer with every day that passed. She still hadn't started on the nursery, which would be the small bedroom next to hers. She didn't dare, not yet. There was another scan to face before she'd do that.

'So how many weeks are you?'

'Seventeen.'

'Right.' He loosened his tie and dragged it off, giving her the impression it was too tight around his neck, binding him like he maybe thought she was trying to do with this news. 'So when do you think?' He paused. 'I mean how? We were always careful.'

'Except that morning when we weren't.' It felt strange, taking them back to those days when they'd made love so often after their first time. 'We ran out of condoms and we both agreed we were okay with it. I'm in a different place in my life since I came to Halesmere, and thinking I might ever be pregnant again just didn't feature. Maybe all that helped. Took away the stress I felt when I tried before.'

She jumped as the door opened behind them and Neil stuck his head around, apologising and informing Zac he was required for photographs outside. 'The irony is quite something,' Zac said, shaking his head. 'Finding out you're going to be a father at your godson's christening.'

'Yes.' Alice tried to smile as she left the pew. It was time to leave too; she couldn't hide in the cool church forever.

'Why didn't you tell me?' He halted beside her, and she was surprised to see his eyes shimmering. With uncertainty, fear or dismay, she couldn't tell which. Maybe it was all of them.

'I was going to, today,' she said steadily. 'We're quite far apart, and it's a long journey. I couldn't ask you to come down without a reason and I haven't been feeling that great.'

'But you're okay?' Again his gaze flickered down. 'And the baby?'

'Yes. There's no reason to be concerned right now, other than good old-fashioned worry.' She placed a hand on his arm. All those times they'd touched, hadn't wanted to be apart. 'I would have come up, when the time was right.'

'Yeah. I'll see you later, then.' He let out a long, fraught breath. 'We still need to talk.'

Chapter Twenty

The barn at Halesmere was packed, full of Ella and Max's family, friends and colleagues. Everyone around their community had been invited and the atmosphere was merry as food was served. Alice was hugely relieved that Zac had finally learned about the baby, and she accepted the congratulations of everyone who offered them, wishing she could share these moments with him. Ella and Max had drawn her aside and offered their own support and congratulations, and their words had made Alice cry again.

Zac was seated at another table and whenever she caught his eye, it darted away. She was shocked how much that saddened her, both for the baby as well as herself, but she couldn't blame him. They'd been so close and seeing him today had brought all those feelings she'd had for him straight back. In truth, she hadn't lost them; she'd simply learned to do without them. But she couldn't think about herself now. This was about their baby and how, if, they would parent their child together.

Sandy stuck close and Alice was grateful for her support as she picked her way through the food. Her appetite was really good now but today she didn't feel like eating much. Her stomach was churning and this time it wasn't carrying a baby that was causing it. Ella stood to thank everyone for coming and the special gifts they'd brought for Isaac, and a few guests wandered off.

Alice caught Zac's eye again and this time he didn't look away, tilting his head in the direction of the door. They met outside and she pointed to the Flower Shed. 'In there? At least we won't be interrupted.'

'It looks great,' he said quietly as he took in the latest improvements after she'd let him in and closed the door behind them. Stan had built more shelves, and each was full of gardening and nature books, tiny bud vases she loved to collect and refresh every couple of days, and the decorations she kept for making wreaths and arrangements. Three vases filled with yellow daffodils were bright on the huge table and she pointed to a sofa.

'Tea? I'll make some.'

'I would've brought milk just in case if I'd known.' Zac's smile was wry as he sat down, and her laugh was a quick one. Humour was something in this moment; at least he wasn't in a towering rage. But that had never been his style. He was easy-going for the most part, great company and still learning not to sweat the big stuff quite so much, like her. Did that a good father make? Alice wondered. It didn't matter; she wouldn't have chosen a different one for their baby even if she could have.

'Thanks.' He accepted the mug she offered, and she curled up with ginger tea on the other sofa, legs tucked under her. She didn't often wear dresses, given the work she did, and this one was stretched over her stomach, revealing her bump. His gaze was on it again and she wished, hoped, prayed, that their baby might know their father in some way. So much rested on what they would say next.

'How long have you known?'

'Since January, about a month after you left. I was feeling off and did a test. I wasn't certain, far from it, of a positive result, so it was still a huge shock.' And a miracle and a joy that still sometimes stopped her in her tracks to marvel.

'Left? I moved, Alice, for a job I'd signed a contract for.' His words were hollow. 'You make it sound like I walked right out of your life because what we'd shared meant nothing.'

'Sorry. I didn't mean to.' She still thought of it as 'left' but he was right. It was his own new start; it just happened to be six hours away from hers.

'Why didn't you tell me before? January was two months ago.' Zac's voice was strained, as though each word needed more breath to release its meaning.

'I was so thrilled, Zac, but I didn't exactly expect you to feel the same.' Alice attempted a smile. 'You were just starting out with your new life, and I didn't want to throw a bomb under all of that.'

'No, Stan did that a couple of hours ago.' Zac rolled his eyes, and she raised a shoulder.

'We had a wonderful time,' she told him softly. 'But we both knew it was going to be over at some point and I had no idea how you'd feel about this, whether you'd actually want...'

'A baby? To be a father?' He sighed. 'One day, probably.'

'Exactly. Not now, not like this.' Alice didn't add *with me*; they'd neither of them ever imagined it was even possible. It was one of the reasons she'd refused to try to hold him back from his move, because she couldn't give him the family, or so she'd thought, that maybe he'd eventually want. She'd been concealing her true feelings

273

about him for months and it was crucial to keep doing that in these next moments. This was about their baby, not how her heart felt about Zac. She was still learning how to live without him.

'What about you?'

'Our circumstances aren't ideal but they're not unusual. Some people have babies when they're no longer together.' She paused. 'And I needed time to reassess my future and plan how I'll cope, on my own.'

At first she'd lain awake at night worrying about this. For all the joy and the anticipation, it was a long road ahead and she was thirty-eight. This would probably never happen again, and she'd thought of how far she'd come since her first loss, the end of her marriage and her move. But those nights filled with anxiety were gone; she was starting over again and this time it was very different.

'On your own?' Zac's head jerked up. 'So you've already decided that, have you? Decided what role I can play in my own kid's life?'

'What? No! I want you to be involved, of course I do. It's just…'

'What?' His gaze hardened on hers. 'I know what it's like to grow up without one parent being around. I never thought I'd do that to my own child.'

'I understand, but I know I can do this,' she rushed out. 'I've had time to think it through and I've learned so much about myself these past two years. I was half of a couple for so long and I wasn't sure I knew who I was outside of my marriage. I've come a long way and I can feel my own strength now, like a band of steel running through me. I'm not saying I'm naïve enough to think it's all going to be a bed of roses, but I'll be okay. Me and the baby. It's my future but it doesn't have to be yours as well. You and I were wonderful while it lasted, but…'

Alice couldn't continue without wanting to confess how she still felt, and she reached across to touch his hand. 'I want you to be part of this, Zac, I do. And I'm sure you need to think about it too and decide how that might look for you.'

'So how do we find a way to take care of this child together?' He was staring at her fingers resting on his and she slid them away.

'Are you serious?' This was more than she'd dared hope for but maybe it was just high emotion talking, and he'd reconsider when he was three hundred miles away. 'There's no rush. Go home and let's talk again when you've had time to process it.'

'Home?' Zac sighed as he glanced at the antique clock on the wall. 'Right. I've got to leave soon – early start tomorrow.'

'I understand.' Alice stood up, hand on her bump. She touched it often, reassuring both of them. 'I am sorry about how you found out and that you've landed in the middle of something with me you never expected.' She took a breath. 'But I'm not sorry about the baby. There was no decision to be made about that once I knew.'

'I would never have asked that of you, no matter what it means to me, or how we're going to cope,' he said sharply. 'Never. I know how much you wanted a family.'

Her hand was on the familiar wriggle inside her that became more insistent by the day.

'What?'

'Just the baby moving. I'm used to it now.' She hesitated. 'Do you want to try? They might not do it again, though, or are still too small for you to feel it. They're about the size of a pomegranate now.'

'Can I?' he asked hoarsely, and she nodded. His hand curled around their baby's emerging bump and a rush of tears followed as her eyes met his. Whatever the future might be for all three of them, this was a moment she'd always treasure. The baby wriggled again, and he didn't need to utter a word to let her know he'd felt it. The wonder of it was in his eyes and he nodded fiercely.

'What did you want to talk to me about, Zac?' she asked quietly, aware that time was passing, and he needed to go. 'You mentioned it this morning, at the church.'

'Just a catch-up, nothing much.' He removed his hand and neither of them knew quite how to say goodbye. 'I'll find a way, Alice. I promise.'

–

Three weeks later, Alice had agreed to meet Zac at the hospital for her scan, hopefully just a routine appointment. She'd tried to suggest that he didn't make the journey in the first place, but he was having none of it. She'd offered him the guest room at home, and he'd refused, saying he had to get back and he'd catch a kip in his van when he needed it.

They were in touch every week, sending one another polite messages. Ones when he would enquire how she and the baby were doing, and she'd let him know things were fine. He was in the car park when she arrived, and he came over, holding his arms out for a stilted sort of a hug she wasn't expecting.

'Thank you for doing this.' Sandy had been prepared to come instead but Alice was glad Zac was here. 'I hope you won't be too tired by the drive later.'

'I'll be fine.' He glanced down. The weather was improving all the time and her cardigan was unfastened. 'You've grown.'

'You mean the baby has!'

'Yeah, sorry.'

'Good job it's a summer baby,' she said lightly, trying to ease past the emotion of seeing him. 'I can't wear my waterproofs now; they're already too tight.'

'Shame. You know how good you look in them.'

'Funny, you're the only person who's ever said that.'

'But you're okay? You and the baby?'

'We're fine, at least I hope so.' She bit her lip. She just needed to get this next appointment out of the way. 'I can feel them moving more every day and my bump has definitely expanded.'

'I saw.' Zac smiled and her heart jolted at the sight. 'I looked it up – more like the size of a banana now.'

'Yes.' She hadn't expected that, imagining she was the only one who'd bought books, been online and was making a wish list of items for the new nursery. She spent part of her evenings outdoors in her garden when she could, enjoying this first glimpse of spring in her new home. She wanted the baby to grow up in nature, to run around and feel the rain, the wind on their face, and she wandered in the woods most days, hoping all this would somehow filter down to their child. 'We're a bit early. I suppose we might as well go in.' Alice checked her phone.

'Have you thought about asking if they can tell what sex the baby is?'

'Yes. But I'm not going to, I'd rather wait until they're born and know then.' That day was still months off, a hazy one far in the future when dreams of her own family would finally be real. 'What about you?'

'I wouldn't mind but it's your decision.' The hospital corridors were busy as they walked along, following another couple who were hand in hand. Alice had to quash the moment of sadness. Zac was here, he wanted to be a good father and they'd gone into their time together knowing it would end, never imagining that they'd always be linked by this baby. It would have to be enough.

'You're the one who's doing this every day, Alice. I'm the one who's miles away, just checking in.'

They sat in silence until she was called for the scan and a blast of nerves had her finding his hand. He gripped it, not letting go until she was comfortable on the couch, tissue tucked into her newly purchased maternity trousers and her stomach exposed. He was at her side and this time it was his hand who found hers to hold it.

The gel was cool on her skin as the sonographer smoothed the probe across her stomach, and Alice saw the very obvious black and white outline of their baby on the screen. A head, arms, legs, even a cute little nose. She couldn't help it: tears were hovering, and she glanced at Zac, who was staring with equal awe at this first sight of their child.

'We don't want to know what sex the baby is,' she said hastily. 'We're going to wait.'

The sonographer assured them that was fine, and she was quiet as the scan continued, pressing the probe more firmly on Alice's bump from time to time. The screen was slightly angled away from her, and she concentrated on steadying her breathing. Then it was over, and she heard Zac's rushed breath escape when the sonographer confirmed that all looked fine and the baby was progressing as normal, as far as it was possible to tell.

Alice wiped the gel from her stomach and stood up slowly. She laughed at the wonder on Zac's face, certain it must be on her own, and this time their hug was a tight, totally natural one. Back outside in the spring sunshine, they paused, about to say goodbye and head off separately, and Zac spoke first.

'Would you like to have a coffee or something, before I go? We should maybe talk about August and what's going to happen when the baby comes.'

'Are you sure you've got time?'

'Another hour's not going to make much difference.'

Zac followed her into town, and they parked in a supermarket. The café inside was busy, bland, and she settled on green tea as there was no ginger. He brought their drinks over, along with the toasted teacake she'd requested.

'Thank you. I'm so hungry these days. If I didn't know I was pregnant, I'd definitely be suspicious about eating for two. It's probably all the hours I spend outside.'

'You look amazing.' His lips were smiling but he wasn't quick enough to disguise a glimmer of sadness in his eyes. 'Have you made a start on the nursery?'

'I've chosen a few things but not ordered them yet. I was waiting for the scan to be over, so I'll get on with it now. Stan's put his name down for decorating. I've found a calm pale green, almost white, and he's itching to get started.' Alice laughed and it faded as she caught the suggestion of hurt in Zac's expression. 'I'm sorry. It's just, time doesn't stand still, Zac, and I can't expect you to give up your weekends to do stuff with me.'

'You haven't asked me.'

'Well, there's plenty do to,' she said lightly. 'If you're up for building furniture, then… My flat pack skills aren't the best. You'll always be welcome, I promise. I'm not trying to shut you out.'

'I know, and I'm sorry.' His hand reached across the table to hers, until he changed his mind and withdrew it. She was glad and sorry all at once; it would be too easy to fall back into what they had once shared only to have to give it up all over again.

'How are things with work? I know you've found someone to take care of the meadow.'

'Good,' Alice confirmed. 'They're going to look after the garden as well, at least for the rest of the year. I'll still be running courses until the baby comes and then I'll take some time off. I've had plenty of offers for babysitting, and my mum wants to come for an extended stay.'

'That's great. I'm glad you're happy. And you finding your way was never in doubt; it was only a matter of time.'

'Thanks, Zac.' Alice knew she was doing a good job of assuring him that she was settled if he didn't suspect how she really felt about him. How happy it made her, that he was here now; how difficult she found every goodbye. The first half of her teacake was gone, and she picked up the second. 'I've spoken to Lizzie and Ella about my taking over the mindfulness sessions next year. They were really keen, and I can train online when I'm ready. I use it every day and I want to combine it with nature and the forest bathing. It's another line of work outside of the garden.'

'I think you'll be perfect. It's great, how you've made Halesmere such a home.'

'Thank you,' she said wistfully. 'But what about you? I've barely heard you mention your fabulous new job.'

'That's because we've had other things to talk about,' he said quietly.

'True. But how is everything, really?' Suddenly Alice didn't want to know all about his new life. What if he'd met someone else and hadn't found a way to tell her? And what if he wanted to take their child hundreds of miles and six hours north for a long weekend, and she'd be left at home fretting about how he was coping? Or shared those times with a new partner, someone who'd be a stranger to Alice and yet a step-parent to her child?

But she'd just have to cope; those scenarios came with the territory, and they weren't here yet. Maybe she could bring the baby up for those first faraway visits, and stay somewhere close at hand, if not actually with him. There was going to be so much they'd both miss, parenting separately.

'It's fine,' he said. 'Busy, long hours.'

'Okay. And the house, have you found anywhere else yet? It's not that long until your first six months will be up.'

'I've viewed a couple, but they weren't right, not now with the baby. They were both projects and I won't have the time. I don't want to spend every spare minute doing DIY. I'll probably be coming down here, begging for a bed for the weekend. The spare one, obviously,' he finished quickly.

'There'll always be room for you at the barn,' Alice offered. 'We'd love to see you.'

'I think you'll be an amazing mum, Alice. You have so much love to give.' His voice caught and his hand slid over hers. 'The baby's so lucky to have you.'

'And you too.' She swallowed. 'You'll be the one teaching them how to climb trees and drive a car and ride a bike down a mountain. And so much more.'

'I hope so.' Zac's eyes were bright. 'My dad's over the moon; he can't wait for another grandchild.'

'I know, he keeps asking me how I'm doing and if there's anything I need. He's so sweet. I heard his house has sold and he's found a new one, near Halesmere.'

'Yeah.' Zac sighed. 'Weird, isn't it, him being the one to move up here right after I've left. He and Sandy seem really happy together.'

'It's wonderful.' Another family thread binding Alice and Zac together.

He checked his phone. 'I'd better make a move. I've booked a couple of weeks' holiday around the end of August, so hopefully the baby won't be too far either side of the due date.'

'Let's hope so.' Alice gathered her bag and stood up. 'I probably won't have much say in it.'

–

Four weeks later, Alice was in the Flower Shed, the door wide open to allow in the spring breeze. May was a glorious month and she loved every moment of it. Lush new green life was exploding everywhere, and the days were bright, easing into mild nights. All her hard work in the autumn had paid off and the meadow was thriving. Cold gloomy hours planting hundreds of bulbs were worth every minute when she caught sight of the array of colour greeting her each morning. She loved to wander among it all and pick the flowers and foliage she arranged in the house for guests. The annuals in the polytunnel would go in the ground soon, and she had some help lined up for that.

She was almost six months pregnant now and flourishing, thankful there had been no real complications so far. She made sure to eat and drink well, and she walked every single day, no matter the weather. Since her scan, Zac had been down for a weekend and he'd stayed at the barn, which had been both wonderful and desperately sad as they navigated this different relationship.

She'd lain awake thinking of him across the house, wishing he was beside her, their baby between them. The nursery was finished and they'd gone shopping, choosing the last few bits together. The musical mobile to hang above the cot, with its furry grey elephant and cuddly friends; the matching sleep bag and a pushchair they'd spent hours over, trying to decide what would be best.

'Hey, Alice.'

Alice looked up from the table and the list of bulbs she was planning to add to the meadow in the autumn. Ella was at the door, Isaac swaddled against her chest in a baby carrier.

'Are you busy?'

'Never for you and that gorgeous little guy.' Alice swallowed; it still hit her every time she saw Isaac that he was Zac's godson and she got to spend more time with him than Zac did. 'Please can I have a cuddle?'

'You definitely can.' Ella unwrapped Isaac and handed him over to Alice, whose heart expanded with love. It did that often, these days.

'Gosh, Ella, he's such a sweetheart. So like Max, and his hair's so blonde.'

'He really is.' Ella laughed as she tugged Isaac's coat off and he beamed at Alice, making her heart flutter again. One day her baby would smile like that. 'I'm off to the vet's to pick up something for the sheep; we can't stay long. There was nearly a riot first thing because one of them needed the vet and Arlo did not want to leave it.'

'Oh dear.'

'Exactly. I've just checked again and it's fine now it's had a jab of antibiotics.'

'How many has he got now they've all lambed? I can't keep up and the lambs are too quick to count, the way they leap about!'

'Sixteen. Quite the little flock now, and he's desperate for his own sheepdog.' Ella tapped her nose. 'It's his birthday soon and he has no idea that Luke has his present down at the farm. He'll be one very happy little boy and that's another animal to add to our growing menagerie. How are you doing? You look fabulous.'

'Thank you.' Alice was pulling faces at Isaac, loving the smiles she was getting in return as he waved a chunky fist in the air. 'I feel so much better now the sickness has passed.'

'Yeah, it was horrible.' Ella rolled her eyes, laughing as Isaac tried to grab Alice's hair. 'But so worth it.'

They chatted for a few minutes and Ella checked her phone. 'I need to make a move; Prim will be waiting for her walk when I get back, before we head down to school later. She knows better than me when it's time to pick them up.'

She held out her arms to Isaac and he giggled as Alice handed him back to his mum. 'Alice, forgive me if I'm speaking out of turn but I wondered if you'd heard from Zac recently?'

'Yes, a couple of days ago. We message quite regularly and we speak every week. I'm not sure when he's planning to come down again now we've finished the nursery.'

'Right.' Ella fastened Isaac back into his carrier. 'It was just a thought.'

'Is there something the matter?' Alice's pulse spiked with worry. Ella was always very friendly and generally direct, but she'd never discussed Zac with her before. 'Ella, is he all right? I'm worried there's something you're not telling me.'

'Okay, I'm just going to come out and say it.' Ella took a deep breath. 'Max had a message from Zac over the weekend and he's a bit concerned. I think he's going to go up and see him, have a chat.'

'What about?' Alice gripped the table. Had Zac changed his mind about the baby, decided he couldn't be involved after all?

'I don't know the specifics, but I do know that he's unhappy. He hasn't settled into his new job and he's thinking about his future there.'

'What? Why? He hasn't said anything to me.' But why would he? Alice reasoned. They were connected by their baby, family and friends, but nothing else. Not like they had been, once. If he didn't share her life, then it didn't exactly matter where he lived; they could travel anywhere to meet up when they needed to.

'He doesn't want to worry you, plus he thinks… Never mind.' Ella was at the door, and she looked back. 'It's not Max he wants to see, Alice, it's you. Max can't help him with this.'

'Me! But Max is his friend, the person he's closest to, apart from his dad. If he's concerned about something, then surely he'd tell one of them?'

'True but then they're not you. I know it's a long way and I wouldn't have said it if I didn't think it was important. I think you're the only one who can help him this time.'

Chapter Twenty-One

After Alice left Glasgow, the drive alongside Loch Lomond towards Glencoe was spectacular, and if she wasn't in such a rush to reach the tiny village where Zac lived, she would have loved every second of it. She pulled up, parking outside his house, shattered, seven hours after she'd left Halesmere. She'd had to stop three times for the loo to accommodate her pregnancy and the water she drank.

She tapped nervously on the front door but the lack of a nearby van suggested he hadn't made it home from work yet, and she needed the loo, again. She drove to a little café still open and busy with tourists. Thirty minutes later, after a cup of green tea she couldn't finish, she was back at the cottage. Alice parked outside for a second time and prepared to wait.

It was almost six p.m. when she saw his van approaching in her rear-view mirror and the snacks she'd brought were long since gone. She got slowly out of the Porsche, new fears chasing through her mind. What if Ella was mistaken and Alice shouldn't be here? What if Zac wasn't pleased to see her or had plans this evening? What if she'd got this whole thing wrong and she'd be turning tail in five minutes? She couldn't face that drive again tonight; she'd have to find a hotel and eat, and…

'Alice? Is there something wrong?' Zac had slammed the door and he ran over, skidding to a halt a few feet away as his eyes leaped to her stomach. 'Are you okay? The baby?'

'We're fine. I'm sorry, I didn't mean to give you a shock. Another one.'

'That's okay, now I know you're both all right.' Zac let out a relieved breath and a smile was hovering on his lips. 'So why are you here on a Monday night without letting me know you were coming? It's a long way. And I've run out of milk.'

'If I'd known I would have brought you some. Got any ginger tea instead?' She was smiling too, and a glimmer of hope was flickering inside her. He looked so good, and she just wanted to hold him. 'I don't drink much milky tea right now.'

'Sorry, no. I'd go to the shop for you if there was one still open.' His eyes narrowed and Alice was drinking in the sight of him. Her life was fuller now, especially with the baby, but it had been so much richer when he'd been in it. 'So why are you here? I missed that bit.'

'Ella mentioned you were unhappy, and she thought I should find out why.' Alice lifted her chin. She'd worried about this nearly all the way here. 'Is it the baby? If you've changed your mind, then it's fine. I thought maybe you'd met someone else, and she wanted me to hear it from you. It's okay if you have, you can tell me, you know I'll…'

'Alice, I haven't changed my mind and I haven't met someone else.'

'You haven't? But one day you will.' Her pulse was thudding, and she touched her neck, trying pointlessly to calm it.

'I won't.'

'So are you unhappy, then?' She raised her hand some more to shield her eyes from the evening sun behind him.

'Not any more.'

'Oh!' The car keys in her other hand rattled nervously. 'Right, well, that's great. I can go then, and let Ella and Max know you're all right.' Alice paused. 'Why aren't you unhappy? Not that it's a bad thing, of course! I just wondered.'

'Because I've left my job. I sent the email today.'

'What? I've driven for seven hours and that's it? You've left your job?' The hope was already disintegrating, and she glared at him. 'Well, if it's career advice you want then I'm definitely not the right person. Max should be here, not me.'

'It's not just about the job and I'm not sorry Max isn't here. Alice, why did you drive all the way up here?' Zac glanced at the bright yellow Porsche parked beside her and his own smile was back. Hopeful, like hers.

'Because I... Because Ella said I should!'

'So there was no other reason?'

'I was worried too,' Alice shot back. 'I don't want you to be unhappy either.'

'Because?' He was walking very slowly towards her.

'Because I care about you! What is this, twenty questions! I'm here because...' Again the words faltered in her throat.

'Say it.'

'Say what?' She had to dredge up every ounce of strength not to reveal the only words in her mind. The ones she'd really driven six hours with three loo stops to tell him. 'Why did you leave your job?'

'Because I don't really like it. Because it's not hands-on enough for me. But mainly because it's here. Not where you and our baby are.' Zac halted right in front of her and took her hands. 'If you need me to tell you first that I'm love with you then I will. If you need to know I've missed you every single day since I've been here then I have. If you want to know that leaving you was the hardest thing I've ever done, then it's true. Walking away from racing having achieved what I'd set out to do was enough. Walking away from you when my heart knew we weren't done was worse. Alice…' He squeezed her hand, laughter brightening his eyes. 'The moment I saw that crazy yellow car I knew why you'd come. No one, not even a person who adores driving, sits in a car for six hours for someone they don't care about. You can give me all the career advice you want, and I'll listen but we both know why you're really here.'

'I told you, because I'm worried about you!'

'That's not it.' Zac gently pulled her nearer, shielding out the sun. 'Wow, that banana has really grown. How am I going to hold you close now, Harvey?'

'You want to hold me?'

'Every day,' he said simply. 'Every day and every night, always. And this one.' A hand went to her bump, and he laughed. 'I didn't miss that kick. Do you think we've got a footballer in there?'

'Or a rugby player?' Alice was laughing with him, certain now, happy, home. She could tell him what she'd really come to say.

'What about cars? It's in the genes.'

'Definitely cars, especially bright yellow ones. My Porsche is a family heirloom.'

'Alice, I love you.' Zac raised a shoulder and a tear escaped from his eye. He tried to laugh as he brushed it away. 'I've loved you since that night Isaac was born and I fell asleep in your arms. I knew it when I woke up and saw you beside me, and I felt like my future was right there. But that wasn't supposed to happen and I was afraid of letting you know and getting us into something we weren't looking for. I thought moving away would change how I felt but even that didn't work. I was shocked about the baby, we both were, but I want to share every part of their life with you. Together, as a family.

'I grew up with a mum who left me and Hayley behind and Dad was brilliant; he was always there for us. But home didn't feel quite right afterwards and whenever I went to see my mum, her place wasn't home either. It was like having a foot in two camps and not quite belonging in either. I thought I'd found a home with Serena but looking back it was just an illusion. It was all about the racing and what we felt didn't exist beyond our careers. I clung to the idea of being in love with her for a long time; I just didn't know what else to do.'

'Oh, Zac. I'm sorry.'

'It's okay, you don't need to be. I was planning to tell you how I felt at the christening and then Stan dropped our bombshell, and everything changed. You made it clear you were fine on your own and I thought it was just me who felt that way. I didn't think we had a chance.'

'I needed time to know I would cope on my own before I told you,' Alice whispered. 'I needed to be certain if you walked away.'

'You thought I'd do that?' His eyes were shimmering.

'It was a massive curveball for both of us and I wasn't sure,' she told him seriously. 'But I want our baby to know their father more than anything. More than you and me.'

'You're amazing and I love you.' Zac placed his hands on her shoulders. 'There, I've said it twice. Three times, in fact. Now it's your turn because however much you love that car, you didn't bring it all the way up here to ask me if I'm okay.'

'I didn't?' She was teasing him now and she missed it, and him, so very much. Some of the laughter had left her life when he'd left too, and she wanted it back.

'You definitely didn't.' He bent down to whisper in her ear. 'Go on, say it. Our banana wants you to.'

'They're not a banana now, more like a marrow.' Alice slid her arms around him, pulling him as close as she could. She'd missed his kisses as well, his energy, his everything, and she put the first one to rights immediately. 'Okay, I did come here to tell you I love you too. I felt the same, when you left, and I was afraid of holding you back. Happy?'

'I am now.' He hesitated. 'I haven't really been happy since I got here. All I could think about was you and me, and how we were crazy to let go of something so incredible. I was planning to quit my job and ask you for a chance, but once I knew about the baby, I felt I couldn't, that we needed the security.'

'So why have you done it now?' She tilted her head back to stare at him, loving the new exhilaration in his eyes.

'Well, I've gone and bought a wood instead of a house.' He laughed, astonishing her all over again. 'The one next door to Halesmere. Max was interested and he stepped back when he knew I wanted it. I'm going to manage his alongside ours. I completed the course while I've been up here, so I know what I'm doing. Some, anyway. There's lots to learn.'

'A wood! Zac, that's wonderful; think of everything we can do with it.'

'Exactly. We can't live there but I'm going to build a cabin where we can hide away when we want to, the three of us. I'd love it to be a place where kids can run wild. Ours, Isaac, Lily and Arlo, our girls, the lot of them. I've been thinking about the idea of a forest school as well, and I'm planning to start training.'

'I think it's perfect. You'll be perfect.'

'It won't be enough on its own,' Zac said quickly. 'I'll still need work. But Max and I have talked and I'm going to set up my own company. I'll work with him when he needs me, but I'll be freelance too, taking on other contracts. Alice, I'll do whatever it takes to look after our family, I promise.' His hold around her fingers was tight, eyes blazing with love and hope. 'So what do you think?'

'I think you need to pack up that cottage and come home with me,' she whispered.

'I haven't got a home at Halesmere,' he reminded her. 'The flat was only temporary.'

'Of course you do.' Alice shifted his hands, holding one and putting the other on their baby. 'We're your home.'

Epilogue

August, three months later

Crowds had been building all morning, swelled by holi-daymakers passing through, and the weather was ideal: the sun not too hot with a gentle breeze helping keep the competitors cool. The entire Halesmere team, plus Alice's mum, Steven, Jenna, their girls and Zac's family, had all turned out to support him. Alice's friend Kelly and her partner, Damon, had sent their apologies, delayed on a flight from Dubai.

It had been Zac's idea to enter the triathlon and he'd devised a training plan and stuck to it. Alice had been lost for words when he told her he'd entered straight after Isaac's christening, knowing she wouldn't be able to continue. He'd explained he wasn't doing it just for her, but for the same reasons she had wanted to enter in the first place. To say thank you for the support she'd received and to help those who would come after her. And not only that – and she'd laid the blame for crying again firmly on her hormones – but he felt braver because of her and their baby.

Ella had organised a giant picnic and people were still trickling in long after the competitors had finished their swim and the cycle and were out on the run. Alice had been here all day and she'd seen Zac enter the lake first thing before he was lost in the flurry of swimming caps and arms in wetsuits arcing through the water.

She was near the transition area to clap him through when he emerged from the lake, pulling off his wetsuit as he ran and flashing her a grin. He'd created his own fundraising page when he'd moved back to Halesmere, and Alice found she minded much less about people guessing why she'd had the idea in the first place. Their baby's due date was less than two weeks away, and she had a check-up appointment with the midwife on Monday.

Lily and Arlo were wildly excited when they arrived with a dog each. Prim was much better behaved, being a very grown-up two years old, than Arlo's adored collie, Fly, his birthday present back in May. Fly was learning to be sociable as well as useful, and he and Arlo were both in training with Luke down at the farm. Max had to make a grab for Fly's lead more than once when it seemed he'd settle for herding children instead of sheep, and Noelle had joined them with a friend up from London. She was sketching baby Isaac as he giggled on his nana's knee, charming everyone.

Lily and Arlo soon handed over the dogs to Max so they could take off and play with Alice and Zac's four nieces, who often came to stay with them at the barn. The sight made her heart bump with love – such a simple thing and one day their child would join the gang with Isaac. Mates, all mucking in together.

The sale of the wood was complete, and she and Zac spent much of their free time there, working sometimes but also coming to understand the land and the trees. What grew and flowered where and when; land that held the water after rain and swelled the stream gushing through the wood and out into a river; the birds and wildlife that called this place home, just like they did. He'd already picked out a spot for their cabin, which he planned to build himself with a bit of help from Stan, and then there would be a treehouse for wild adventures and long days outdoors.

Neil had moved north too, dividing his time between his two children and their families, and he and Sandy were regulars at the barn. He'd taken up photography, encouraged by Lizzie, and loved his early morning starts in search of the golden hour and a perfect shot. Lizzie and Cal's wedding was planned for next summer and everyone was invited, including the reality television star who'd become a friend, and who Stan still insisted on calling 'that daft lad'.

The television series about the Lakes and the Dales was going out next month and Stan took all the teasing about the potential for becoming a TV star in his own right with endless good humour. Max's hotel project was complete, and the garden was breathtakingly beautiful, constructed from local and natural materials with abundant, joyful planting, and he was booked up for the next two years as a consequence. His current project, and one he considered at least as important as the hotel if not more so, was redesigning the garden at Lily and Arlo's primary school. He'd promised the head teacher he'd do it and the full weight of his landscaping team was on it through the holidays.

Zac was working through his forest school training and he would be running sessions in the autumn, allowing children to set their own pace as they learned how to take risks, create their own ideas and adventures in a safe and supported environment. Alice loved sharing the barn with him, and it had never felt more like home. She'd found the strength to start over at Halesmere and knew she had friends and family alongside her when she needed them. She and Zac would both be taking some time off when the baby arrived, and they planned to work around each other's commitments as much as they could. His own company was just getting going and projects were filling his calendar months in advance.

She had begun her mindfulness training and, once complete, they planned to combine this with the forest school and the Flower Shed, helping to connect people with nature and bring a little of it into their everyday lives. Halesmere was growing and evolving, and the house was booked for retreats for the next twelve months. The reality television star was staying for Christmas and Lizzie had arranged a butler after he announced he never wanted to see the inside of a tent again.

Alice, their four girls, Lily and Arlo were waiting for Zac when he returned from the cycle and set out on the final stage. The children all ran alongside him for a few yards, and he managed to high-five everyone before they abandoned the chase. Lily had a job holding on to Prim, who was used to running with Ella and very much wanted to continue.

Zac had been concerned about Alice sitting out for hours today and she'd told him she would be fine. She'd been having Braxton Hicks contractions for a few days, all perfectly normal as her body prepared for their baby to be born. Even though she was apprehensive about the actual birth, she couldn't wait to meet their child. Sleeping was difficult now and she was tired more often but none of it mattered, not really. Just a safe and healthy delivery.

She was feeling much less comfortable as the first runners returned and was at the finish line with the children to cheer and clap Zac as he crossed it. He hugged her in triumph as best he could before bending to catch his breath, hands on his knees. He accepted a medal from an organiser, along with some goodies, water and an energy bar. He wanted Alice in the official photograph with him and everyone else had their phones out.

'You'll be happy to hear we've saved you some food. Even though Ella brought masses, six kids have had more than their fill.' Alice caught Zac's hand, drawing him to a halt before they reached the others. 'Thank you,' she said simply. 'It means the world and I know why you did it.'

'How could I not?' he said softly. 'I was thinking of you both the whole way round. Well, that and how I'm never going to do it again. I hate running.'

'Me too. I'm not built for it.'

He laughed, murmuring his agreement as they shared a kiss. The whole gang was waiting, and they stood to give him a cheer, which he tried to laugh off as he flopped onto the grass. Stan was rocking Isaac in his pram and told Zac he'd better get a move on if he wanted help with this cabin malarkey now the triathlon was over because he had *The Repair Shop* in his sights and once he was on the telly, it was only a matter of time.

Alice needed the loo again, a constant these days, and she didn't fancy wedging herself in one of the portable ones brought in for today. A café was across the road, and they kindly let her use theirs. She'd barely locked the cubicle before a weird rushing feeling was followed by a blast of liquid running down her legs. Excited and worried all at once, she cleaned herself up as best she could and tottered back to the picnic.

'All right?' Zac was sprawled on the ground with another bottle of water, still in his running kit.

She shook her head faintly and realised her smile might not have been that reassuring when he leaped up. 'What is it?'

'My waters have just broken. I've been having some pains all morning, but I didn't think they were anything. They're a bit stronger now.'

'Bloody hell, Alice,' Zac roared, scattering alarmed children, food and two excitable dogs. 'Are you having the baby? Now?'

'Not now, no.' She tried to laugh as he grabbed her arm. 'But maybe in the next day or so. We should probably go to hospital for a check-up at least.'

'Right. Hospital, yeah.' He glanced wildly around as though an air ambulance might have suddenly dropped in to help, and Ella and Max were on their feet.

'We'll sort everything here; you two just go.' Ella hugged Alice and Zac was swapping keys with Max so he could bring Zac's bike back in the van. 'We'll be thinking of you all, lots of love.'

'Thank you.' Alice winced as another contraction came. 'It'll probably be nothing and they'll send me home again.'

Zac helped Alice into Max's pickup and he drove to the hospital like any ex-racing driver about to become a father might, yelling at the tourists pootling along in front and overtaking when he could. Alice was white, wanting to tell him there was no rush but the contractions were definitely stronger and quite a bit closer together. He drove expertly, making her feel as safe as ever and once they arrived, they went straight to the maternity unit. Her bag had been packed for weeks and she was very relieved she'd brought it with her today.

'Is this it?' He grasped her hand, eyes alight with exhilaration and wonder. Alice was attached to a machine to monitor the baby's heartbeat and her first observations had already been done. 'Alice, love of my life, is our baby really going to be born today?'

'Hopefully.' She clutched Zac's hand as another contraction came, trying to smile through her grimace as the midwife reappeared to check the monitor. 'I wouldn't mind this bit being over.'

Twenty-four hours later

'Hey.'

Alice was vaguely aware of voices, melting the moment she fixed her tired gaze on Zac, sitting beside her bed with a bundle wrapped in white safe in his arms.

'How are you feeling?' He stood up to kiss her forehead.

She offered a weak smile. 'Like I've just had a baby. How is he?'

'He's perfect. Asleep but I think maybe not for much longer. He's been a bit restless.'

'I can't believe I fell asleep again.'

'I can; you needed it. You were amazing. Do you want to hold him? I think our son wants his mummy.'

Alice carefully sat up and held out her arms. Zac placed the baby in them, and her eyes welled up again. Bloody hormones. Or maybe not. Maybe it was just overwhelming, overpowering love for this tiny, new person in their lives. Their baby was staring right back at her, and she gulped. 'He is perfect and I'm not at all biased. Do you think that's my nose? It's very cute. And he's definitely got my hair, from what I can tell. Gorgeous.'

'Are you talking about me or our son?' Zac leaned over to kiss her again and her laugh was light.

'Definitely our son but you're wonderful too. I'm sure he'll take after his daddy in lots of ways.'

'So you mean he'll be handsome, funny and clever?'

'I was thinking more hungry, demanding and noisy. But hey, if you say so. Maybe it's time we tried another feed.'

'I'll never get tired of watching you with him.'

She laughed, full of love for Zac and their son. 'I bet you will. Hopefully this will be pretty routine stuff soon.'

'I won't.' Zac smoothed a gentle hand over the baby's head as Alice prepared to feed him. 'Theo's a gift, Alice, one who brought me back to you. And I wouldn't change a thing.'

Acknowledgements

Alice's story has been with me since the earliest days of planning the Love in the Lakes series, and I always knew that growing and gardening would be a theme that suited Zac's story too. Many thanks to Alison of Yewbarrow Flower Farm, who showed me around her own burgeoning flower meadow and provided such inspiration for Alice's own. It's wonderful to see your meadow flourishing and the barn is such a welcoming space to learn a new skill and take home something beautiful.

Thank you to Susan Yearwood for giving me that first professional writing opportunity. To Emily Bedford and the brilliant team at Canelo, including the cover designers, thank you! A seventh book is so much more than I ever imagined, and I'm very grateful to be writing stories about all kinds of love. Thank you to readers and bloggers everywhere who champion our genre. I appreciate all the support and everything you do to help readers discover authors.

Thanks as ever to my wonderful family for keeping everything on track when I'm on a deadline, and when I'm not! Your encouragement means the world and I'm thankful for all you do, not least inspiring me to take opportunities when they come along. Those few days in the Dales made all the difference to this book.

To Ali and Jo, fellow dils, thank you for your love and support. We're always there for each other, through everything. Love and laughter really do make our world go around.

Like Alice, whilst writing this book I've come to notice so much more about the natural world. I grew up in the landscape and love it still, but sometimes I forget to look. Alice's story taught me to slow down and take a breath every day; to feel the breeze, listen to the birds and so much more. I wandered in a lot of woodlands when writing and there I found my inspiration as I planned Alice and Zac's future; one of hope, growth and love. I'll miss everyone at Halesmere, but I think they've found their place and Stan will have his eye on them all.